RANGE

THE METCALFES || BOOK 3

RONIE KENDIG

TASK FORCE press

© 2022 by Ronie Kendig – A Rapid-Fire Fiction Novel

All rights reserved. No part of this publication may be reproduced or transmitted in any form or by any means without written permission of the publisher.

Scripture quotations are taken from the HOLY BIBLE, NEW INTERNATIONAL VERSION®. NIV®. Copyright © 1973, 1978, 1984, 2011 by Biblica, Inc.™ Used by permission. All rights reserved worldwide.

Additional scripture taken from the King James Version of the Bible.

This book is a work of fiction. Names, characters, places, and incidents are either products of the author's imagination or used fictitiously. Any similarity to actual people, organizations, and/or events is purely coincidental.

For more information about Ronie Kendig, please visit: www.roniekendig.com

Cover design: Jennifer Zemanek/Seedlings LLC

Author is represented by Steve Laube of the Steve Laube Agency, Phoenix, AZ

DEAR READER ...

The contents of this book will not be easy to read.
Readily I admit—this story was hard to write, finding that delicate balance of sharing the brutal truths behind human trafficking and respecting the survivors. Between helping people understand the depths of depravity, yet not glorifying the shadows.

You may find this story *too* hard to read, but I hope you will brave the journey and allow your heart to be moved by the plight of so many. If you need a breather in the midst of the trials happening for the characters, take it—and in the pause, I beg you to remember those trapped in this nightmare and *pray for them*!

Ronie

Defend the poor and fatherless;
do justice to the afflicted and needy.
Deliver the poor and needy:
free them from
the hand of the wicked.
Psalm 82:3-4

CHAPTER ONE

Kandahar Province, Afghanistan

MOST INFURIATING WAS the breed of animal whose fierce self-preservation instincts aroused very mercurial behaviors when said instincts were poked. Men. Nothing they did surprised her. They were predictable, pathetic, and predatory.

Not that she was bitter. Simply ... well informed.

Since men could not control themselves, she was outfitted in a hijab and abaya in the unrelenting heat—not as bad as summer months—but still smothering. Regardless, she would not be diverted from her purpose or the hope tingling in her veins. Not today. If she was careful enough, she could send a message at the café to one whose name never crossed her tongue. It had been her last chance.

Kasra surveyed the paltry offerings of her favorite produce vendor and sighed at the limited selection. Drought and fighting had threatened crops over the last few years, then add to that the unpredictable border closures into Pakistan restricting fruit exports, and it left little and even less variety. Then again, she should only take what would not spoil quickly. That alone limited her choices.

And somehow reminded her of an encounter some weeks back.

A man approached the stand, his gaze skimming over hers. She need not look to see it happen; she felt it. Always had. It prickled the hairs on the back of her neck. He picked up a pomegranate, popped it in the air, and caught it. Grinning at her—something that somehow threw light into the prettiest of blue eyes she had seen in ages. "Khayista." After a wink to her and tossing an afghani to the vendor, the man moved on.

Beautiful, he had whispered.

Ignoring his open innuendo, Kasra cursed herself for slipping away without her bodyguard. Too many men flirted, especially Americans like him. It was as if she had a sign over her head declaring her profession. Like bees to honey.

So why was she still wondering if he'd meant her or the pomegranate?

Were Americans so bold when they were in *their* country? She had yet to meet a man—of any nationality—whose eyes did not narrow in thought when he learned her ... profession. The one she had not chosen.

Time is short, Kasra. She must keep the timeline or eighteen months of planning and preparing would be destroyed.

She rubbed her neck and handed twenty afghanis to the vendor with a nod. "*Manana.*" At another shop, she picked up another disposable phone. Plucking more afghanis from her purse, she made her way to the vendor to pay.

A small purple and yellow stuffed bear lured Kasra from her mission. Throat constricting, she touched the bear. Traced its large black nose.

Would she like this one? Does she even like purple? Her birthday was soon. Perhaps—

A vise clamped her wrist. "*Ma aladhi tafealuh huna?*" a man growled lowly, yanking her around, outrage radiating off him.

Taken by surprise, she stumbled, his grip shaking the phone

and money from her hand. That cold, iron rod slid into her spine as she met the pocked face.

A frequent visitor to the compound.

"Release me," she hissed at him in their native Pashto. "Or all who are even now staring will know *your* business, Halim Alikhel. What would your wife say? Your children?" Rising into the confidence she had been forced to adopt after years of dealing with hypocritical men, she pressed into his personal space. "What will the mosque say? The other imams, when they find out that one of their own—"

His hand flew hard and fast across her face.

But this, too, she was used to. This, too, she had learned how to handle. When he went to strike her again, she flicked her hand up. Used a slice-hand to nail his wrist, which she then grabbed, bending the thumb back toward it with her other hand.

When he cried out, she stilled. Shoved him back several steps.

"*Khuda hafez.*"

Rage twisted his face into a knot. "You will regret this."

"No, it is you who will regret this if Taweel learns what you have done here."

At this Alikhel paled.

Though Kasra hated invoking the name of the man who controlled her and the compound, she took great pleasure in the way this fool scampered away.

Delivered of the insipid man, she slowed her breathing. So much for a respite. She retrieved the phone, money, and paid for them—minus the colorful bear. She could not do much for *her*, except spare her the disgrace of being associated with the notorious Madam of Kandahar.

Ache raw, she headed to her car and set the items on the passenger seat. She made her way around to the driver's side when something cracked against her temple.

Kasra yelped and covered the spot, turning to see what had

happened. Two youths ran away from her, laughing as they aimed straight for Alikhel. Stoning was a justifiable punishment for a woman caught in adultery, as was one-hundred lashes. But what of the men who tasted that fruit? Like him.

On any other day, she would make sure he knew the full weight of her fury. Today, however ... not even he could ruin the defiant streak of hope that shoved through her hard heart.

CIA Safehouse, Kandahar Province, Afghanistan

"Hey, Pretty Boy—clearance came through to hit the compound."

Sweating and out of breath, Range Metcalfe swiveled on the weight bench and glanced over his shoulder. Spotted the two-twenty barrel-chested owner of Omen Tactical Group stalking across the gym, his reflection skipping along the mirrored walls.

"You know better than to taunt me."

Former Navy SEAL Master Chief Pike Auberon, now CEO of Omen, was notorious for yanking chains. "Just heard from Eclipse—we're hitting it tonight."

Toweling off, Range grabbed his shirt and hustled after him. "What changed?"

"Someone's mind," Pike grunted as he hiked up to the Command center on the second level.

Finally. After all the innocents this woman had trafficked, he'd end her despicable trade—at least here. It was a beginning.

Following him around a corner, Range nearly collided with a thick wall of muscle named Luther Landry.

The big Southern guy slapped his back. "See? Dreams do come true, Pretty Boy."

Shouldering away, Range veered into the operations hub of

the safehouse. Monitors and systems lined every table and hung from the ceilings. Screens mounted against badly papered walls were alive with various feeds from around the city. A long, rectangular table littered with tablets, laptops, and phones sat crowded by the half-dozen members of Omen.

"Okay, boys," said Dade Tycho as he clapped, as if this team needed any more enthusiasm. "OTG is officially OTG."

Laughter filtered around the room at the double entendre—Omen Tactical Group was officially On The Go.

"Took 'em long enough," Brick Archer groused from where he adjusted his ball cap, a Glock holstered to his thigh. "I mean, we couldn't do nothin' despite having our eyes on this chick for how long?"

Too long. Range stretched his neck as he scanned the latest intel logs and information streaming across the monitors.

"Listen up." Pike planted his hands on his belt. "Our objective is one Kasra Jazani. As many of you know, we've had eyes on this madam for a long while."

Screens around the room lit with an oval-faced woman. Green-brown eyes. Roughly early thirties. A complexion that indicated mixed heritage—not quite olive, yet definitely not Caucasian. She wore a teal hijab and knowing smile. Like she wasn't worried about getting taken down.

Dade gave a sexy whistle. "The hottie from Kandahari." The bad rhyme earned him both chuckles and smacks from the guys.

Range scowled. "This sick witch has been trafficking women and children up and down the Mideast Trench." The name given for the hole she'd buried too many innocents in with this disgusting business.

"So, wait—we're hitting the Roud Compound?" Luther's tone betrayed the ominous truth of that site.

"That is correct. Couldn't make this easy on you." Pike nodded. "And as we all know Roud is essentially a small, well-fortified and well-armed city. HUMINT determined this three-story structure"—he used a laser to point out a large, square building dominating the walled-in compound dotted with dozens of squats—"is where Jazani and her minions play office. You will infil at zero five hundred."

"Nearly dawn." Landry cocked his head in a nod. "Gutsy. Light hits and we could be exposed."

"Necessary," Range said. "Daytime puts us at risk and night is when they are infiltrated with buyers. We need as little interference and as few innocents onsite as possible."

Pike folded his arms. "You'll go in, locate Jazani, and exfil."

Landry grunted and scowled. "Are we putting sex buyers in the innocent category?"

"Right now, they don't matter." Range nodded to the screens where the woman sneered down at them. "*She* does. We take her no matter what."

"I wouldn't mind getting some of that," Tycho grinned.

Not trusting himself to speak, Range stared—hard—until the guy faltered.

"What?" Tycho motioned to the monitor. "Look at her. She's hot."

"She's *repulsive!* So are you, if you're okay with sex trafficking."

Tycho balked. "Never said that."

"Take a walk if you can't get your head out of your—"

"*Easy,*" Pike intervened, giving Range a pat on the shoulder. "Guys are just riding adrenaline, ready to get to work." He indicated to the screen, addressing the team again. "This man is her personal bodyguard, Razam Osuli. There's nobody she trusts more, so if you find him, likely you've found her or at least have a bead on her location. We don't want a body count, but we're also not leaving without her."

"Boss." Landry studied the map and satellite images of the compound. "Roud is looking heavily fortified … Like more than usual."

"Correct. SATINT has seen increased security measures and a bigger presence of well-trained security belonging to Taweel Abdul-Ghulam." Pike scratched his jaw. "The guy has invested millions in protecting his merchandise via security, sensors, tracking systems—you name it. There are at least a couple dozen well-armed guards inside."

"Maybe because of Pretty Boy's tête-à-tête with the Madam a few months back," suggested Tycho.

"Don't give him too much credit—he'll get a big head." Landry grinned.

Pike's expression never shifted. "This isn't anything you haven't tackled before."

Range had no doubt they could handle it.

Landry rubbed his hands together. "Need to hit the pit, lay out that compound, and figure out our infil and exfil. Do that till go-time"—he nodded—"we should be solid."

"Simple and fast," Tycho said with entirely too much bravado. "Get in, grab the lady, and get out. No complications."

Which meant there would be. And Range wasn't going to let cavalier attitudes jeopardize his chance to take her down this time. "Keep in mind that the madam is very skilled in CQC, so be ready."

"He's right," Pike said. "This woman is not the type of girl you'd take home to Mom for Sunday dinner. She's had to protect herself, the brothel, and those girls."

Teeth gritted, Range didn't like the way the chief portrayed her. "Don't think of her as a victim—that'd be a deadly mistake," he warned. "She works with and for Taweel Abdul-Ghulam. That should tell you something."

Turning, Pike nodded to one of the analysts, who sent the intel to their devices. "Metcalfe has lead on this op, so respect that. I've sent pictures of Osuli and the Madam to your devices." He glanced around the men and landed on Range. "Anything to add?"

"The Nigerians," Range said, then stood and flicked data to the screens. "These girls are Adesina and Ginika, both kidnapped from one of Cord Gatlin's safe-haven compounds in Nigeria. Watch for them. I promised my sister we'd keep an eye out."

"Your sister—now *there* is a—"

Range speared him with a look, arms maneuvering to his sides for a fight. "The priority"—he bit out—"is Jazani, but if we can find these girls, it'd give us a big lead in connecting the business to its source. It'll mean Nigeria is part of the same region and route as the Trench. That could aid in finding and cutting off the head of the dragon in this global ring."

"AKA Viper," Luther Landry muttered.

"Okay, Ladies," Pike said. "Head down to the pit and start familiarizing yourselves with the layout of the village to help us review contingencies."

Crammed into the narrow stairwell of the converted home, Range hustled down with one man who hadn't commented in the briefing.

Former Iraqi soldier and interpreter, Tariq Wadi had joined the U.S. Army, then earned his citizenship for his meritorious service. "This is good thing," he said. "This *business*"—his lip curled at the word—"of hers is dark stain on my country."

"On many countries."

"There was time these women would have been stoned or give one hundred lashes." Even with his broken English, he was still well-spoken. "Now, we free them. Help them."

Was the guy annoyed or pleased?

They slipped into the basement-like pit, which was noticeably cooler as it welcomed them into its musty embrace.

"Pretty Boy," Tycho called.

Irritated with him, Range noticed the guy had at least two meters, a scaled-down model of the village, and two operators between them.

Tycho had taken protective cover to avoid getting punched. Smart. "What's your beef with this chick anyway?"

Range gritted his teeth and chose not to entertain the idiot. The answer was obvious, and if Tycho didn't get that, he wasn't worth the breath wasted trying to explain it.

"Hey." Tycho closed a few feet. His pursed his lips, then closed a few more feet. "Pretty Boy …"

Keep coming, and I'll show you the pretty side of my fist.

Tycho bobbed his head. "I want you to know I wouldn't do that—you know, prostitutes." His expression seemed sincere. "It was a joke—but I shouldn't have said that. It was wrong."

Jokes about trafficking weren't jokes. They were indicators of bad mojo. "People who joke about the skin trade are the same ones buying favors."

Tycho's eyebrows shot to his hairline. "You—serious—that—" He patted Luther Landry's shoulder. "D'you hear what he's saying about me, man?"

Range stared at him, hard. "She's selling her own people, innocent girls—*children*—and you said you wanted some."

Palms up, Tycho lifted his eyebrows. "I was mouthing off. Got out of line." He held out a hand. "My apologies. Peace?"

Not hardly. He couldn't shake the one seven-year-old girl they'd found six months ago, one of Kasra Jazani's victims. The trigger that made him vow to end this woman. Wishing he could get away from that sight burned into his mind's eye, he turned to look out the window. Ran a hand over his face. Sick, dark … Horrific.

"Hey." Tycho patted Range's chest.

Range grabbed the guy's wrist with his left hand and yanked him into his personal space, jabbing his elbow into his throat and pinning him. Glared at the bulging eyes. "Stay out of my way."

"Hey!" Pike shoved them apart, hand landing on Range's shoulder.

Instinct and anger had Range clamping onto his friend's hand.

Pike's gray eyes nailed him. Brow furrowed and mouth tightened in warning.

Cocking his head, Range did his best to shed the need to crack skulls. Huffed a breath. "I'm good."

His buddy shoved in closer. "Are you?" he hissed, shouldering in. "Because this op can't go wrong. Eyes are watching us. We screw up, *we* are screwed."

Range balled his fists.

"You're throwing attitude around like smoke from a frag. It's blinding you to the fact we're all on the same side." Pike shouldered in. "Get it together or get on the next plane out."

CHAPTER TWO

Roud Village, Kandahar Province, Afghanistan

HER EVERY MOVE WAS MONITORED. From the second she drove back through the compound gate until this very moment as, arms piled with packages, she strode up into the main house. Every step tracked and logged. Every word recorded by some faceless entity miles from the compound. It was a wonder she had managed to put this together. Eighteen months of careful, meticulous planning, preparation, and maneuvering. Working around unexpected changes, like Taweel on an unscheduled visit and bringing in new girls.

And tonight, it would happen.

Tall, lanky Razam paced her down the long hall. "Did you get everything?"

"When did I last need your guidance in ensuring I shopped correctly?" She strode back to her office with the purchases.

"You know what the imam says." Razam was always so good at the pretense, but today, he wiped his hand over his mouth. Then down his shirt. Through his black, unruly hair.

"Mm, indeed I do." She thought of Alikhel in the market,

who had dared to challenge her, only to have her set him straight.

Razam leaned against the credenza, then straightened and paced. His nerves were going to boil over onto hers if she did not refocus his energy.

"How are the new girls settling?" She set her packages on the table in her office, then removed her hijab, taking in the air conditioning she had convinced Taweel would go a long way in keeping customers comfortable. "Have they eaten?" With her back to the door and mirror, where she knew a camera had been installed, she lifted her eyebrows in emphasis. "I would not want them to go hungry tonight."

"I will check on them."

"Oh," she said, motioning to the packages on her desk. "There are the last of the supplies needed for them. Please be sure each girl gets what they need." It was not, of course for the new girls. It was for all the girls. The last of what was necessary for tonight.

A smirk in his cheek, Razam nodded.

She wished she could reassure him, tell him things would be fine. Truth was, every second that brought them closer and closer to their very dangerous exit felt like a miracle. Years spent in this trade taught her mastery over facial expressions, body language, and words. But she could not deny the nerves rattling through her, since it would quite literally be her head if they were discovered. Months ago, she thought the plan ruined when Aqbari had been taken. But she, Fatina, and Razam adjusted and continued with the plan.

For that very reason, she sat at the desk and forced herself to review the ledgers, the appointment books, check email. She drew out the sweets she had purchased for herself—one last reward, since she knew not what would come once she entered the tunnels.

"Madam," Fatina appeared in the doorway, her face nearly white. Eyes wide and mouth ajar. "The gate. He's coming!"

"Who?"

"Taweel!"

Breath jammed in her throat, Kasra ignored the buzz of adrenaline and stood. "He was just here a few days ago." Surely he does not know. He could not. They had been so careful.

The walk into the halls seemed to take hours with the way her legs trembled, but here, she knew she could relax because there were no cameras.

Behind her, Fatina hissed, "He knows!"

Kasra turned into her dear friend and decoy. "No." She caught and squeezed her forearm. "Listen." When brown eyes met hers, she nodded. "Razam is in the cellar stuffing the backpacks. Get him out, make sure the door is shut and covered. Dust on the floor. Yes?"

Understanding, Fatina drew in a sharp breath and blurred away from her.

Taking a moment for courage, Kasra fixed her gaze not on the end of the hall that led to the foyer, but to her future. To what she was fighting for. Nobody else would help her. It was time to make freedom happen. For herself. For the others. No matter the cost.

What if he *does* know? What if he had hidden cameras in the cellar after all?

She faltered inwardly. Swallowed. No, she must remain strong. Shoulders straight, she raised her chin and strode to the front of the house, where three armored SUVs barreled to a stop.

As she watched through the open door, she swallowed. A metallic taste hit her tongue—fear. A flavor that had not filled her mouth in many months.

Taweel's bodyguard, Abdullah, flung open the door and stepped out, as did six other guards, checking the perimeter.

Accursed Taweel, always changing his routine to avoid predictability and attacks, emerged. Afternoon sunlight caught his thin hair that was slicked back as if he were some movie star. Aviator sunglasses added to his superior air, as well as a silk button-down shirt, slacks, and shiny black shoes that were even now coating with dust from the road. Strutting like a peacock, he gained the third step of the house and removed his sunglasses, gaze tracking over the foyer and stairs.

His glower struck her. "Where are the girls? Why are they not presented?"

Donning contrition like armor as always, Kasra followed him inside. "They are in Comportment and Etiquette with Hana. Since you were here not three days past and this visit unannounced, I thought they should continue with their le—"

His hand rose.

She saw it. Knew what he intended. Knew she could stop him. Level, if not kill, him. But she must not. For the girls and the many, many weapons trained on her around the compound itching to spill her blood. So, Kasra let the blow land.

It wracked across her cheek. Snapped her head back. She stumbled backward—partly to gain more distance. But he flew at her. Cuffed her throat and pinned her against the still-open door. *"Never* think you know better than me." His grip tightened and he bared his teeth. "Or I will gut you, Kasra. Am. I. Clear?"

You can try. Face tight, she nodded. Even managed to produce tears. Hands fisted, she told herself to remember … *Tonight.*

With a shove that smacked her head against the door, he stalked from her. "Where are the African girls?"

Kasra started. "The Niger"—she faltered, knowing *he* hated being corrected—"*new* ones?" *What was this? Why would he ask after those girls?* When his rage registered again, she lowered her gaze. "In class with Hana."

Razam manifested in the hall—dust on the knee of one pant leg, making Kasra tense. Pray it was not noticed.

Taweel's gaze locked on him. "Razam! Bring the African girls at once."

What was so special about the Nigerian girls that he would return for them? Mind racing, she could not help but notice he had not left the foyer. Usually, he would move into the parlor and have a drink, be attended by Fatina or one of the older girls.

Crying erupted and grew louder, the girls' cries growing piqued as they were delivered to the foyer.

This ... this is what Kasra hated. Dreaded. If they did not cease wailing, he would make sure they were quiet—or worse. He had no compunction against beating them. Or raping them. He didn't care. They were his property and they would submit.

Kasra stepped between his fury and the girls. "They are new. I have not had time to teach them—"

"Take them out."

Silenced, Kasra startled. Watched as Abdullah grabbed them by the arms and dragged them through the door. She fought the twitch to tell him to be careful or he'd bruise them. Taweel hated the girls bruised or injured for the clients.

If he was taking them to the SUV, then Taweel would not stay ...?

Mastering her poise, she hid her reaction. "Will they return? Their rooms—"

"No."

Heartbroken for the girls—at least here with her, they had a chance—she also felt hope that this monster before her would soon leave. But then ... he seemed to be hesitating. He always availed himself of the services of at least one girl—or her, though that had not happened in a year—while at Roud, and his desire to do that now seemed to war with some tight schedule.

"Shall I have your room prepared?" Kasra asked.

Nostrils flared, he pivoted to the door. "Do better next time or I will teach you a lesson."

"Of course." It was the only acceptable answer.

Kasra stared holes into his back as he stomped down the steps and climbed into the first vehicle again. She watched to the last possible moment as Fatina closed the door. Then through the lacy curtains monitored the exit of the vehicles. Waited as the gate opened, the SUVs pausing for the lumbering barrier. Held her breath as the leaches slipped through and the dark wood gate swung shut.

Kasra finally expelled that trapped breath. Strode past Razam. "Your slacks are dusty." Calm and composed, she walked to the kitchen, snagged a scone, and continued to her room. Set the scone on the dressing table, then slipped into the bathroom where she entered the shower, clothes and all. She slumped against the wall and fought the tears.

Such hope existed that she could help those girls. Hated that she had lost the chance to save the two Nigerian girls, who had been so sweet and clearly traumatized. She had seen it in their eyes. A look one cannot describe other than to call it haunted.

As dusk settled that evening, she did her best to stay distracted. Not think about the fact that Taweel would chop her into a hundred pieces if she failed. If they were caught. It was one thing to escape alone. Quite another to strip every source of his income here in the province. It would devastate his estate. He would cut her up into pieces and send one to every other brothel he owned as a warning. She knew because it is what he had done to Basima two years ago.

A knock interrupted her dark thoughts. "Come."

Fatina's oval face—a mirror of her own—appeared in the crack of the door. "Madam, the rats you suggested Razam deal with? He said you would want to see it."

It was time.

Allah, keep us safe.

Private Airstrip, Kandahar Province, Afghanistan

The armored vehicle whipped onto a private airstrip where a Blackhawk waited, engines warm and pilots in the cockpit ready. Range threw open the door of the armored SUV and hustled with OTG to the bird. He tucked in his comms piece as he sat crammed between Pike and Landry. Airborne two mikes later, he closed his eyes. Mentally walked the compound and the plan they'd developed in the pit. Thought of the woman who had passed girls—children!—off to older men. What kind of sick b—

"Two klicks," one of the pilots comm'd. "Going silent."

Adrenaline jacked, Range drew into himself. Thought to pray, but he'd been beyond that for a few years. Still, he hoped God appreciated what he was doing here, snatching innocents from the manicured nails of this vile woman. He recalled the verse written over the orphanage door where they'd found that girl. It'd seared into his brain, along with her body.

"Defend the poor and fatherless; do justice to the afflicted and needy. Deliver the poor and needy: free them from the hand of the wicked."

Right there in that village, mud and blood on his boots, he'd taken that Psalm to heart. Bled it. Fed it.

When the chopper hovered five feet off the ground, he hopped out. Took a knee, scanning the area down his M4. The open area and road lay awash in green from the night-vision goggles mounted to his helmet. Pulse amped, he was ready to do justice.

A pat to his shoulder indicated OTG had formed up behind him. Like a deadly viper, he snaked through the field. Along a wall where they hunch-ran up to the compound wall, still warm from the Kandahar sun.

OTG flanked the south door. Two and Four scurried in and placed plastique on the door over the lock and hinges, then backed aside.

Range turned away and clenched his eyes so he wasn't blinded by the blast.

Boom!

The concussion thumped his back, bringing him around, weapon up. Knowing they had the advantage of surprise, he slid through the smoke and dust. Through the door and down into the tunnel that banked to his nine, setting bathed in the green glow of his NVGs.

"Contact rear!" Luther announced amid the crackle of gunfire as he brought up the tail of their insertion.

Aiming toward the rear entrance of the building, Range hurried forward, scanning shadow and every juncture between buildings. They scurried up to the building. Even as he steadied himself, he nodded to Pike and Brick flanking the door. Stepped back, and drove his heel into it. The flimsy barrier flipped backward.

As his boot landed, he spotted a weapon swing around a corner. "Contact, hall." He squeezed off two rounds. A body slid into his path. "Target down." He moved in, ready—so ready—to get this woman. He stepped over the body and aimed for the office.

"OTG, you have eight local fighters headed your way," sniper Crow Rawlins said from his nest on a rooftop." A resonant crack punctuated his warning, evidence he'd taken a shot. "Make that seven." *Crack.* "Six."

Huffing, heart thumping, Range rounded the corner. He could feel it. So close. A little more and she'd be done.

And yet ... something felt ... off. He treaded quietly down the hall, snapping his weapon at one room—empty. "Clear." Moved on. Kitchen, empty.

A vibration started at the back of his skull. Told him to pay attention. He hesitated, glancing back down the direction he'd come. Found himself facing Landry.

The big guy cocked his head. "What?"

He hadn't gone the wrong way, had he? Frowning, he scanned the passage. Glanced to the ceiling, listening. No creaking. No voices. That was it—nobody was here. It was quiet. Entirely too quiet for a house full of girls. "Something's wrong." He keyed his mic. "OTG, sit-rep."

"One here," Pike responded. "Negative one HVT."

"Same for Three," Brick comm'd. And on down the line.

"Where are they?" Range growled, shoving his way back toward front, keying his comm again to talk to Crow. "Three, do you have eyes on anyone?"

"Negative, One. We have—" He cursed. "OTG, you have a problem. Car pulled up south of your infil point. Six … seven women just came out of the ground and got in a vehicle."

"Tunnels!" Fury ignited in Range's gut as he pitched himself back out of the house. "OTG, converge on the south side. Stop them at all costs. Go go go!"

"Three," Pike comm'd. "Keep the guards busy and pinned down on that side of the compound."

"Good copy," Crow reported.

Perfect. While they chased Jazani, at least the guards wouldn't interfere. Range slid out into the open, sweeping left and alleys as he backtracked to the south door. Pike was already there, doing a quick look-see, then moved into the open.

Range stalked to his side. "Anything?" he asked, probing the area again.

"Nothing," Pike growled, shaking his head. "Freakin' noth—"

A shadow moved beneath a small copse of trees. Then another.

"There!" Range snapped his weapon there. "Two o'clock, beneath the trees." Fast-walking, weapon tucked to his shoulder, he advanced quickly, sights trained on the emerging figures. He signaled Tycho and Landry up from the rear and over to the other side. Hurrying toward the escaping persons, he hoped he hadn't missed Jazani.

A man turned to help others up out of the ground. A gun in hand.

"Weapon!" Range recognized Jazani's bodyguard as the gunman. "Osuli, drop it!"

The man jerked, twitched as if to run, then motioned whoever was in the tunnel to go back.

Erasing the last half-dozen paces, Range shouted in Pashto, "Razam Osuli, drop the gun! On your knees."

The Afghan man let the weapon tumble to the ground.

As Range kicked it out of reach, Landry drove a knee into the man's back—forcing him to eat grass—and pinned him in place but did not impede oxygen flow.

"Where's Kasra Jazani?" Range demanded, looking to Pike, who shouted at someone in the tunnel. "Where is she, Osuli? Where's Kasra?"

Hands over his head, the man didn't move. Didn't answer.

"He won't give her up," Pike muttered as he dragged two girls from the tunnel.

"Squirters! Headed east!" Brick shouted as he gave chase, followed by Tariq.

Turning to eyeball the action, Range spotted the squirters emerging from tunnels at the gate door. Dark hair. "Jazani," he whispered.

"Go," Pike barked, apparently having seen the same thing. "Don't let her escape."

"Landry, on me!" Weapon in hand, Range sprinted back into the compound. Wove left, down the alley. Past one building. This was getting crazy tight with time, but he wasn't leaving or letting her escape.

C'mon, c'mon. Where was she? Let me do justice ...

Ahead, a shape vanished back into the building where they'd started this game. He sprinted after her.

Dark hair, hijab sliding free as she leapt for the door.

"Stop!" He fired, hoping to tag her leg. It splintered the door. He moved after her, heartrate jacked. Saw shadows shifting at the far end of the hall. "Target contact. Sector Blue Two. Moving to second level." As he reached the door, he slowed. Felt the breath of Death skate down his neck. Braced, then did a quick look—

Crack!

Splinters spat at his face.

Range jerked back with a curse. Knew Death had a thing for him. "Contact, last door."

From another juncture came Landry, who negotiated the stairs with him. Nodded.

Holding up three fingers, Range started the countdown: three ... two ...

Tink-tink. Tink. Thunk.

"Grenade!" Range pitched himself away from the explosive. He'd no sooner dived for cover than the blast punched his spine. Felt fiery heat scrape the back of his legs and neck. The concussion rang his bell and sucked out his hearing. He shook his head. Shrugged it off. Knew she'd come on its heels. As he whipped over, he felt the air stir.

Jazani.

He snapped out a hand. Met bone, the impact vibrating down his forearm, and flipped her.

She thudded onto the floor. Not willing to lose this target, he grabbed through the haze at the dark blur. Found a leg. Clamped onto it.

A grunt issued from the woman.

He saw her heel a second too late. It connected with his jaw. Whipped his head backward. But he had the wherewithal to know if he lost his grip, he'd lose her. She knew this compound and no doubt they had hidey holes. And fighters.

With a growl, he hoisted himself toward her at the same time he yanked her leg to himself. They collided in the chaos. Her limbs flailed as he anchored her with his own body, positioning himself to lock her legs in his own and coldcock her as he had two months ago when he'd come looking for Aqbari.

She did her best to scissor her legs to free herself.

But he'd been prepared after their last CQC.

Her fist found his nose.

Pain wracking his skull, he tasted the blood, but didn't care.

A burst of shots erupted nearby.

"Keep still or the next one will be in your head," Landry shouted in Pashto.

The madam ignored it. Kept fighting.

As you wish ...

Range had her pinned and reared back with his Glock.

"Okay," she breathed. Chest rising and falling raggedly, she went still, hair askew, eyes wide. "Okay."

Surprised she had surrendered, he frowned down at the woman.

Her lip was split at the corner. Cheeks flushed from the sparring. A knot rose on her temple.

Pike and Landry moved in, grabbing her hands. Flipping her over.

Range shifted back onto his haunches as the men secured her. Put a sack over her head. Propped against the wall, he wiped his nose on his sleeve, ticked. Found his feet as they dragged her onto hers. Funny, he'd expected a harder fight. Not surrender as easily. Or at all.

Between the two special operators, the madam seemed unusually small.

Range started for the rear door again. Glanced at Landry and Archer. They had a handful of females on their knees under a tree. He angled to the side, catching an exchange of glances between Osuli and two women hugging each other.

"OTG," Eclipse said, "you have two vehicles inbound with at least twenty fighters. Recommend immediate exfil."

"Good copy," Pike replied, shaking his head. "Base, we are exfil-ing now and heavy six packages."

CHAPTER THREE

CIA Safehouse, Kandahar Province, Afghanistan

"SOMETHING EATING YOU?"

Arms folded as he propped against the wall outside the interview room, Range trained his focus on the woman sitting on the other side of the one-way glass. "She gave up too easy."

Pike joined him. "Who cares as long as we have her, and now a couple dozen women and children freed of her."

Though Range nodded, it still didn't add up.

"What?"

"Something's not right." He peeled off the wall and faced the onetime master chief. "You've seen it—these women are terrified to flee. Yet we infiltrated a heavily fortified compound and find them ... what? Escaping." He shook his head. "Doesn't add up."

Pike studied him for a long second.

"I'm not overthinking it."

"It's what you do best." Laughing, he slapped Range's shoulder. "Relax. We got them—her. She's there and she's not going anywhere."

Hijab back in place, Jazani kept her gaze down, her mouth closed as she sat alone in the interview room.

"We've got people working to get the girls to safe havens until they can be reunited with their families," Pike said. "Meantime, we'll get the madam talking once we let her sweat it out a while. Find out who's who. Make some connections to the supply chain."

Ranged wanted to reach through the glass and strangle her. "Then burn her at the stake."

Pike snickered. "Clearly, the people who said you were the nice Metcalfe were wrong."

"Being nice doesn't get results." Pushing off the wall, Range slid his hands onto his tac belt. "How much longer? I could go in there—"

"Relax, Landry's bringing an interpreter."

Range frowned, knowing they wouldn't bring in just anyone. "Why aren't you using analysts?" And he'd thought he'd read something about the madam being bilingual or multilingual.

"Out on another op," he said.

"Does it seem strange to you that the Madam of Kandahar, responsible for trafficking dozens, if not hundreds, across the province, doesn't speak English?"

"Yep." Pike was unfazed. "There's a local one we've used a few times at the base. She's here—rounded up with the others."

"Wait—she's a—one of *hers*?" Range stabbed a finger at the glass. "And you trust her to talk to the madam?"

"We've used Malala before."

Range straightened, scowling. "Do what? How could you trust her? Why would y—" The explanation formed before him.

Pike grinned. "See? There's that reason I wanted you with Omen."

Again eying the woman, he considered the chief's play. "You really think she'll tell the interpreter something?"

"Counting on it."

"And you know Pashto, too."

"Pretty boy, and smarts?" Pike clicked his tongue. "Definitely Omen material."

Range studied the woman who still seemed shorter than he remembered. Then again, they hadn't been standing side by side. She'd been a flurry of strikes and kicks that had kept him on his toes—and on his butt a couple of times.

Scratching his jaw, Pike eyed her. "Gotta admit, she's impressive. I mean, look at her—pretty face, got those ninja skills she used on you"—he made a few corny knife-hand strikes—"and she runs that whole compound. Incredible, all things considered."

"All things considered, she's the spawn of Satan." Fed up with people only seeing her beauty, Range glanced out the door. "How's Brick doing with Osuli?"

"Nothing."

"Hey, Boss," Luther said, guiding a woman into the room. "Terp's here."

Pike nodded, his expression suddenly different. "*As-Salaam alaikum*, Malala."

Range shifted around, stunned at the women before him. Something about her ricocheted through his mind. *It's her!*

Thick, dark hair framed an olive face with full pink lips and—*brown* eyes. She had brown eyes. But Jazani had hazel eyes—like the woman in the room. The likeness between the two was crazy.

"*Wa-alaikum salaam.*" Malala smiled. Cheeks pinked, she inclined her head. "With so perfect a greeting, I wonder why you would seek my help."

"No hijab," Range noted.

Her brown eyes hit his. "Since the American military has left, the Taliban has risen back to power and now insist I must cover myself because Muslim men cannot control themselves."

She seemed amused as she met his gaze. "Must I wear one here, too?"

Luther barked a laugh and slapped Range's chest. "Ouch, Pretty Boy."

"What happened to your cheek?" Range wondered if she'd gotten that sparring like Jazani.

"Sometimes," Malala said quietly, "what we are made to do in Roud comes with … abuse."

Landry gave him a disgusted look for asking the question.

"Malala," Pike said as he motioned her out of the room. "You know her, yes?"

The woman glanced at the interview room. "Of course. She is Madam."

Pike shared a glance with Range, then refocused on the terp. "We need help translating, and you've done that before. Can we trust you to translate for us?" He inclined his head. "Would it be too difficult, considering her position?"

"No … I would be glad to help. What she has done …" She hunched her shoulders.

Range's left eye twitched as she went with Landry into the interrogation room. He returned to the glass and tucked his hands under his armpits, watching Jazani as the door opened. No reaction. She kept her gaze down.

Pike joined him as Landry positioned himself with his back to the window, forcing the terp into the side chair. "Miss Jazani, you can call me Luther. This is our interpreter, Malala."

The Madam kept her chin tucked.

"Is there anything you would like to volunteer?"

Malala repeated the question in Pashto.

No response.

"We can help you, arrange for possible immunity if you can tell us who you were working for, and who his boss is."

Again, Malala relayed the words. Again, no response.

"Listen," Landry said, his broad shoulders leaned forward,

elbows finding the table. "We know the john who runs Roud isn't kind to the girls. Malala's face is proof."

For the first time, Jazani's gaze lifted. Concern etched itself into her expression as she looked at Malala, then washed away. Head went back down.

"You realize, Kasra," Landry went on, "that if you do not help us, we will have no choice but to turn you over to the authorities. You will be prosecuted to the fullest extent for the sex crimes committed under your forced direction."

Still nothing.

Landry laid out a folder. "What about this truck and the girls who went to it? Are they are in trouble?"

Even before the interpreter finished, the madam's gaze flicked to the photo.

"Interesting," Pike muttered from beside him.

The interview went on for another couple of hours in which Range had settled against the wall again, watching.

"Can you tell me if they are in trouble, Kasra?" Landry leaned in. "If they are, we can help. But we can't do that unless you talk to us."

Her gaze stayed on the image that showed a truck with girls climbing into it. It seemed her finger itched.

"That's important to her," Range said. "And the interpreter's busted cheek."

Pike grunted. "Like she almost cared."

"Don't read into it. Battered face doesn't sell."

Malala bent forward and spoke in their language, "It's okay to tell them. They can help."

Tentative eyes rose to the terp's. Locked. Then she curled a lip. "I do not need you to tell me what to say. They will use you like every other man!"

"Okay," Luther said, touching the terp's shoulder. "That's enough for today."

Malala eased back, but there was not concern or even anger

in her eyes. There was ... something else.

As Luther and the terp exited, Pike glanced at Range. "Thoughts?"

"I'm going to walk the terp back to the others."

Pike struck out a hand, catching his arm. "Malala? But nothing was said ..."

"Not verbally."

His mere presence jammed her heart against her chest. She recognized him and when the man first brought her to Fatina, was certain he had recognized her as well. He had stared hard into her eyes—but thankfully the contacts had worked. While he may not remember her, she recalled too well fighting this man with the fierce anger and beautiful eyes when he had taken Aqbari. Where was the traitor now?

As he walked her down a long alley toward the building where she and the others were being kept in a large, well-guarded warehouse, he kept his arms at his side. Hand always near that thigh-holstered pistol.

She doubted she could reach it if needed.

"What do you think?" His voice had a nice sound to it, but then, even knives had a pretty song when sharpened.

Thankfully, Fatina had been well-trained as a decoy and would hold the line as long as possible. Kasra had tried to let her friend know it was okay to give them some information, and had done so in a manner that seemed to draw no attention. Yet, Fatina remained quiet. "She will not say much."

He did not respond, though she could tell he was thinking deeply.

Long had she prided herself on being able to read people, and this man had skills that could dismantle everything she had worked for, her entire plan to free the girls. Already he had interrupted it, and she despised him for it. Every second in this place made it more likely that Taweel would learn they had been taken by the Americans. He would come, and she would be murdered. Because of this man.

"You're angry."

Startled that he so accurately read her, she looked up—straight into those blue eyes. Her nerves rattled and caused her breath to struggle up her throat. She focused on the gate to the walled-in area where she and the others were allowed to get fresh air and the children to play, shaded beneath a large canopy that likely prohibited satellites from seeing into the yard. As for his statement, it would be better, easier, to own the feeling than keep track of another lie.

"I am," she finally conceded. She slowed and glanced back in the direction they'd come, searching for some plausible justification to give him.

He reached out and caught her arm, directing her back toward the enclosure, perhaps mistaking her intent as one to return to the other building, or worse, to flee.

Kasra would use his concerns. "She ... she sits there in silence as if she has all the time in the world, yet"—she slid her gaze to those beyond the iron gate that barred the others from leaving and her from entering—"if they learn we are here, the punishment ..."

Allah, have mercy on us!

"Won't be pretty."

She sniffed and shook her head. How much should she betray? "This life ... our lives," she corrected, "is not pretty. Not one that any of us chose."

"Can't fathom your own people abusing you so horribly."

"Can you not?" she challenged, knowing this was not a problem isolated to one people, but to the entirety of the human race. "Roud was not frequented by only Afghans ..."

Something dark slid through his gaze. "Americans went to Roud."

The way he said that somehow embarrassed her.

"Despicable."

Did he mean her, or the men …?

With a terse expression, he nodded, understanding parked on his furrowed brow. "I have a feeling not much gets past you."

He had no idea.

"Since you live there, surely you've seen the boss come and go … I mean, clearly you know Americans are coming, so you see a lot. And you're smart."

Flattery. Designed to ply words from one he deemed innocent. It should not surprise that he would work her for information as well. "I see much."

Head tilted to the side, he paused in their trek. "Can you give us a name?" He indicated back to the other building where Fatina was held in isolation. "Help us put her and her boss away. For good. Shut down Roud."

Only a fool would believe that could happen. If not Roud here in Kandahar Province, then Roud elsewhere. Taweel would simply relocate and the girls would still be forced to give their bodies to men. That had been why she worked for a year to put together an escape that should have worked. *Would* have worked. Had it not been for this man.

Anger sprouted through her chest. And she wondered why—it was an ineffective emotion. Only served to muddle the mind.

"Fatina," he said, inching nearer and lower his gaze to hers, "use that anger and turn it against these people who have so horribly abused you. Help us help you."

Smooth, masterful words. "It is dangerous …" Hope. This conversation. The Americans. "If we are returned …"

"That won't happen."

He meant well. And merciful goodness how she wanted to believe him. A decade spent trapped in this world proved no one could fulfill a promise like that. But the way he watched, the intensity in his beautiful eyes, told her this man would not easily give up. That, at least, they had in common.

Regardless, she must feed him something to turn that hunger for justice in another direction. "Taweel—"

Fool! What had she done, speaking that name!? It had been her intent *not* to mention him. If it was learned she had given them his name—

He nodded, a smirk sliding into his handsome features. "Good."

It dawned on her that the name had not surprised him. "You know him?"

Another nod.

So perhaps it was not so bad as she had anticipated. Still ... she must be more careful. Kasra hugged herself, trying to look demure. Insecure. "What does your boss think?" she asked, and when he frowned, she clarified. "About Madam?"

After a sidelong glance, he squinted out at the paved parking lot in the center of the block. "We need her to talk."

"Your boss is ..." She tried to leave an opening for him to fill in the name, but he did not. "He knew of Taweel. Has he ... Is there proof?"

Was it possible they *could* take him down for good?

Curse you, Kasra! You know better!

"Is he the one who did this?" His fingers reached toward her cheek and lower lip.

Even as her stomach fluttered, she batted away his hand. Then started at her bold move and tucked her chin. How did she keep making so many mistakes with this man? Batting his hand away was not the action of a girl who had been trafficked, but of one who was in control. She stared at the dirty road, yet could sense his discerning gaze on her.

He was dangerous. Far too dangerous for her to remain here.

"I should return to the others."

But he angled his head, reaching for her shoulder, but stopping. "Hey. Nobody is going to hurt you here …"

Relief swarmed her—not at the empty words, but that he had not realized her mistakes. Kasra reminded herself that, to him, she was not the jaded madam; she was an innocent girl. "You cannot promise that. Nobody can." With that, she turned toward the gate where an armed soldier stood guard.

He didn't open it.

The soldier glanced to the man who had escorted her back. A man she had heard the boss call Pretty Boy. Needing to be freed of his presence, she looked back as well, putting as much pleading into her gaze.

He jutted his jaw to the gate, and the guard swung open.

Kasra hurried in, not surprised to see Razam striding toward her. Pretty Boy was too keen, too perceptive. With the slightest shake of her head to warn off her bodyguard, she went in a different direction. Spied little Iamar and lifted her into her arms. Surprising how good it felt to hug her, to restrain her need to pace or panic.

"R'augh!"

The shout drew her around. Shock pinned Kasra to her spot at the sight of Razam fighting with Pretty Boy. The confrontation was fierce, a flurry of fists and moves. But the blond, blue-eyed operator was a blur of rage, and quickly gained the upper hand. Gripped Razam by the shirt. Drew him up. Slammed him against the concrete wall, his arm still well in the man's grasp, eliciting a howl from Razam.

"Don't move," the American growled, "or you'll have an extra hole in your head."

"No!" Kasra started forward, even as those words registered. As the weapons drawn on Razam stilled her.

Two men burst into the yard from the other building. Luther, who had been in the interview room, and the one they called Chief—their boss.

"Range," the chief shouted. "Stand down!"

Arms hooked beneath his, they hauled him backward. Face red, eyes ablaze, he scrambled at Razam, who slid down against the wall, shaking. Bleeding.

Her gaze connected with his—*what they called him, Rage, seemed fitting*—and then wandered to her friend. She hurried to Razam's side and squatted next to him. "What did you do?" she hissed as the chief all but pushed Rage through the gate. She helped him on his feet.

Blood sliding from his busted lip and quickly swelling eye, Razam huffed. "I saw him *touch* you, and—"

"You fool!" She peered through the bars of the iron gate. Across the way. Saw Rage stalking away from the chief, but then his gaze skidded to hers. And he slowed. Stilled. Frowned.

Of all the men for Razam to pick a fight with, it had to be with the one man who could figure out her secret and steal it from the cage in which she'd locked it.

CHAPTER
FOUR

CIA Safehouse, Kandahar Province, Afghanistan

NOTHING TORMENTED HIM LIKE SLEEP. Or the lack thereof.

Of course, this would be where Mom told him he wouldn't have sleep problems if he'd read his Bible.

Dragging himself off the vinyl mattress, Range groaned. Sat, elbows on his knees, as he roughed a hand over his face and yawned. He stared at the concrete floor, frustrated he couldn't connect the dots and get some shut-eye. Hated this—the pieces were right there, lurking in the shadows of his mind.

Shoving to his feet, he snagged his shirt. Headed across the courtyard. Punched in his code to the main building, and threaded his way to the gym. He flipped the switch, throwing light across the workout equipment. Most places he'd been deployed to and ships he'd been on had workout rooms that were all dingy and smelly. Not this one. At least the CIA had done one thing right here.

After stretching, Range spent fifteen minutes jump-roping, then moved to the pull-up bar and did twenty reps. Then a variety of push-ups and planks to build his strength. Beat his body into submission, since his mind seemed unwilling to submit and surrender whatever truth it held hostage. He wasn't one to give up easily. Never had been. Especially when he was right.

And he was—something was off with the madam. Or the interrogation. Maybe they just weren't asking the right questions.

He prepped a stack of 450-lbs on the bench-press bar and secured them, his thoughts flicking back to the terp and her brown eyes. Laying back, he thought about the way that guy in the yard had come at him. Punched him—not the worst he'd taken one from, but no featherweight either. After a quick confrontation, he'd subdued the guy, flatting him against the concrete block wall. Drove his fist into his face.

Didn't make sense for the guy to sit in lock-up all day then suddenly fly at Range.

Unless there was something between him and the interpreter. Likely possibility. She was attractive, intelligent ... Men here had a sense of honor that was quickly vanishing back home. Had to admire the guy if he was defending her. Respected it. Couldn't blame him either. She seemed a caring, compassionate woman. Stepping in to help.

Yet ... hadn't there been a strangeness between her and the madam in that interview room? Almost like the madam felt bad for Malala's injuries. Not something he'd expected, since the girl was one of her captives. The seeming concern, he guessed, could be attributed to the madam wanting her property undamaged.

Settling back against the vinyl bench, he adjusted his spine and lifted. Grunted through a handful of reps. Recalled the way she'd watched him after he'd subdued the guy. Nah, it wasn't the way she'd watched him—though, maybe in some way it was, but more than that ... The way the *others* in the yard had held back. Watched her. Eyes shocked. As if it'd been something they'd never seen before.

His arms trembled as he tried to lift the bar. With a few staccato breaths, he readied to exert his strength and land the bar in the braces. But it didn't land there. The left side missed. Canted.

"Whoa!" Pike was there, catching it. "You idiot—why don't you have a spotter?"

Relieved as the bar clanged in the brace, Range pried himself up. Grabbed his sweat rag and wiped his face. "That'd defeat the purpose."

The chief glowered. "Of?"

"Working out alone."

"Something bugging you?"

Range sniffed. "Yeah." He shrugged. "This whole thing."

"Something's missing."

"Yeah …" Range's gaze bounced around the gym. "I guess. Not sure what. Something's definitely off, though." Noting Pike wore his tac shirt and pants, Range squinted up at him. "You need something?"

With a huff, the chief yanked his head toward the door. "Come on. Need to show you something."

Range stood to follow, then got a whiff of himself. "Give me five to shower."

"Make it ten. Your stink led me right to you." Pike grinned and stalked out.

After a quick shower and change, Range headed upstairs. There were always a couple of analysts working round-the-clock to monitor intel, security detail walking the U-shaped buildings and courtyard, and at least one watching the security cameras.

This morning, the latter was Luther Landry. "Kinda early for you, isn't it, Pretty Boy?"

Range banked toward the aroma of strong coffee that filled the mostly quiet Command center. "What've we got?" Taking his first slurp, he angled toward Pike.

The smattering of silver along his temples and threaded

through his tight crop were the only signs that Pike Auberon had hit his forties. Like him, most in the special ops community had more than their fair share of gray hair and heartburn. But that was the extent of the chief's age markers. Fit, trim, and sharp-witted, he had developed his own team that earned the respect, not the derision, of the U.S. government and military. The fact that the CIA worked so closely with Omen spoke of that long-standing respect.

"Casey there"—Pike jutted his jaw toward a plain female analyst with straight blonde hair tied into a tight bun at the base of her neck—"has been monitoring Roud."

"In case they come looking," Range muttered, one arm over his chest, the other propping up the coffee mug. "Knew extracting her would tick them off."

"And it has," Casey said. "It's been twelve hours and there are already more vehicles in that village and compound than we've tracked in weeks."

Range smirked. "Good."

The chief snapped a gaze to him. "Good?"

"Tick them off, they want to act now." He shrugged. "They make mistakes."

"They're gearing up to make the kind of mistakes we can't come back from."

Now Range hesitated.

"Tell him, Casey."

"So far, we have identified several AK47s—"

"They had those when we hit it."

"—and about four RPGs, and three technicals, specifically trucks with RPKs mounted on the back."

Okay, that was a lot of firepower. Too much for a search. This was an attack party. He frowned. "They can't know where the women are …" Unless— "Freak." He glanced at the chief. "Trackers."

"Our best guess, too," Pike said with a nod. "Crow is down

there now, running the scanners over them and will neutralize any tracking devices." He moved to a monitor on the right. "Wanted you to see this."

Range shifted to eyeball the screen.

"Video during the night in the bunkroom."

The imaging turned the sleeping forms into faint blue ghosts. The nine members they'd brought in slept soundly … save one male figure that moved through the dark room and knelt beside a bed.

"That's the guy who tried to pound your nose into your skull sneaking over to talk with the interpreter." Pike jutted his jaw again. "But watch."

The woman wrapped the blanket around her shoulders and the two moved to a corner … right below the eye of the camera. "Casey, the other one." The screen flickered to life with the view of another camera. "She knew there was a camera there, but hadn't spotted the one in the A/C vent."

Range grunted.

Luther joined them. "Only person who searches for cameras in rooms is one who's guilty."

"Or one who has had to live with them." Range watched, and despite no sound, it wasn't hard to figure out there was an argument.

"You're defending her?"

"Stating facts," he countered, left cheek twitching as he took in the body language on the screen. Watching as the woman maneuvered her way out of the corner in which she'd been backed. "Do we know the relationship between these two?"

"Negative," Pike said. "We believe he's the madam's bodyguard, but no connection or relation to the interpreter."

"There's a connection," Range countered. "That's too intimate of a fight to not have one."

"Not our concern," Pike said. "We need actionable intel from Jazani. I'm already getting heat from higher-ups."

Scowling, Range straightened. "We just brought her in!"

"And she's a hot target—you knew that. Time is limited."

"Then yank her back into the tank and apply pressure."

Pike grinned. "Already happening. Started at the top of the hour."

Before he went through more hours of watching her evade questions, he had one of his own. "Hey, Case." He angled toward the CIA operations officer. "Can you send me the package you have on the HVT?"

She pursed her lips. "Sure."

"And the interrogation video?"

"It'll cost ya," she flirted.

He worked what little of the Metcalfe charm he had and winked. "My treat—your choice ... of any frozen dinners in the breakroom." Her laughter followed him down the stairs even as two chirps hit his device, indicating she'd already made good on her end of the bargain. Making his way down the hall, he felt his phone buzz and answered. "Yeah." He saw Crow bringing the interpreter across the yard.

"Found those girls yet?"

Jaw tight, Range angled to the side, regretting that Stone had given Canyon his number. "I would've called if I had."

"Willow asked me to check."

He huffed.

"Keep me posted."

That's what he'd promised to do after the interdiction in the Canary Islands.

"Mom wants you to call."

That was low even for Canyon.

"Thought you should know Stone's going to be a dad again." What was Canyon doing? Trying to rub it in his face that Range was the black sheep of the family? "I wouldn't be surprised if Willow is a mom soon, too." Road noise filled the connection. "You're probably wondering why I haven't hung up yet."

"Always were smart." He clamped his mouth, afraid to say more.

"We haven't heard from Brooke."

"Nothing new." She was worse than Range at keeping in touch with family.

"We're not sure about that. Things were strange with her—Cord said she showed up in Nigeria, and she's gone silent since." Canyon huffed. "Look, one last thing. Cord's doing all this trafficking work as you know. Got wind from Pike about what's happening there. Just wanted to say … Range, I know you got an iceberg-sized chip on your shoulder, so you won't want to hear this—but what you're dealing with, *who* you're dealing with … you have an opportunity to be the difference … or the destruction in her life."

What the heck was Pike doing talking about his mission with Canyon?

"I saw that real clear about a year in with Dani after her captivity."

Range exhaled sharply. Just the sound of Canyon's voice pitched him back to that godforsaken year. To the rescue of Dani from that yacht. To the powerful hope that God had put her in his path to be *his,* not Midas's. Never had Range wanted a family as badly as he'd wanted it with her. But Canyon …

"Tread carefully, little brother."

He hadn't needed Canyon's advice or input in a decade. Didn't need it now. Besides, his brother had no idea what he was talking about. Range wasn't trying to make a difference in her life but in the lives of her victims.

"I can feel that cold shoulder all the way across the Atlantic. Stay safe, brother." The call ended.

Range pivoted and threw a fist into the wall. Heard a distinctive crack and cursed the pain that spiked across his hand and wrist.

Dang, he brought out the worse in Range.

"Are you okay, Rage?"

Startled at the soft voice, he shifted to the side. Saw the interpreter standing there, Pike just outside the door, talking with Landry. Had she called him Rage? He must've misheard.

"Fine." He shook out his hand and strode toward her. "Do you need coffee or something before getting started?"

"Anything to get my attention off you?" Her expression was amused.

Range faltered. Couldn't believe she'd be that direct. "Excuse me?"

She inclined her head. "Coffee would be nice. Usually, I stay with tea, but"—her gaze hit the door to the interview room—"today feels like it needs more." Her head came to his shoulder, a notable size difference, though he knew better than to expect weakness.

"Agreed." *Not a good sign when Canyon calls before sun-up.* "What do you take in it? Creamer? Sugar?"

"Nothing."

Why did that make him proud? "Done." Except he shouldn't leave her until Pike returned. "D'you sleep okay?"

Brown eyes widened, his question taking her off-guard it seemed. "Honestly, no."

"Not surprised—the bunks weren't made for comfort."

Her eyebrow arched. "And did you?"

"Not in a decade," he laughed, but then sobered. "I would've thought not having to worry about being ... abused, you might have slept easier."

"It will take more than one night to erase that fear."

Range felt like a heel. He donned some contrition. "Of course. Sorry."

"Please do not. You are neither the cause nor can you alter what has happened."

"But it's an evil I want eradicated, for no one to ever again endure it."

Keen eyes assessed him. "That sounds like a wound deeper than just your encounter with Roud." Her words thudded straight through that ballistic-grade reinforced steel barrier he'd erected around his heart.

He found himself staring into warm, caring eyes.

She stepped nearer. "I would ask—please get us out of here."

He drew up sharp and scowled. Was she working him? *Is that what this was?*

"I do not mean from your people, but out of this place." Her words were soft and lilting. "If it is learned where we are, he will come for the girls—us."

They'd already seen evidence of preparation to do exactly that. "Taweel."

She inclined her head. "And if he takes them back, they will be brutalized."

"They."

Something twitched in her cheek, a schism of worry. "Us. All of us."

"The best thing you can do is help us get her to talk. That is what's keeping you and the others here." It wasn't wholly true. Their CIA liaison was neck-deep in arrangements to move everyone to a safe location far from Taweel's grasp. But it took time. Still, he could use her anxiety to benefit everyone.

"Malala?"

They both flinched at Pike's voice, and she offered Range a smile as she stepped around him. He shifted and spotted Landry stepping out of the interview room, where he'd anchored the ankle bracelets to the floor of the Madam, who had been forced into a plain brown dress. No shoes. Anything to make her as miserable as possible so she'd cooperate.

"What are you doing?" the interpreter snapped. "You should not be alone with a woman!"

Surprised at her outrage, Range angled in. Caught her shoulder. "Hey, easy. It's his job."

Her expression convulsed and contrition once more slid into her features. "Forgive me. I ... we must protect each other—women. You understand, yes?"

He did. But it seemed ... more.

Like the eruption of relief in the madam's eyes when she saw Malala.

Fatina was wearing down, and in turn, it was wearing down Kasra, mostly her patience. Not even twenty-four hours had passed and already her decoy seemed willing to surrender. They could not let their ruse fall so soon. Just a little more time. They had endured longer the time Taweel sought to rout who had been an accomplice in injuring one of the clients who had come. The man had beaten a girl unconscious, so Razam had repaid the favor. And every girl held the secret, but ultimately, Kasra had paid the price, since she had been in charge.

It was so very hard to keep up the pretense while sitting across from her sweet decoy. To not speak out, urge Fatina to be stronger. Her weakness would betray them. That or Razam's impatience and impudence—first he attacked Rage, then last night she had to force him into the corner to hide from the camera. He was so angry that they were still here, that she was not getting them out of there. It had taken her last ounce of civility to point out things he should have seen, but his distress over his sister's unknown location—she had been in the second group who escaped—and their predicament at being in American hands had strangled common sense.

"How long have you been at the compound?"

The change in the direction of the questioning caught her off-guard. But Kasra scrambled and presented the question to Fatina.

"*Thamani sanawat.*"

Kasra faltered at the wrong answer. Not eight years—it had been nine. Silently she debated: should she provide the incorrect number Fatina had spoken, or correct it and pray no one noticed? The latter was too risky—most elite soldiers like these men knew the language. Which would beg the question of their use of an interpreter. Was it possible none here knew Pashto?

No. She would not believe it. Nothing would she put past Rage. Every little thing she had spoken to him in the hall he seemed to absorb. Ready to pounce, like a panther stalking his prey.

"Malala?" the chief prompted.

She smiled. "Sorry." A smile. Did it seem nervous? "Eight years," she finally repeated, praying no one would know the real answer. They had not caught on that the real Kasra Jazani spoke five languages, so it was possible they would miss it.

"And have you always been the one forcing the girls to have sex with men?"

Guilt harangued Kasra as she stared across the table at Fatina. One of the girls she had forced … Had she not, they could have both been killed. Their families killed.

She then saw the uncertainty in Fatina's eyes, which looked bloodshot.

"*Something is wrong—they burn, Kasra.*"

"*They are fine. The more you wear the contacts, the more your eyes will adjust.*"

Apparently not.

Fatina rubbed her eyes.

"Tears are too little too late," Rage barked from behind the boss. "Answer the question."

His terse words made Fatina jump and earned a reproving look from his boss, but Kasra again wondered what made him so very angry. What wound?

Her decoy rallied and answered.

And Kasra translated. "She was brought to Roud like most of

the girls, but she earned the favor of the boss. Other madams through the years either died or were relocated, and she became madam." This simplest of answers was devoid of the horrors endured to step into a position where she could do good. One *ser* of good for a *khawar* of evil? It was a terrible imbalance that shamed her.

The questions went on and on. How could she betray her own people?

Give them names of those involved and they would help her get a light sentence. Who was the man who attacked Rage? On and on.

"Who does Taweel answer to?" Rage spoke again.

The question slammed against her ribs, but Kasra braced herself. Could not say the same for Fatina.

The girl sucked in a breath. Shot wide, red eyes to Kasra. "*Qult lahum?*"

Kasra felt her insides quake, the girl not realizing in that one moment how many mistakes she had made.

"Take Malala out," Pike said to Rage, who drew her out of the chair.

She stumbled, trying to keep her balance. Though she wanted to offer reassurance to her decoy, she felt it better to maintain the ruse. Long ago, she had learned to not offer information that was not specifically asked for.

He led her down the hall and around a corner. Swung her toward the wall. "So she speaks English."

Pretend... Kasra frowned. "I am sorry?"

"You didn't translate that last question before she answered."

"I did not have to—you spoke his name." She shrugged, each word infusing her with confidence. "No matter whether in English or Pashto, it strikes terror in all our hearts." With everything in her, she prayed the truth of that convinced him.

Mouth tight, he stared. "C'mon." Grip again tight, he turned toward the courtyard.

The door at the far end opened, an explosion of light making silhouettes of three men who entered. That manner of their appearance scalded Kasra with recognition that lit fire through her lungs.

No. Breath stolen, she slipped behind Rage and ducked. Prayed the officer there did not look in their direction. Did not notice her. She waited until the hall quieted, until she heard doors open and close elsewhere, then braved a glance.

And those forbidding gray eyes condemned now even as they had then. Her heart lurched and she could not move. Could not think. How …? *How* was he here? She turned toward the courtyard doors, head tucked even more, hoping he had not truly seen her face. Would not say anything. He could upend her ruse. Ruin everything. Again.

"Captain," someone called from another passage, drawing him away.

Kasra touched her temple, her fingers trembling. She snatched her hand down, even then feeling a certain pair of blue eyes on her. "I … should return to the others." She inched nearer the barred window, waiting for him to enter his code into the keypad.

He shifted next to her, his presence so devouring. No doubt he had not missed the split-second reaction between her and the captain. His hand hovered above the security pad … and stilled. His other hand touched her shoulder.

And she felt something in her shrivel.

"Are—"

"Please," she whispered, her voice raw, wavering. "Please do not ask."

The vacuum beneath them snapped closed. He entered the code and the *shunk* sounded.

Anxious for air, she shoved the door out of the way. Nearly

tripped into the open. He caught her elbow, but she shrugged it off. Kept her gaze on the path forward. Wanted to run. Should have. But did not. She moved a little faster, hoping to avoid any more conversation. Afraid he would ask about the captain. Terrified he would seek the captain out. If he did, he would know she was not Malala.

The revelation made her stomach churn. They must prepare. She had been a fool to think she could make this work. Convince him to release them. She hurried into the yard and into the building where the others were eating. After accepting a bowl of meat and rice, she went to her bunk. Hunched there, thinking.

"What is it?" Raz asked, joining her.

"You were right. We have to get out of here. Tonight."

"What about Fatina?"

Her insides squeezed. "We'll find a way." They must. It was impossible. It was all so very impossible and the thought nearly choked her. Her breath shuddered.

I am so sick of my life. It must end. All of it.

"I'm worried about you."

"Do not."

"I've never seen you like this."

Never again will you either. Even then an idea stole into her dark thoughts. "I might have a plan." One that depended on blue eyes.

CHAPTER FIVE

CIA SAFEHOUSE, KANDAHAR PROVINCE, AFGHANISTAN

IT WAS TOO much like Dani. Way too much.

Palming the counter as his stir-fry reheated in the microwave, Range plowed through the last few encounters with Malala. There was a whole lot of rotten happening here. So many things that didn't connect, so many indicators that said this was a major snafu. Lies buried among lies. And the way she reacted to the captain ...

"It is not only Afghans who ... come to Roud."

Was it possible? Had the captain frequented the Roud brothel? Americans stationed here were supposed to make things better, not worse. Fists balled, Range wanted to hang the guy out to dry. Or just hang him. Quicker.

What was he even doing here? Leadership and troops had drawn down more than a year ago. He shouldn't even be in-country.

"You trying to burn the place down?"

"What?" he groused, looking over his shoulder to the door.

Landry stood there, frowning. Jutted his jaw. "Dude, it's smoking."

Range straightened, only then noticing the smoke streaming from the back of the microwave. With a curse, he hit the door button. Smoke and acrid fumes billowed out. He yanked out the now-blackened stir-fry and dropped it in the trash with a huff.

"What's eating your gray matter?"

Range grabbed a bottled water. "Nothing. Just need a face for a punching bag."

"Sorry, not volunteering."

Jaw clenched, he decided to hit the gym again. He shoved past Landry, who caught his shoulder. "Not now."

"Sometimes it helps to talk it out."

Range stalked a few more steps, then hesitated. Glanced back. "Before the draw-down, you ever hear of brass hitting Roud ... after hours?"

Luther considered him. Shrugged. "Honestly, I don't know many who *didn't* visit one brothel or another."

Dade Tycho showed up. "What're we talking about?"

"You ever visit one?" Landry asked.

"Look," Tycho said, already sounding defensive, "I might've hired a prostitute on a night or two when I was having a hard time being away from my family—and by family, I mean Mom, Dad, sisters, brothers, cousins. But those girls—it's different, right? It's their work. How they earn money."

"Is it?" Range challenged. "Did you see where the money went after you gave it to them?"

"Besides in her bra strap?"

"I really need to deliver you of some teeth," Landry said.

"No," Tycho huffed. "I didn't. But—c'mon. You can't tell me it's the same as locking them up and forcing them into sex. You know?"

"Consent draws the line," Range said, feeling the steeled edge of his voice against his throat. "If there's a pimp, they're being controlled. Forced to perform. And no matter what label you use to justify it, you're as bad as the johns and that madam."

He stalked away before he did something he regretted. Needed to talk to Pike, all the missing dots blurring the big picture here. As he hoofed it up the stairs to the Command center, laughter trickled from somewhere. When he reached the main level, he noticed the window was cracked a bit. He peered out and found a perfect view overlooking the yard. From the roof to the fifteen-foot concrete wall that enclosed the space, a canvas tarp hung at a steep slope, protecting the area from the sun. It'd become the garden, though only defiant weeds shoved up through the rocks and hardpacked earth, but the tables and chairs somehow invited people to linger. Nothing fancy.

There, huddled to the side, directly below the camera again, were Malala and the madam's bodyguard, Razam. The woman talking with him was not the same one who had shrank and cowered from the captain. She was possessed once more of confidence and strength. And … authority.

Interesting. Why would she be in authority over the bodyguard?

Raised voices came from the Command center—including Pike's. Range strode into the room. "Hey, Chief. I—"

"Not now, Pretty Boy."

Range started, not only at the snapped words from Pike, but that the three men from earlier, including the captain, stood with their arms folded and whatever message they'd delivered thickened the tension in the air.

Steely eyes held his, narrowing and judging him.

"You have your orders," a short, squat man said. "Understood?"

Pike looked ready to toss a grenade. "Sadly, sir, my team is not under your purview."

The captain shifted, positioning himself as one in charge. "But you are working in cooperation with the DIA and the

Agency. Pending analysis of your gathered intel from the raid on Roud, which is still under review to see if Omen exceeded its granted authority in the region, that cooperation is withdrawn."

"Bullspit!" Pike barked.

"Reinstatement is possible, depending on what is found in the AAR of the raid."

"You don't have the authority—"

"Oh, I do." The squat man spoke up again and pointed to a file in Pike's hand. "Right there. Like I said—you and your team have twenty-fours hours to provide actionable intel, or you're out of here."

"What about the victims?" Range inserted himself into the conversation.

"I don't think we answer to you," the captain snipped.

"If, as you state, OTG disregarded clear Agency and DIA guidelines in executing the Roud raid, then you have a responsibility to the people of this country—and there are nine of them onsite—to ensure they are safely returned to their families."

"Families," the captain spat. "You do know what you raided, don't you?"

"Maybe you should enlighten us," Range said coolly.

"What does that mean?"

Range feigned ignorance. "Maybe I misunderstood. I didn't realize you were legitimately asking what we raided. It was—"

"You smart a—"

"Range!" Pike shot him a glare, warning him to stand down. "Take a walk."

Problem was, Range had given up subservience long ago. He'd taken enough grief from Canyon to last a lifetime. But to be fair, he also didn't want to make life difficult for Pike or Omen. Tucking his anger into his fists, he started for the door.

"Range."

Hearing the captain mention his name, in a curious way that

was more informed than he'd prefer, Range told himself not to turn back.

"Can't be a Metcalfe. They have class. Know when to keep their noses clean."

Biggest lie on the books. None of them knew how to keep their noses clean. They found trouble without looking for it. That was part of the Metcalfe brand.

That and the attitude.

He kept walking. Felt good to give the captain his backside instead of dignifying his stupidity with a comeback. Proud of himself, he huffed off the need to rearrange the guy's face. It was progress, being able to walk away.

A hand clamped onto his shoulder. "Where is she?" Pulled him around. "Tell me! I saw you with her."

Range shoved himself into the captain. Slammed him against the wall. "Your mom? I wouldn't—"

"Kasra. Where is—"

"You sick—you were supposed to *protect* the people here, not rape them!"

The captain's fist collided with his jaw. Wracked pain through Range's neck, which whiplashed. He threw his own. Nailed the guy solidly. Threw another. A flurry of strikes and he had the guy on the ground.

"*Range!*" Hands hauled him backwards.

Huffing out his breaths, knuckles bleeding, he stopped wrangling. Wanted to spit something at the guy.

"Get out of here," Pike bit out and got in his face. "Stay out of sight until they're gone."

Knuckling away the warmth slipping down his jaw, Range eyed the captain whose left eye was swollen shut, his nose and mouth bleeding, then slid his gaze to the chief before he started down the back steps. As he took to the stairs, he shifted from a walk to a jog, his irritation flaring. His anger baiting him.

Where is she? … Kasra.

Range stopped at the bottom of the stairs. *"I saw you with her."* In the hall. Son of a ... Range slumped back against the wall. That was it ... Wasn't it?

Kasra. She was Kasra, not Malala.

Why hadn't he seen it?

"Whoa, dude." At the bloody sight of Range, Tycho rolled aside. "What happened?"

Range kept walking, then pivoted back. "Do me a favor."

"You do know I don't work for you."

"Never said you did."

Stretching his jaw, Tycho nodded. "What?"

"Bring the interpreter to the interview room. Tell her I want to talk to Kasra."

Tycho gave him a weird look. "Seriously?"

"Was I stuttering?"

"No, it's just—Dude, she just asked to talk with you."

Okay, he hadn't expected that. "Interview room 1." Once the guy left to retrieve her, Range diverted to the bathroom and cleaned the blood from his face. Red smeared his shirt but he didn't have time to change. He needed to be in the room when she arrived.

He entered the room and flipped on the light, wincing at the telltale migraine brewing from the fight. Leaning against the wall, he mentally reviewed the facts. The ones that had been dangling in front of him the whole time. Some had even slipped off his tongue but the connections weren't there.

Now they were.

Voices came from the hall, and he heard her.

Since when do you recognize her voice?

The door creaked open and she entered, wariness thicker than that hijab. She glanced around and started when she saw him. Her eyes widened. "Your face! What happened!"

"Have a seat," he said gruffly.

She frowned, glancing around. "I was told you wanted to talk to Kasra …?"

Gripping the back of the metal chair, he stared at her. "I do."

A nervous laugh trickled up her throat. "It will be hard to without her here."

Range cocked his head, noting for the first time her eyes were no longer brown. Rather, the left one was still brown. The right was hazel. "Isn't she, though?"

Guilt slid off that gentle, pretty façade that had been Malala and revealed the harder-edge, coldhearted shrew who had sold girls and children for sex.

He was going to enjoy shredding her

Vulnerability slipped into her bones like a winter chill she could not shake. It was both familiar to her, and yet completely new. How long had it been since any man made her feel vulnerable?

She had been a fool to think he would see past … everything to the real her. She had expected far too much of this man. Why had the curl of his lip as he'd asked that question—*isn't she though?*—hurt so very much?

Kasra cursed her slowness. She should have thought to seek him out earlier, but doubt and this repugnant vulnerability kept her in the yard, alone with her thoughts and fears. Had she sent word for him sooner, he might have believed that she sought his help. Now, anything she said would be deemed manipulative and conniving. It was written all over his bruised and bloodied face.

Oh, Allah, please help.

Arms folded, he flared his nostrils.

"How did you sort it?"

"Does it matter?"

She lowered herself into the chair and sat back. Mostly to put the table between them but it served well in feigning more confidence than she felt now. "I suppose not." She drew off the hijab and folded it across her lap. Could he see her hands shaking? She crossed her arms, knowing those pale blue eyes did not miss anything. "It took you long enough to figure it out."

Still standing, hands hooked in his pockets, chin tucked, he stared.

This would not work—her defiant persona. They must get to the heart of the situation. What he thought of her—his disgust was clear enough—did not matter. "Did the other soldier tell you I asked to speak with you?"

Lips tight, his brow furrowed, he remained unmoving.

"Hate me if you want, but there is a problem. One that is *very* dangerous"—she swallowed, thinking of the captain's terrible eyes, but knew that would not remove this mountain of disdain from the conversation—"for the others."

He hadn't moved still. Nor spoken.

She bounced her gaze to his. "What do you want me to say? Ask what you will of me, but this"—she motioned between them—"is ineffective and puts the lives of my people at risk."

"I'm listening."

She sniffed, resenting how much his hatred of her hurt. It shouldn't. She'd endured much worse. "As I said to you before, Americans came to the compound. *He* came to the compound."

"That's why you were scared earlier—you knew he'd recognized you." He shook his head. "But if he was a customer—"

"He was more than that," Kasra said, looking down. "He had befriended Taweel. Ensured security looked the other way while American soldiers came to Roud."

"And you were afraid he would betray you, tell me who you were."

"No." But wasn't it? "Yes ... A little. But I speak truth when

I say I worry for the others. If Captain Hellqvist knows they are here, too—and he likely does now that he has seen me—it is very probable that he will tell Taweel. And it would put everyone at risk." She abandoned her ambivalence and confidence. "You saw the others who escaped. We were *all* supposed to escape. But now that he has seen me …" She leaned against the table, her hijab in hand. "Tell me—have they pressured you to return us?"

He was difficult to read, and yet she could read him like a book. Though she could not say what changed, there *was* a change. A near-lightening around the eyes. Maybe a loosening of the knot that held his shoulders so taut. Though, with those muscles, she was not sure that could be accurately described as "loose." She hated the way he studied her, despised her.

"Do not speak—fine. But I see in your eyes they have," Kasra said. "And they will continue until we are forced to return or leave. Either way, Taweel and his men will be waiting. The longer we are here, the more time he has to rally men. Wait too long, and they will attack this very place." She balled the fabric in her hand. "For everyone's sake, we *must* leave here."

He considered her for several long seconds, then shifted his stance. Lifted his hands. And in a slow manner, clapped. Smirked. "You're a very good actress."

Futility coiled around her and squeezed. "You cannot be this stupid!" she growled, banging her fist on the table.

He resumed his position. "Who do we have in lock-up?"

She deflated, desperate to get past his mistrust. "Fatina, my"—he would not appreciate the term decoy—"assistant."

"Uncanny likeness between you two." He stayed on his feet. Was it designed for a sense of power and control? Or was he afraid she would use the table to pin him to the wall and attempt an escape?

All of the above.

He stretched his jaw—and winced at the injury to his mouth.

"Here's what I can't figure, *Madam Jazani*." The way his accent dragged over her name made her angry and sad at the same time. "You act like you are a saint who cares about her people—"

"I do!"

"—and yet you slept in that comfortable bed among *friends*, eating hot meals, having a modicum of freedom, while *your assistant* has been isolated, deprived of food and water, interrogated for endless hours …" He gave her a cockeyed nod. "And I'm supposed to believe you care about anyone but yourself?"

"Allah have mercy, are you so thick?"

He smirked.

And she could tell he was deliberately working to get under her skin. He had done that the first time they had sparred in her private apartment in Roud. "You do not need my word."

His eyebrow lifted, amused. Or confused. Maybe both. It was hard to focus when *he* was so wholly focused on her.

"You know the captain is dangerous—I saw it in your eyes." She eyed the cut lip and reddened spot on his jaw. "Are those from him?" She stretched her neck and pulled at the collar of her blouse, revealing the cigarette burns. "This is what he gave me once." She stabbed her finger on the table. "Whether I speak it or not, your heart knows these people must leave here before it's too late. The longer he is gone, the faster their fate comes."

He sighed and leaned back against the glass she knew to be one-way. "Let me get this straight—you have given us exactly nothing and I'm just supposed to let everyone walk away?" He bobbed his head. "Oh wait, you have given us a lot of lies. You've been very good at those."

Desperation choked her.

"And now you want our help …?"

She saw his point. Felt the pain of the ruse and its

repercussions. "I do—but not for me. For the others." She wanted to strangle this arrogant, gorgeous man. "Please."

"Why'd you do it?" he asked with a nod. "Sell them for sex?"

Now she must return the favor of silence.

He sniffed. "Madam, cooperation is a two-way street."

There was nothing for it. Kasra would either die here or at Taweel's hands, especially now that the captain knew her location. But she did have one thing the Americans wanted. "If you get the others to the north side of the city," she said, finally braving his eyes again, "I will give you the name of the man Taweel answers to."

CHAPTER SIX

CIA S<small>AFEHOUSE</small>, K<small>ANDAHAR</small> P<small>ROVINCE</small>, A<small>FGHANISTAN</small>

TWO RAPS RATTLED the glass at his back as he considered her.

"No." It had been too easy. No way she'd give up this easy with so much at stake.

More raps on the glass.

"What else do you want?" she asked, eyes blazing. "I will give you whatever you want, only let them go."

Desperation. No, this wasn't how the madam worked.

Or maybe it *was* how she worked. Playing men. She knew how to get her way. "You could hand us any name and your friends are free."

"I could," she said, her one hazel eye sparking with defiance. "But you would still have me as your prisoner and could beat me to your heart's content."

Inwardly, Range winced. Was that what she thought they'd do?

The door to the interview room flung open. Pike glowered at him. "A word." He stepped back.

And all over the madam's face was the glee of triumph.

"Shackles," Range grunted to Landry, who stood beyond the chief.

Though he scowled, he produced them from a nearby storage room.

Taking too much pleasure in her irritation at the metal cuffs, he clamped one into the floor hook and the other end around her wrists.

Her hand, cool and delicate, caught his wrist. "I swear to you, I only ask for the others. Please. I am no harm to you."

He slid his gaze to her as he remained ready for her to strike. Erupt at him. "Said the serpent baring her fangs. The same one who gave me this." He pointed to the scar on his cheek. "Yeah, not buying it, Madam." He tightened the shackles and tugged on the chains to insure they were taut. Angling away, he couldn't resist taunting her. "Don't go anywhere."

He stepped in the hall and closed the door.

"Okay, I'd ask how this all happened, but we are out of time." Pike stroked his salt-and-pepper beard. "Take the deal she offered. Get the name."

"You—what?" Range balked. "You're out of your mind. No way. She's not going to give us legit intel. Just like faking her role as the interpreter, she's faking that. Looking for her Get Out of Jail Free card."

"I don't care what she wants—we get a name." Piked nodded. "At least we have something to hand up the chain." He stepped in. "Your little stunt with the captain? It cost us."

Range faltered.

"Yeah, about time you took a step back and thought beyond yourself."

"That captain," Range hissed, "frequented Roud." He stabbed a hand toward the door. "And her. He knew. Came at me, demanding to know where *she* was."

Now it was Pike's turn to hesitate for a second. "All the more reason to work with her."

"Work with—"

The chief thumped his chest, silencing him. Backstepped, motioning him to follow. "Hear me out: Tell her we'll get the others to the northern part of the city—but not free. To our Secondary. We hold them there, and she stays until we verify the intel. If it's true, we'll release the others. Her? We turn her in."

Range worked his jaw. "Her bodyguard … and the assistant. I don't think it's wise to let them go."

"If you think it's possible to make that deal with her then do it. But we need to get the heat off us."

"What if she's legit?" Landry asked. "What if they really are in danger?" He indicated to Range's face. "The captain had something at stake to come at you like that."

Range couldn't argue that, and it ticked him off that he knew what she'd say to a half-cocked offer. "She'll insist all or nothing."

Pike shrugged. "That's what I'd do."

With a huff, Range nodded. So would he. "She said the captain would alert her owner … handler …whatever he is. Said the longer they're here, the more danger they're in."

The chief raked a hand over his head. "I'll have Crow and Dade take—"

"Not Dade," Range snapped, glancing at the chief. "He's a problem."

Pike hesitated, though it wasn't for long. "Brick and Crow will take the others to our Secondary. You work her."

"Done." He wheeled around. Though he knew he'd anchored her to the floor, she was Kasra Jazani. He gripped the knob and flashed open the door—if she had been waiting, she'd have eaten the door in the face.

But she was still seated, head down. The epitome of contrition. She'd even reddened her eyes—fake crying. What a master.

As he planted himself in the chair, he leaned back. Considered her for a moment. Had to admit, he was impressed with all she'd managed to control and maneuver as Madam Jazani. "Against my vehement disagreement," Range said, amping up the truth a bit to sell the golden opportunity she was being handed, "the chief has decided to accept your offer."

Tears turned her hazel eyes into a mossy-like pond. "Thank you."

"Yeah, wouldn't do that yet." He sniffed. "The others will be taken to the north side of the city as you asked, moved to an alternate safe house, but you'll stay—"

"No." Her lips flattened. "And I'm not leaving them."

"I think you misheard me," Range said. "They're leaving *you*."

"No. It's too dangerous. I must go with—"

"Hey!" He pushed in, scowling. "I thought this was about *them*. Thought you wanted them safe, but there you are negotiating for yourself."

Her chin worked overtime to control tears. She drew herself straight.

Masterful, masterful. Almost convinced him.

"Fine."

That sounded like it hurt.

"Swear to me—the north side of the city. They'll be safe."

He stood and started for the door.

Chains rattled and she lunged upward.

Instinct snapped Range into a fighting stance even as the chains yanked her back.

"Please," she pleaded, half growling, her hands yanked down. Tears slid down her cheeks as she tried to angle around to reach him. "Tell me they will be safe. That I can trust your word."

Something about the hoarse way she begged reached up inside Range and grabbed his gut. Sure wasn't his heart because he didn't have one. But he tucked his chin and seared her into silence. "I never said anything about trusting me. But you can trust the chief."

"You don't scare me, Rage."

He twitched back. Scowled. "What?" She *had* called him Rage? He sniffed. Apropos

She shifted, glancing to the door. "Your anger, I know it masks a wound. A deep one. It does not scare me."

With a mental shrug, he smirked. "I don't care about scaring you, Madam. Only about ending your depravity."

Everything was a disaster.

No, she could not say that. Twenty girls were on their way to freedom. Twelve others would be soon. If Razam could get them to the northern edge of the city, they could reach one of her contacts. Razam had the information. The plans. Granted, they were now two days behind, but she prayed Allah looked favorably upon her efforts to free them.

For her? Chains. Whether these that yet bound her arms in this cold room with its hard, metal chair and table, or the mental ones that would forever bind her to the very depravity Rage had named.

Elbows on the table, she held her face in her hands. Imagined Razam free. He was a good, good man. He deserved to find a wife and have a family. Always had he favored Fatina. Perhaps the two could find solace in one another.

The girls ...

Allah, forgive me. I know I cannot undo the past, but with all that is in me, will I ensure they are free. If I can give my own life, then I do. Please—take it.

Life was too cruel and more times than not, she did not want to live. Then she would remind herself that the girls would have no one to defend them. They could not break free of the prison that had entombed their lives …

Until now.

At least for them.

Watching the first van drive away with 6 girls … then the next two with the others … it had worked, and she was both exultant and terrified. Then it was her turn. Yet as they slunk through the tunnel came the strange glow of green. Pop of gunfire. Allah had shown her that freedom was not to be hers. It was her penance.

But Atia …

She folded her arms on the table and buried her face as tears threatened.

No, do not show them weakness.

Kasra lifted her head again. Glanced at the mirrored glass. Were they watching? She could not tell, but she also could not doubt they were. Then to the wall by the door. If she stretched out her leg, could she toe the light off?

Angling out of the chair, she moved herself as far from the anchor hold as she could possibly move, then stretched her leg … her slipper reaching … reaching. The chains tugged. She slowed her moves, deliberate. Swiped the wall. Missed the switch. With a grunt, she tried again. And again. Until she scream-growled her frustration. Somehow, the chains yanked her backward. She landed hard on her hip, daggers of pain knifing her back. She arched her spine, then curled in on herself. Drew her hijab over her face. Let herself cry.

Except … she could not. Tears were as elusive as sleep.

In a fetal position, she stayed there. Rested. Or tried to. Her hip hurt and the cold of the floor made it ache.

The door thudded open. She need not look to know it was Rage. He was the only one who opened the door that way, like he expected her to be poised to attack.

"Up." His deep voice echoed. Then his boots thumped closer. "Let's go, Madam."

She really hated that he kept calling her that, but she deserved it.

His firm grip caught her arms. Pulled her up.

Something defiant wormed through her, making her give no strength to her legs, so she wobbled and went down. Which was stupid—she hurt her knees that time.

"Okay, sleep on the floor."

When he opened the door, she heard steps. Voices—Fatina!

Her friend appeared there and peeked in. Her face came alive. "Kasra! We leave—"

"Get her out back," Rage barked at the other man.

Greedy, desperate for the touch of a friend, Kasra lunged forward, cared not how the chains tore at her shoulders and arms. "Be free, my dear friend."

Fatina found her. Wrapped her in a hug. Cried against her ear, "I am so sorry. I failed you—"

"Get her out!" Rage shouted, thrusting Fatina backward. "*She* failed *you!*" he shouted, pointing at Kasra on the floor.

"You don't know what or of whom you speak," Fatina spat back. "She is our savior!"

"Go, Fatina," Kasra said softly, heartbroken she would not see her again, yet so very relieved at the same time that they would not see each other again. It was a good thing. A very good thing.

As the door came between hem, Kasra exhaled heavily. Was grateful to have seen her friend, the woman who had so often put herself in harm's way to protect her. *A friend I did not deserve.* She pushed her gaze to the gray floor ... and saw his boots there. He hadn't said anything.

She had no fight in her. Not now. So she climbed to her feet, chains still anchoring her. Kept her head down.

He stepped closer. Caught her hands. "You mentioned trust,"

he said, guiding her by the restraints back to the chair and motioned for her to sit. "I'm going to extend you some of that." Hand never leaving the crossbar fastened to her wrists, he went to a knee at her side, his gaze sliding into hers. "Don't make me regret it."

Those eyes held her hostage. Communicated a depth she had seen in few people. Were he any other, she would have already knocked him back. Tried to flee the danger yet breathing down her neck. But he held her. Not by physical force. But by something else she could not understand.

She was keenly aware of him, of the way his knee touched hers. The piney scent of deodorant or shave cream wafting off him. Then how his muscles strained the fabric of his black, long-sleeve shirt with a camo pattern over the broad shoulders. That jaw muscle twitching as his fingers traced her ankle to unlock it.

She held her breath, surprised at the skitter that spirited up her leg. Marveled that despite his rough words, his touch was gentle. Though he meant business—she had no doubt—he was … different. She could not say "nicer," because there was obviously a reason he was called Rage.

Any attempt at an escape would be met with violence. Perhaps those pretty eyes even now begged her to try. She recalled fighting him. He had a violent grace about him. His strikes practiced and polished. To match his determination. This man did not do anything halfway.

His hand found her other ankle, snatching her breath.

His gaze struck hers. "Easy …"

No. No it was not. Nothing about this or this man was easy.

She looked away, fighting every instinct to kick him in the face. Plow into him. Never had she taken manhandling well. But this was for Raz and the others. The children. *Free them.* The hope reverberated in her soul.

"The hinge is tight." He caught the one around her wrists.

It would be so simple to break free …

He cocked his head, which invariably made her smile. "Don't think about it."

Holding his gaze, she mused, "Too late."

Gripping the crossbar again, he straightened to his full height. Wrapped the chain latched to the crossbar around his waist. Locked it. "Now, if you try to get away, we're both going to get hurt—but you won't get far." He started for the door.

"What's a little pain?"

His gaze cut to hers again. "Who said anything about a little?"

She could not help the barest of smiles that defied her willpower. Even when he held her elbow again, she tensed. "Wh-where are we going?"

He side-eyed her as he led her to same door where she had seen the captain and indicated to the courtyard. "Thought you'd want to see."

Chain rattling, she slipped closer. Peered through the glass and wrought-iron decoration on the door. Saw a beat-up blue van in the middle of the courtyard, and— She stilled. Felt an eruption of surprise and relief as she watched Raz lift a defiant Iamar into his arms. He moved toward it, and the little one looking over his shoulder somehow spotted Kasra at the door. She shoved out her arms and released a piercing cry.

Starting forward, Kasra felt the link between her and the American grow taut and knew he would not let her go out there. Would not let her leave his side. So, she shook her head, trying to encourage the little one to leave with them. Used sign language as she had taught the girls to communicate when words were not acceptable. Told her to find Yasmine.

Find freedom, little one. Far from here. Far from me.

Somehow, Raz saw her too. Inclined his head slowly, his gaze shifting to her captor beside her. His expression tightened, but he whispered to the girl who now reached for Fatina. Only as she felt the touch of her fingers against her own lips did Kasra realize what she did in front of this man—nearly blowing a kiss to Iamar. He would capitalize on weakness. All men did.

She lowered her hand, watching through tear-blurred eyes as the three climbed into the van. Watched the door close. The van pulled through a gate and stopped. Was something wrong?

The gate closed, but the van had not moved forward.

Had it been a trap? Make her think they were …

Movement on the far side stilled her frantic thoughts. Another gate … The center was a security measure. The roof of the van slowly eased away and turned left.

"Let's go." Rage shifted and that invariably tugged the shackles.

"They are not necessary."

He kept walking. Down past the hall and break room. Turned left to another long hall. As they moved down that one, she glanced back. At the far end was a door. The one the captain had come in through. Was that the front of the property?

"Mapping your escape?" He'd stopped and stood staring at her. Judging.

Kasra half expected him to tug the chain as one would a dog's leash. "An old habit."

"Just remember, they aren't free until you give us that name."

"Of course," she said with derision, "I forgot Americans only care about what they get out of things. Humanity and compassion are lost to you."

His brow rippled. "That's sharp irony coming from you, *Madam*." He flicked open a door and nodded her toward it.

A room. Correction, bedroom. A bed with a nightstand. No lamp.

What … was he implying? She could not meet his gaze.

Irritated, he sniffed and moved into the room. The chain yanked her in with him.

"You did that on purpose."

He grunted. "Wish I had." Unlocking the chain, he coiled it around the bar of the bed. "You'll stay here until you give us the name."

Kasra started. It wasn't a luxurious hotel, but it was a vast leap from what they had in the large warehouse. "Why am I not being put in isolation?"

"First place someone would look if they came for you."

She snapped her gaze to his. "You believe me?"

Blue eyes tracking over her, he shifted. "No windows. No pipes you can break off and use to render me unconscious. If you want to escape, I will likely put lead between your eyes."

She lifted her jaw, trying to push off the way those words wounded. "I gave my word."

At the threshold, he paused, hands on his tactical belt. "Pardon me if I can't trust the word of a madam who has sold kids for sex." He stepped out and closed the door, leaving her alone.

Yes ... Alone. Very alone. Raz and Fatina were gone. The girls were gone. She slumped against the mattress. Loneliness she had known her entire life. Even being despised. Neither were new to her.

So why did she feel as if he'd just delivered the cruelest of blows? Why did she care so much about this American with his blue eyes, big muscles, and churning anger?

CHAPTER
SEVEN

CIA S*afehouse*, K*andahar* P*rovince*, A*fghanistan*

WHAT WAS he supposed to make of her tears as she watched the others leave? Was it fear of her own outcome? Manufactured so he'd go easy on her? And what was with the look she'd thrown him as he closed the door earlier?

Range flipped through the dossier Casey had put together on Kasra Jazani. Saw the facts there that he'd wondered about—she spoke several languages.

Called it.

Brown hair. Hazel eyes.

That didn't really fit the color—they were brown with green and glittery-gold flecks rimming her iri—

What the heck?

Sliding a hand down the back of his neck, he flipped the page. Scoured the known intel for family—parents, brothers, sisters ... Extended family. None.

Even though he'd distanced himself from his family, he couldn't imagine not having any. What an empty existence. Then again, her family would likely never again claim her after sexual immorality. While Westerners had shirked biblical values and made excuses for sex before marriage, Muslims did not. He had to admit ... he agreed with them—to an extent—on this one. Sex was a tangled, messy conversation no matter which way you came at it. Stepped on people's toes. Crushed dreams and lives.

To this day, he still remembered that moment in Mom's living room when Canyon had told the family he'd gotten Dani pregnant.

On a mission. A freakin' mission when he was supposed to be *protecting* her and keeping her safe.

While Mom had given Canyon a mild rebuke, everyone else had hugged Dani, welcome her. Got excited about a baby in the family again. Forget that she'd been with Range just before that mission. Attended his Coast Guard ball with him.

Nobody had even seen Range leave. He hadn't looked back since.

His phone buzzed on the table, and he glanced at the screen. Dani.

What the ...? Seriously? It was like she heard his thoughts all the way across the globe. Stunned, he answered it. "Yeah."

"Hey, just saw that I missed your call."

"Right." He'd forgotten about that. On the chair, he swiveled toward the door, mentally jogged down the hall to her room. "I ..." He'd wanted to ask her how a woman held captive and sexually brutalized behaved. But now that he heard her voice, thought of what had happened to her at the hands of the Venezuelan general, he realized he was an idiot. "Yeah. Never mind. Problem resolved."

"You certain?"

"I am. Thanks."

"It's been a while. You doing okay?"

It was some kind of twisted weird, chatting as if he hadn't been MIA for the last decade. "Yeah, sure."

"Okay, I don't believe that."

Danggit. He wanted to talk. Tell her what was happening. Get her thoughts on Kasra and what he should expect. But … "Maybe later."

"Deal. But not two years later, okay?"

He spotted Pike heading his way with a grim expression. "Gotta go." He ended the call and came to his feet, ready for whatever was about to get thrown at him. "Problem?"

Lips taut around that carefully trimmed beard, Pike seemed to chew some facts. "Might have a problem."

Range had learned long ago that keeping his mouth shut could be more effective thank talking.

Gray eyes hit his. "Thinking maybe Hellqvist or one of the VIPs sold us out."

Something savage rose through Range. "Definitely Hellqvist."

"Analysts picked up some heavy chatter on long-quiet channels. Seeing movement inbound."

Range lifted his eyebrows. "Here?" His gut churned. "They're coming here."

"That's our guess. Timing is too much to deny." Pike considered him. "We need that name if I'm going to get some brass back-up against Hellqvist." He scratched his beard. "It'll take hours for the others to reach the Secondary, so ask her. Put the fear of God in her—"

"A woman like that doesn't fear God."

"*Make her*. There's only one reason to keep her close: that name. Without it, she's—"

"Expendable?" Why did it tick him off?

"—just like the rest of them." Pike glowered. "Look, if you can't get the name, I'll send her with Casey and—"

"I'll *get* the name," he gritted out.

Pike huffed, eyeballing him through a stern brow. "Okay." He smoothed a hand over his beard. "I'm sending Casey and Phil to the Secondary with the victims. Then I'm rerouting everyone to another location."

And why wasn't he telling Range where that was?

"We're readying to vacate the premises."

"You think they're coming."

"I know they are. Get your gear together. When the time comes, I want you to take the girl and—"

"*Take her ...?*"

"If we effect a family reunion between her and the others, we'll get squat out of her! And I need that name to remain viable." He stabbed a finger at Range. "She's soft on you—"

Range barked a laugh. "That's a load of—"

"Tell me what I saw in that interview room wasn't some connection between you and her, what with all the googly eyes you two were shooting at each other."

Range scoffed. "What you saw was me expecting her to knife-hand my throat or gouge out my eyes."

"Yet she didn't. She just ... stared at you."

"We made a deal." Dang, that sounded just as pathetic as when she'd said it. "Besides, she's not a woman I'd ever consider in that way." *Change the topic before you perpetuate the idiocy.* Pike clearly had a plan. "What're you thinking?"

"Dinner." He set it on the table next to the bed.

"No fork?" she asked, feeling like a dog chained to a post.

"So you can stab me?"

"It would make it easier." When she noticed him moving back to the door, she stood. "I would use the restroom."

He caught the knob of the door and pulled it closed.

Kasra sat with her legs folded and drew the box of food onto her lap. She opened it and smiled. Naan, lamb, and rice. No fork needed. Oh how her stomach rumbled at the aroma—even though the food was barely warm now. She did not care. It was wonderful, considering what had been served in the big room.

Once it was finished, she really could not wait to use the restroom. She banged on the door she could barely reach, thanks to the chains. And banged and banged.

"What in the blazes do you want?" Rage barked as he flung open the door.

It caught her off-guard, making her stumble back. Anger spiraled and threatened her control. But she wrestled it into submission. Fisted her hands. "I must use the restroom."

He huffed and stalked to her.

She cried out and raised her hands, cowering.

He drew up straight, something feral in his expression as she steadied. "What do you think I am?"

"The man I fought in my apartment."

He grabbed the bar on her hands, glowering at her. Unlocked it. "Let's go. I've got things to do." He escorted her to a bathroom.

She availed herself of the facilities, then took a few paper towels, wet them, and gave herself a semblance of a bath.

Thud-thud-thud!

"Hurry up."

Kasra caught her reflection in the mirror and ... stilled. The dark circles under her eyes. Sallow cheeks. The bruise and cut on her cheek from— "Taweel."

Was he as angry as she imagined he would be? What had he thought when he discovered her missing? The girls gone. His income gone. He would not go quietly into poverty or disfavor with the boss.

He will kill me.

The sound of gunfire erupted through the house.

Taweel! He had found her!

Kasra moved away from the door, staring at it. Expecting him to come through it.

Bang-bang.
She jolted.
"Out! Now!"
At Rage's barked commands, she whipped open the door. Found his back to her, weapon aimed down the hall. "Ready?" he asked, never looking back or taking his eyes off whatever threat he had perceived.
"Ye—" Her throat cracked. "Yes."
"Hand on my belt," he instructed.
Numb and shaky, she faltered. Caught a belt loop.
He set his over hers and squeezed. "Tight. Keep your head down." And he was moving.
"Who is it?"
"Didn't ask for ID." With skill and stealth, he negotiated the darkened hall. Night had fallen, yes, but the darkness was from loss of electricity. Tremors slivered through her spine and arms as she kept a death grip on his canvas belt.
They moved quickly down the passage that led to the front. He scurried up to a corner. His stop was so sudden, she nearly collided with him. "Hold."
"I *am.*"
He huffed. "I mean—don't move."
Oh.
He bobbed a look around the corner.
Crack! Ping!
Even as he shoved backward into her, Kasra felt the bite of tile from the wall next to her eye and jerked away. Heart pounding, she fought a whimper. Rage leaned into the open and fired down the hall.
A response of bullets came from the other end.
"Back! Back!" Even as he uttered the command, he was backtracking, weapon facing forward.
She had seen the men of Roud doing this, and the one behind always faced the other way to be sure nobody came up

behind them. But she had no weapon. Still, she should watch … Fingers coiled around his belt, she shifted sideways and squinted through the darkness.

These men are going to die because of me.

The thought stopped her cold. No. she could not let that happen.

Rage bumped into her. "Move," he hissed.

"They are here for me." She let her hand slip from his belt. "I should—"

Rage whirled on her, his body a barrier. "You're smarter than that."

Defiance flared. "I am smart enough to know that if I do not surrender, you and your men will be killed."

He bared his teeth. "You give us too little credit and yourself too much." He caught her shoulder and pitched her down the hall. "Go."

The manhandling ignited her anger. "I am not—"

His left arm came up, pinning her to the wall. He fired several times, each trigger pull throwing a brief illumination across his intense, focused visage. He was raw, powerful.

Scared yet relieved he had seen the threat her arrogance had missed, she had the good sense not to fight the way he barricaded her. Understood pinning her had not been to demean her, but to protect her. When had anyone done such a thing … for her?

Still eying the passage, he angled his head to her. "Hand," he demanded.

Embarrassed she'd forgotten to maintain a grip, she flinched. Felt a flare of anger. Obedience had never been one of her virtues, yet her hand found his belt.

"Move," he ground out even as he was stalking forward.

Wait. Forward? "B–but were they not this way? Should we not go anot—"

"Quiet." How he charged through this passage … toward the

danger, toward the threat ... unafraid. A few more steps and he diverted into a room, pulling her in with him. Walked the pitch-black room.

Kasra stood against a wall, unable to see, unsure what was happening. What he was doing in here. Faint green cast its dull glow over his face. He wore a headset as he came toward her. "Put this on."

She felt something thrust against her and caught it. "What ...?"

"Vest. Now."

Understanding what was in her hand dawned, a bulletproof vest. She did her best to figure it out and finally slid it over her head. Secured the sides. It felt awkward, heavy, and that somehow made her feel safer.

His strong, capable hand closed around hers as he drew it his side, to a hard surface—a vest. "Hold tight. No talking."

She found a nylon strap on his right side and curled her hand into it.

A ground-shaking boom punched through her chest. Kasra gasped and instinctively took a step—whether to escape or be closer to him, she wasn't sure. Maybe both. Her shoulder bumped his back ... pack.

"Let's go." They snaked through the passages and out a side exit. Staying in the shadow of the building, they hurried across the length of the courtyard. Headed to a small door in the concrete wall.

Shots peppered the air, concrete spitting at her. She yelped and ducked, pressing her face to his pack and doing her best to stay in tandem with him. He swung around, movements strong and intentional. He engaged the enemy. "The door," he ordered. "Unlatch it."

Terrified to move and get shot, she hesitated.

"*Now!*"

At his anger and sharp tone, she surged forward. Thankfully, the safehouse's lights helped her find the latch. She slid the crossbar up and over, felt a definitive *shunk*.

Rage backed toward her, firing. "Out. Left. Hug the wall."

Kasra complied, kept a hand on the wall, rushing forward, listening carefully. Heart racing so violently, she wasn't sure she would hear him anyway. The wall ended and she faltered, wondering whether to go—

"On me. Hand." He darted across a shadowy section of the road, their intrusion into the street earning a harsh rebuke from the fighters pursuing them.

Even as they gained more distance, her heart pounded more. Instinct wanted her to break away.

Trust him. Stay with him.

He was, after all, the only one with a weapon.

"Run!" he grunted.

The surprise command jumpstarted her heart. She burst forward, keeping him in her periphery as they zigzagged up and down the street. Across to a new one. Turned right, then left. Through a residential neighborhood. Down a market. Running. Running.

Legs aching, lungs burning, she stumbled.

Hands caught her. "Just a little farther." He drew her on. Rage stalked forward, powerful and focused. Endless energy and strength.

Slowly, she began to recognize the buildings, the streets, the market ... Sounds. "It's not safe here."

Huffing, he seemed to already know that and kept moving. Entire body taut with readiness. Always anticipating with his weapon. Never tiring.

She knew not how much longer they hurried through the streets, but her calves were cramping and felt leaden. Her arms like anchors. "I ... I can't." She glanced back. Saw nothing, heard nothing. Stopped. "I need—" Sucking in a breath, she realized he was ... gone. "Rage ...?"

Fear trickled through her veins as darkness and smells closed in on her. "Rage." Her voice echoed down the endless street. She rubbed her palms, turned. Searched the shadows. He'd left her ...?

Crack! Pop!

She whipped to the right. Saw a man charging her. Face contorted. Weapon spitting balls of fire.

Abdullah.

Oh, merciful Allah ... Kasra pitched herself around. Ran, though her legs felt like jelly. She sprinted, terror nipping at her heels. Her foot hit something. She pitched forward. Scored her knees and palms on the road. Though she shoved up, she heard more shots. Felt something burn her shoulder. She glanced back again.

Crack! Crack!

"Did you think we would not find you, whore?" Abdullah growled, bearing down on her. "You are dead!"

Crack-crack-crack! Crack!

Abdullah crumpled, blood smearing his kaftan.

The bullets had come from behind. Rage was there, clasping her arm. Hauling her up. "C'mon."

Holding onto him as if it meant her life, she ignored the burning in her knees, hands, and shoulder. Clung to him. "Wh-where did you go? I could not find you." Her eyes burned but she blinked away the tears.

"You stopped."

It felt like an accusation—because he was right ... she had been so tired—but he did not seem angry. "I was tired. Am tired." And in pain now. "I cannot believe they are here. They found me ..."

It seemed hours before Rage directed her down a particularly quiet and dark street. No lights. In the distance, she saw the fields and hills. "There." He pointed across the road ... to an open field. "That hut. We'll hideout there."

Under the gentle caress of moonlight a hut beckoned. Or threatened. Gave her chills. "It looks abandoned."

"Exactly," he said with a near smile as he struck out toward it.

Kasra hurried after him. "Meaning, no roof."

"Just need walls to stop the bullets if they come." Hiking with intent, he crossed the road. How was he not out of breath or tired?

She scrambled to catch up, too afraid of repeating her mistake from earlier. "Why would we hide? Should we not find your people? Figure out what happened, where they are?"

Hunched against a bitter wind raking the long grass that had grown up over the field, he said nothing. "We all scatter when there's a breach."

Hugging herself, Kasra abandoned the questions, since he would not answer.

The lean-to was quite literally leaning to. Worn and torn, the sheet that covered the door let more wind in than it kept out.

He shrugged beneath it and glanced around. "You were wrong."

Kasra slipped in and frowned.

He pointed up to a wood-and-thatch roof that slumped wearily toward one side. "Half a roof."

"But only three walls."

He shrugged. "Three *and half*."

"Do you think this is funny?" she demanded.

Rage pushed into her face. "No. In fact, I'm ticked off. Because of *you*, I got separated from my team. Because of you, I nearly ate lead. Because of you—"

"Okay! I get your point."

"Do you?" he challenged. Then nodded. "Good. Because this is a major snafu. If you want to go back and find a comfortable place, be my guest. *After* you give me that name."

Wind gusted through said hole, and he lifted a dingy, nasty

gray feathered mattress. Mice squeaked and squealed, scattering.

So did Kasra, watching the rodents rush out of the hut. Thinking to do the same.

Rage set the mattress against the hole. The chill seemed to abate a fraction. He shrugged out of his pack, tugged open a compartment and drew something out. "Here. You'll need this."

Surprised that he handed her sweatshirt, she took it. "I … don't understand."

He looked up at her. "It's a sweatshirt. You put it over your—"

"Why are we here?" She hated that he would make sport of her. "Why aren't we trying to make it back to your team? To the safehouse?"

"Besides the fact you were already so exhausted you nearly got us both killed?" On his haunches, he stared at her. Pushed to his full height. "C'mere." He stepped out and that wind snapped at her. "See that?" He pointed to the city.

Lights and buildings. "Yes?"

"No, *look*."

"I am!" She scanned, lost for his meaning, what he indicated.

With a huff, he stepped up behind her. His chest pressed into her shoulders as his right arm slid around into her periphery, pointing toward the city. His cheek nearly against hers, he repositioned her.

Allah, forgive her, but awareness flared through her. His smell. His presence. His strength—

"There." His chest rumbled when he spoke, a deep sound that trilled against her spine.

Forcing herself to focus, to prove she had a brain in her head, she blinked. Looked across the field. Saw buildings, stars, clouds … No, not clouds. "Smoke."

Thick and gray, a column rose in the distance.

"*That's* the compound."

She drew in a breath, looked to the side where he remained close. So very close. "How … do you know?" Beautiful the way the moonlight caught his pale eyes and danced in them.

"You doubt me?"

She angled more toward him. "No, I—"

Disapproval sharp in his gaze, he turned and ducked back inside.

Did he think she cared about his approval?

Kasra wilted. Of course she did, though she could not fathom why. He was arrogant, hostile, and so very … *American*. Already made that mistake once in her life and she would not repeat it. Yet, she needed him as an ally.

Or … what if she just started … walking. Would he notice? Care? Her gaze slid to the crumbling structure, probing the gaps and holes. Could he see her? Why was she considering this? But then a shift of shadow stabbed her belly with fright—he was there, positioned to see through a narrow gap between the canvas over the door and the stone jamb. Watching her.

Of course he was. She turned back, hating that he did not trust her. Hating that he was so completely disgusted by her.

Why? Why did it matter? He was American. Did not know her.

Impulse twitched to start the journey. Reason and honor held her in place. After all, she had given her word in exchange for the safety of Raz and the girls.

He thinks you void of honor.

She moved a few paces farther away, hugging herself against the wind. Testing him. Wondering—

"Inside," came his low growl.

His tone made her want to disregard his instructions. But like it or not, her life was in his hands. Not giving him the pleasure of her gaze, she lifted her chin. "Are you afraid I will run?"

"If you think you're safer with a goat farmer, have at it."

Goat farmer? What …? She scanned the area and only then noticed a tall, lanky shepherd prodding five or six goats down a dirt road.

Her selfish frustration with this man made her make a terrible mistake. Should the goat herder notice them, he could very possibly report them. *How very much I am out of my depth here.* Give her a house with a dozen women and she could manage. This, however …

Every time she thought it could not get worse … it had. Why had she thought *anything* would go right for her?

At least Allah had seen fit to look after the other girls. Likely he thought to save them from her ineptitude. She had done all she could, and in the end, it had not been enough.

Done with the nippy wind, she went inside and stopped short. A nylon rope slung from wall-to-wall with a green canvas draped over it, forming a tent-like shelter.

"Grab some shut-eye," Rage instructed, indicating to the triangle-shaped tube. "We head out before dawn."

"To where?" There did not seem enough room for two in there.

"North."

Hope leapt anew. "Toward the others?"

His gaze rammed into hers. "You will not be reunited with anyone until we have a name. You ready to hand that over?"

Tired, body aching, she *was* ready to give it. Be done with it all. Hand him the name of Taweel's boss and there would be no need to ensure she made it to the other location. Considering the amount of disdain he spat at her, she would need every reason she could get.

Kasra went to her knees, crawled into the tube-like tent, and felt its immediate warmth—the top end protected from the elements. A sleeping bag was unrolled, and she slid into it, knowing the nights this time of year could be very cold. Curled on her side, she peered down the length of her body. Saw Rage moving toward the opening. Was he leaving?

He parked himself against the wall nearest the door and angled toward the hut's opening. To stand watch. While she slept. Why would he do that?

Do not overthink it; he is only doing his job.

CHAPTER EIGHT

Kandahar Province, Afghanistan

JUST A FEW MORE HOURS AND he'd be rid of her. Hook up with Omen at the Secondary and turn the madam over to DIA with that name. Then he could walk away knowing he'd saved thousands of women and children.

He tucked himself into a position that gave him a semblance of comfort, kept the wind from his face, and afforded a bird's-eye view of the road.

Disgusted with himself for losing her on the street. How had he missed that she'd stopped? By the time he backtracked, he saw the gunman. Knew if he was out in the open, the gunman would target him. He used the man's distraction with the madam to close in. His heart had nearly collided with that first bullet.

"She's our savior!"

It was a sad state of affairs in this country when one thought of Kasra Jazani as a savior. How ...? How could that woman think the madam saved them from anything? She *ran* that brothel. Made them have sex with men. Pocketed the money.

Or did all of that go to Taweel?

Nah, couldn't be. Why would she stay if he hadn't given her some of the money? She was pretty well dressed, all things considering. Had a healthy vigor to her face and body, which was not lacking in any respect.

Disgusted with himself for even noticing that, he shifted and pried his thoughts back to the hut. Noted her breathing had evened out. He slapped down his NVGs and peered into the tent, verifying she slept. NVGs back up, he tugged out his phone—set not to light up on use—and found a text from Pike asking for an update.

He tapped out a reply: ALL CLEAR. SHELTERED. RENDEZVOUS AT 0400 AT SECONDARY.

He sighed and rubbed his eyes. The safehouse getting hit was unexpected. Pike had planned an elaborate ruse to draw out the madam, but that attack by her owners did the trick. Maybe.

She's soft on you.

With a quiet groan, he shook his head. Last thing he wanted or needed. His phone thumped. Another message from Pike.

NEGATIVE. PLAN CHANGED. HOLD.

Hold? What the actual heck? He leaned forward, eyeing the words that warned some serious stuff must've hit the fan for Pike to delay him.

HOW LONG?

Supplies weren't the problem—he was trained to live off the land and blend into local populations, but this woman was too well-known around here. And he didn't want to spend any more time with her than was absolutely necessary.

Another text. UNKNOWN.

Son of— Range bit back a curse. Thumped his head against the wall. What was God trying to do to him? Of all the freakin' women to get weighed down with ... It nauseated him, thinking what she had done. How many *men* she had done. How many girls she'd forced—

He punched to his feet. Huffed. This wasn't going to work.

Alone on watch with nothing but his revulsion of this woman as company? What had he done to deserve this? Hadn't he dedicated his life to helping the helpless after—

No. He wouldn't go there.

Clearly he wasn't good enough. Never had been. Not for Dad or Mom. Not for Mariah. Not for Dani. Not for God.

"You know better than that, Range Lincoln Metcalfe!" Mom's words thumped the back of his head from across the pond. That sweet, sage voice always saw through his moodiest, angriest moments. Never gave slack on the lead with which she'd kept her six kids under control.

He did know better. Problem was, he didn't care. God hadn't intervened to help him out any other time. Why should he wait on Him this time?

Range slumped back against the wall and slid down. Did a perimeter check. He looked up through the hole in the ceiling at the blanket of stars. Recalled sea spray and ocean swells that somehow seemed to magnify the stars at night. Though he'd loved that view, he'd decided it was time to put dirt beneath his boots and some meaning to his name. And distance—emotional, mental, and physical—between him and Canyon.

Jazani twitched in the sleeping bag. A whimper. Then a murmur.

Something snagged his periphery. He snapped his gaze to the gap in the curtain door. Saw a shadow moving over the terrain.

"No," came a soft murmur.

Eye on the shadow, ear on Jazani, Range knew the worlds would collide if one of these two did not yield. If she got any louder—

"Please!" she hissed in a half cry, half-angry tone.

He went to a knee. Angled toward the sleeping bag and touched her toe.

She whimpered. "Please ... Atia ..."

With a huff, he edged into the confined space. "Hey." Had to practically hover above her, since being louder wasn't an option. "*Hey.*"

Sucking a breath, she snapped out a hand. Caught his wrist and yanked him forward. Their skulls cracked and Range dropped on her with a curse.

Though he couldn't see her eyes in the darkness, he sensed the way her body went rigid. What likely went through her mind seconds before her hand struck out at him.

Mercifully, he caught it. "Stop," he hissed. Shifted, but there was no way to gain propriety in a one-man tent. "*Kasra,*" he growled. "Someone's coming."

She stilled beneath him, her breath rising and falling.

Just then, they heard whistling.

And somehow … *somehow* he saw the whites of her eyes bulging. "*Don't* move," he whispered against her ear, knowing he couldn't move without potentially giving them away. He pushed his thoughts away from her curves against his, and the uneven rise and fall of her chest. Her wide gaze and shallow breaths.

Deciding the newcomer was still far enough distant not to hear his quiet extrication from the tent, he planted his hands on either side of her head and pushed up, lifting his weight off her. Couldn't help but notice the way she stared at him.

The swish of his tactical pants seemed crazy-loud against the sleeping bag. Slid out of the tent, swiveling around in a fluid motion as he brought up his Sig Sauer. Glided to the entrance and shouldered the wall. Saw the man now less than fifteen yards from their shelter.

Whistling, calling, he was coming straight at them.

Keep moving. Don't look here … don't look here … Range willed the man. He did not want to have to kill this man but neither could he let him compromise their position. Endanger the HVT.

The man stumped closer … ten yards … five …

Range slowed his pulse. Thought through how he'd hide the

body. They'd have to leave immediately. Steal a vehicle. Get as far away as possible as quickly as possible.

Thankfully, Jazani hadn't moved. Or breathed, it seemed. He couldn't afford to look at her, not with the—

The mattress against the window shifted beneath the urging of the wind. Saw the man's shoulder. Tricky shot. He heard Jazani's breath catch. Prayed the guy did not.

As stealthily as possible, every muscle contracted, taut, Range shifted. Eyes locked on the target. Ready to silence him before he could shout for help.

The man snapped his head to the left.

Range applied pressure to the trigger.

A laugh barked into the night. Then the man growled as he turned around, muttering something about a goat.

Easing back, peering through that sliver of space, Range saw the man hauling off a goat.

Jazani huffed a breath. But didn't say anything.

That'd been too close. It was time to move. Once the man was out of sight, Range grabbed his ruck. "We need to go. Now."

"But he is gone," she said, scooting out of the shelter he'd erected.

"For now. But if he's sitting in his house and suddenly wonders why the mattress was against the window, he might come back."

In ten, they were hiking farther west a klick, then he would veer them north. Jazani was stumbling and yawning, both grating on his nerves.

"I thought we—"

"Quiet." He didn't need her thoughts in his head, too. His mind was too crowded with his own. With what had made Pike stall. Delays happened. Things got hot in a location and they bought time. But this ... it felt ... different. "Keep moving."

"I am not—"

He jerked around and shoved into her face. "*Quiet.*"

"No."

Range saw red. "Do you want to die?"

"Why are we going west? You said north earlier—"

"Plans change. Now shut up and move." He started away, and immediately sensed her rebellion. Defiance. Not wanting to glance back, he knew what happened. Knew she was still fifteen paces back where he'd left her. Twenty ... The woman didn't add up. How could someone be so bullheaded and yet people called her savior.

She brainwashed them.

Thirty.

After all, hadn't one of the girls posed as Jazani, taken the isolation, food-and-water-deprivation for her? He'd heard of victims identifying with their captors. Was that what—

Something struck the back of his head.

A rock, he guessed. Though he was ready to rip her a new on, he kept walking. At least she was following now. Wouldn't waste words on her.

Madam Jazani knew where and how to find safety. The woman had smarts, he'd give her that, which is why he hadn't stopped. The attack and the man who'd found them convinced her of the very real danger she was in. Scared her into sticking with him. At least for now.

He tugged his phone out to use the navigation. And in the split-second before the screen changed, he saw a ghostly blur reflected on it—and simultaneously heard a soft thump of her foot.

Dropping his ruck, Range ducked and darted to the side.

Jazani—having hurtled herself at him—vaulted past him. Landed hard on the ground. She didn't cry out. She didn't pout. Instead, she flipped back onto her feet and fell into a fighting stance.

"We don't have time—"

She hiked up and spun, whipping a hook-kick at his head.

Stunned and maybe a little impressed, Range leapt back. Anticipated her landing. Slid in. Rammed an elbow at her face.

Somehow, she avoided the strike. Stumbled back. Tripped over his ruck. Plopped onto her backside. With another grunt, she was upright again. A flurry of strikes and punches. Deflected, both his and hers. Her hijab had long given up on protecting her from men's weakness.

He caught the end of it, twirled it. Yanked it and her toward him. Managed to get her into a strangle hold.

And something went crossways in him at the way she flailed. The way she clawed. Panic. Terror.

He'd never seen that from her. Except with the captain …

Range thrust her forward, releasing her.

She tripped and dropped to the ground. On all fours, her hijab floating away on a chilled wind, she looked at up, dark brown hair wafting around her furious expression.

"Enough!" A strange feeling squirreled through his chest at what just happened. How that made him feel. What thudded in his chest. "We do *not* have time for this."

"I am sick of you treating me worse than a dog!"

"Want something better? Earn it!"

She drew onto her feet. "I should not have to do anything for you to act with honor."

"Why would you expect that from me?" His words faltered, his heart jamming into his throat.

She lifted her chin. "Your bravado and anger do not scare or fool me. Already I have seen honor from you, Rage."

He scowled. "Why do you keep calling me that?"

Eyes darting around, she frowned. "It … It is your name. I heard the men call you that."

Sniffing, he should not be surprised that's what she'd heard. He wasn't interested in correcting her either. It was better that's what she thought of him.

"And I may be the monster you believe me to be, but I am not stupid," she growled, shoving hair from her face. "While you may have the intel to get us to where we're going, it would be poor strategy to have me completely ignorant of what we are doing."

"Not really."

Please," she said with a thick breath, "I thought you were supposed to protect me, get me to the Secondary place?"

Range gritted his teeth, irritated that she had paid so much attention to what they called that location. "As I said, plans change." In fact, he was thinking of changing them again. How much did they really need this HVT?

Looking down, her breathing finally normalizing, she seemed … sad. Broken. Then she jutted that jaw again and all her defiance returned. "What is the new plan?"

Range worked his jaw. Tried to rein in his frustration. "Get a vehicle. Head west till dawn, then bank north."

Side-eyeing him from where she stood, she sighed. "Why did the plan change?"

"The goat farmer—"

"No." She swallowed. "I … I could not sleep. Saw you check your phone. Your expression … changed. You looked upset, worried."

He really did not like that she could read him and he didn't want to tell her anything she didn't have to know. The less she knew the better for OpSec. "Rendezvous time has been pushed back. That's all I know."

She frowned. "But that means we're …"

"Yeah." He shrugged. "I have supplies for two days, but if we don't get clearance to head to Secondary by then, we'll have to consider our options."

The one at the top of his list? Making sure he brought her in, alive or dead. He was leaning toward the latter.

Our options. As if he included *her* in those.

Now Kasra almost regretted going on full attack, but it had seemed the only way this man listened. Allure and candor had no effect on him. He was all that his name, Rage, implied—and now, she wondered if that wasn't his name. The way he'd scowled and asked why she kept calling him that …

"Look," she said, trying to calm herself. "I am sorry for attacking you."

His jaw muscle worked.

"I just … you do not listen when I talk to you, when I ask—"

"The only thing I want to hear come out of your mouth is that name."

It surprised how easily his words hurt her. Abuse and violence had been her existence for most of her life … Yet one little sentence from him was a well-placed dagger to the remnant of her soul.

She recalled awaking in the tent and finding a man over her. Her instincts had kicked in, though dulled a fraction by awareness, and then she realized it was him. The weirdness of him being atop her. The way he'd had to lay there as the goat herder lingered outside the wall. How his breath skated along her cheek.

Clearing her throat, Kasra diverted her thoughts back to finding a way to make him see her as partner in this venture. Not as an adversary. What would convince him …? "Viper."

He snapped to her, muscles taut. "Nice try. Already know—"

"His *real* name is what you want, yes?"

He narrowed his eyes and stepped closer. "Is this a game to you? This man who's running children, robbing them of their innocence and—"

"Do not think to tell me what they are robbed of! I know, all too well."

"Then stop the frickin' games and give me his name!"

Kasra felt something she had not in many years … "I was wrong. You do not have honor. So." Why did her throat feel thick? "What is to stop you from killing me or abandoning me after I give you his name?"

His lip curled. "Guess you'll just have to try me."

At least he had not asked her to trust him. Because she never would. But she needed to get back to the others, which was the only way she could get to Saudi. That was an absolute must. "He is German."

He stared at her, hard.

She felt a pull to give him what he wanted so he would not look at her like that. But that … "That's all. For now."

Shaking his head, he turned away. "You're unbelievable."

"I want to live. And without y—" She felt the 'you' on her lips, her hopes pinned so recklessly to the chest of this man as if with all his military medals he likely had tucked away somewhere. "Without getting back to the others, I have no hope of that."

"Without me, you mean," he snarled.

She swallowed at the way he said that. What he meant by it. Is that what he wanted to hear? Is that all it would take? Others had forced her to admit she needed them and that never ended well for her. But it *had* bought her time … "My life is in your hands, Rage."

He grimaced. Turned away.

"Is that so disgusting to you?"

He jerked back. Frowned. "You know what? *It is!*" He shouldered toward her. "I *hate* that I'm out here, risking my life for someone who sold *children* for sex! For you!"

Kasra drew up straight. "You have no idea—"

"*Do. Not* try to justify what you do." He pressed into her

space. "There is no law severe enough for someone like you. But I vow"—his nostrils flared—"you will feel the full force of my fury when this is over."

Pulse racing, hurting, she stepped into a role so practiced and familiar, she almost didn't notice the shift. "And this is how you convince me to give you his name?"

"*Again,*" he barked, "you prove you're not worth my time and—"

"I wasn't aware this was for you."

"—that you value your own life above that of the innocents caught in your horrific net!"

"It's. Not. My. Net!" Her shrill scream rang in her own ears, startling her.

He snatched up his ruck. Glowered at her. Then struck off in a northwesterly direction.

When? When had she *ever* tried to justify herself to a man, especially one who decided her worth and value based off something he could never fathom if he tried for years. If he only knew what she had risked, sacrificed, to help everyone else. All the hours, the dangers …

What? He would like you? Be nice to you?

She stood there for what felt like ages, frozen in his words, his hatred. Why were they getting in her head? Why did she care what he thought? She should not. Had not—not for any other man who vomited his hatred. She long ago figured out how to be sharper and smarter than any man who came to her …

Until him.

Ruck over his shoulder, he made his way in the light, drizzling rain across the plain.

Watching him move, the distancing growing between them, Kasra felt the raindrops thump against what was left of her courage. The fledgling hope she'd felt back at the safehouse for just a moment ... It had taken on the weight of an anchor and dragged her back into its haunting depths.

Should have known better.

No man would want her. No man would see past the darkness that had devoured her life.

Why do you care? You do not need a man!

Perhaps, but in the safehouse ... when he talked to her as if she were someone worth knowing, smiled at her as if she were someone he found pleasing, inquired of her as if he thought of her as someone intelligent, whose advice was sought ... it had been very nice. That was when Kasra discovered that somehow, in the scorched life that had become hers, a small, raw patch of her once-innocent heart had survived.

A discovery made because of him. Because, the one man who would never want to be in her bed, had somehow found a way into that patch. And the hatred he spat in her face?

Quid pro quo, Handsome.

"There are six things the Lord hates, seven that are an abomination ..."

"No, no no," she muttered, keeping her head down. Those verses needed to take a backseat. For now.

Yet they forced their way forward all the same. *"... a heart that devises wicked plans ..."*

Resisting the urge to stamp her foot or groan, Kasra hugged herself. It was not fair. How many times had wicked plans been carried out against *her*? And those went unhindered.

She wanted to throw a fit. Growl. Rail at the heavens. But those verses ... That little book forgotten one night on her table had gotten her to here. The girls free—most of them, anyway—effectively shutting down Roud. A victory she had not thought possible. And put her in the hands of the Americans.

That American.

Trudging behind him, she watched the morning light tease the glints in his dark blond hair.

It seemed fitting, justice. He had vowed she would pay … Would his thirst for vengeance change at all if he knew all she had done to free the girls? To strike back at Taweel …?

It does not matter.

She did not seek approval or reward for what she had done. It was just … penance, righting all the wrongs. If she survived, if Taweel and the German did not catch her, it would be a miracle. Then … then she would truly know Allah lived. But did she not already? Again, her gaze hit Rage.

Well, she knew the *Iblīs* existed.

CHAPTER NINE

Kandahar Province, Afghanistan

Situation untenable. Sugar Daddy on prowl. Brass ticked. Collusion? Eyes out. Foamy zebra.

"SITUATION UNTENABLE? NO DUH!" Disbelieving the text, Range stared at his phone. What the heck was happening? Collusion—among who? Frustration spitting through his veins, he did his best to maintain his cool. He stopped, lowered into a crouch, and hooked his arms over his head. What were they supposed to do? Options were very limited, considering Americans were no longer supposed to operate in country.

"What is wrong?"

Not now, shrew. Teeth grinding, he just wanted to find a solution. Get the name, get rid of the madam. Foamy Zebra.

Son. Of. A. Biscuit.

He dropped to the ground and peered into the distance. Jazani's escape clearly upset the big guy—big *German* guy, aka Viper, according to her. And now the Brass was ... ticked? Is that why Pike suggested collusion ...? Between the U.S. military and Afghanistan? Or between Viper and the Brass? All of the above?

But ... why would they all be ticked? What about the raid on Roud upset everyone? Bringing down the Trench—that was a good thing. Sure, Afghanistan couldn't be happy to find out there were American operators in-country. But was that all? Or was there more going on here?

He rubbed his thumb over his lower lip, thinking. Jazani had said Captain Hellqvist had frequented Roud. Had other members of the Brass?

"I know you hate me," came her soft voice, "but since we are both in this situation—whatever it is—please tell me what is wrong."

Her words had a strange effect. Pushed his gaze down. "Secondary is compromised." He stared out from their location on a hill. Eyed Kandahar. A small village between them and the city. "We need to get a vehicle." He stood and started down the hillside.

"Wait." Jazani's voice pitched and she slipped and skidded down the dirt to him. Caught his arm. "What do you mean compromised? What about the others? Why are we getting a vehicle? Where are we going?"

He hated her. He really hated her.

Not true. He hated the situation.

Caused by her.

So yeah ... hated her.

"*Hatred stirs up conflict, Son. Love covers all wrongs.*" His mom loved to throw that verse at him every time he'd said he hated Canyon. What would she say about this, about this woman? Surely she wouldn't tell him to cover *this*.

Kasra angled in, prompting him for an answer.

Not trusting himself to speak, he showed her the text from Pike.

She glanced down, dark lashes dusting her olive complexion as she read. Then those brown-green eyes came to his. "What is a foamy zebra?"

"Of all the things to ask about—"

"It is the only one that does not make sense."

He took back his phone. "It makes sense."

She twisted her hair and tossed it over her shoulder. "So, Taweel is making trouble for your friends."

"And for us."

"How?"

Range frowned. "We're on our own."

"For how long?"

"Unknown." Range tugged out his nocs and checked out the nearby close-knit village, bordered by a stone half-wall that sectioned off each home as well. A few vehicles, but he doubted they'd be able to get away with one of them. It was too open. Too few people. They'd be spotted. "We'll need to sneak into the city."

Jazani pulled in a sharp breath. "Are you crazy?"

"I'm with *you*, aren't I?"

Hurt rippled through her but washed away just as fast. She pointed toward the city. "That is Kandahar," she said with emphasis. "I am known there. Their spies are everywhere."

He considered her. Started to say something about her paying for the hurt she'd caused, but something shut his mouth. Tugging out his device, he decided it'd be easier for him to go in alone. Less complicated. "Hide out here, and I'll—"

"No!" She grabbed his arm, fingers digging into his flesh.

Range drew up straight, scowling from her grip to her face. Where he'd expected to find demand and outrage, he saw … fear. "Jazani, what do you want? I say we go in there and you balk. I say to stay and you balk."

She released him and stepped back. Seemed to find herself. "I will wear a burqa."

"And where do you have one of those hidden?" He huffed. "You couldn't have thought of that before accusing me of being crazy?"

"You are ... infuriating. I'll find one!"

"Right back atcha, Madam." He yanked his arm free. "We need a vehicle and we need supplies, so we're going into the city. Want a burqa, then find one."

Again, she paused. "Where will we go after ...?"

Range did not like the answer and knew she'd like it a lot less. "South."

"*South?*" she yelped, shuffling in front of him. "But our deal! I would—"

"Deal's amended due to unforeseen circumstances named Taweel."

She blinked. Faltered. Didn't seem to be able to process things. "But our deal ... I ... I have nothing in the south. I cannot—"

"Great." That was the opening he'd hoped for. "Tell me the name, and you can go wherever the heck you'd like. My infuriating self will be out or your hair." He tucked his chin. "Perfect, right? You get what you want, I get what I need. Just speak the name."

She looked pale. Like she'd be sick. She slumped into a stone wall that bordered the small village and touched her forehead. "What am I going to do ...?"

She said that like she'd had something planned.

Which of course she had. They'd been escaping when the team had interdicted. So there'd been an escape plan ... a way for her to get off scot-free. "You expected to slip into anonymity after ... all that you did?"

Jazani didn't look up. Her gaze darted over the rocks and tufts of grass at her feet. As if she hadn't heard him. Or didn't care. Probably a master at that.

"Like I said," he interrupted her thoughts, which he read as regret that she'd get caught or that things wouldn't be as easy she'd hoped for, "speak the name, go free."

Her gaze stilled. She looked frozen. Swallowed. Then stood,

her face very close to his and set in determination. "I have friends in the city who can help with supplies."

"No friends," he growled, not willing to put his life in her hands or trust anything she said. Wasn't going to come out of this in a pine box or with extra holes in his cadaver.

"How much money do you have?" She shrugged, her dark hair still loose around her shoulders. "I have none."

He wanted to curse her. "There are other ways—"

"If you are caught stealing, they will cut off your hand, but when they realize you're an American, they will cut the rest of you in pieces." She cocked her head. "And I will get to watch."

"That'd make you happy."

"Deliriously." But there was no smile or amusement in her expression. "My friends *will* help us, I assure you. This is my city, and I know how to move through it so as not to draw attention." She arced an eyebrow and cocked her head. "Now, you will need to put your life in my hands."

"Keep dreaming." He shouldered his ruck.

"Hard to dream when you can't sleep."

He frowned. "You dreamed last night."

"No, I never slept—"

"You did."

Defiance glinted in her eyes. "I watched you the whole time."

What did that mean? Scratch that—he didn't care. "Then who's Atia?"

Jazani jerked. Stepped back, her eyes wide. Then she rushed at him and clamped a hand over his mouth. "Never speak that name again." She pushed harder. "Swear it!"

He was so startled by her desperate vehemence, he froze for a second.

"Swear it!"

Instinct said to put her on her backside, knee in her throat. Instead, he flipped her grip and twisted her around, then gave a nudge. Before she could come at him again, he turned toward the city, all the more curious about this Atia.

"Stow your backpack or they will know," Jazani said. "That is too Western."

Irritated that she instructed him, Range knew she was right. But this was all he had. Weapons. Emergency supplies. Clothes. They ducked along one of the walls and he dug a hole while she slipped around a home for a burqa. He was covering the ruck when she returned with the black material and a couple of other pieces.

"What was that you said about stealing?" he challenged.

"*Borrowing.*"

"You intend to return it?"

"When you retrieve your weapons." She nodded. "For you," she said, setting items on the ground.

"What—"

"A kurta and turban. The Taliban insist on a strict dress code, and it will hide your blond hair better than a baseball hat, which makes you look very American and very military."

Right once again. Which was starting to tick him off. Wished he could think of something smart-alec to say. Instead, he finished burying the ruck, spread some scrub over it, then turned.

Jazani was there, hands muddied. She reached toward him.

"Hey! What—"

"You are too ... Women will notice." She smoothed mud into his stubble. Then dusted it off. "And when the women notice, the men will notice."

"And what happens when they see a beautiful woman walking with a dirty, muddied man?"

"Who says they will even notice the dirtied, muddied man at that point?"

He frowned.

"It was a joke, Rage. I will be in a burqa. Nobody will see anything."

Man, he should correct his name, but giving her his real one ... seemed a betrayal. A giving-in.

"There." Her hands rested on his shoulders as she considered him, and forced him to look into those green-brown eyes with gold flecks.

She was beautiful. No denying it. He'd noticed that when she was Malala. Had been intrigued by the interpreter who seemed to communicate so much to the fake Kasra and, now that he considered that time, marveled that she'd made no obvious misstep.

Her expression seemed to soften beneath his assessment. Hesitation perched on her small nose. "I think that ..."

He stepped from her touch and nodded in the direction of the city. "Let's get this done."

Relief washed through her features with a near smile. "Their shop is not far."

Ten minutes later, she had threaded her way into the burqa and negotiated the streets like the professional she was. Which should bother him, but he just wanted to get out of the open before they were recognized. They climbed stairs and made their way down a hall.

When the door opened, Kasra inclined her head. "Gabina—"

"Ah!" A thin, short woman pulled the madam into a hug. A stream of Pashto flew between the two in a merry greeting.

He slid into the flat behind them and checked the hall once more, then locked the door. Did a quick scan of the living space—one large room with two doors splitting off. Bathroom and a bedroom, he guessed. Two children playing on a thick rug with cushions.

Hands behind his back, ready to snatch the Sig Sauger holstered there, Range stood by the door. Had a good line of sight on the street via open windows and could hear voices floating up through the wood floors from the shop below.

"Gabina," Kasra said, pausing with her friend and indicating to him, "this is ... Rage."

He stiffened at the misnomer, but let it go. Nodded at the woman. Better nobody knew his real name anyway.

The friend gave him a hesitant smile, her probing gaze taking him in. Finally, she focused on her friend. "How are you here? What of ...?"

"Roud." The madam gave a sharp nod. "We"—she eyed him, obviously debating how much to say about his role in ruining her chance to flee—"escaped."

Gabina gasped, hand going to her mouth. "How did you do this? With *his* help?" Then she caught her friend's hand and held it close. "It is dangerous, Kasra. You know what will happen—"

"We will not stay long. But I beg for help. We need ... supplies to get away before it is too late. Only a few things, really. Necessities, and I could think of no one I trusted more than you. Can you—"

"Of course!" Gabina's eyes brightened. "Anything. You know this. Come, come." She started for the back room.

The two acted more like friends going on a vacation together than a madam and a friend packing supplies for an escape from the city. The Pashto was too hot and fast to track fully. Range moved around the two-room flat and shouldered up against the shutters to the balcony window. Scanned the street, while listening to the women.

"He is handsome," Gabina whispered in Pashto. "Are you escaping with him? Is that what—"

"No!" Kasra hissed. "Never. I ... I paid him to help me. They are already looking for me. One plan was ruined."

Too much info. Dial it back, Jazani. He slid a glower toward her and found her gaze waiting.

Something quieter whispered between them, and he got the distinct impression she was trying to hide her words from him. Gaze sharp, he sent as much warning as he could not to compromise them.

She met and held his gaze.

But what he saw there was not flirtation or even anger. It was something that went hand-in-hand with that other feeling—fear—he'd seen before: sadness.

Was she planning to double-cross him?

Shadows shifted on the street below.

Range snapped his gaze to the road, palming his Sig. Lifting it from the holster as two shapes bled from the shadows. Strode into the shop below. Two more behind. "Company," he hissed, hurrying to her even as voices echoed in the stairwell. "Move. Now!" Weapon out, he angled toward the door, reaching to swing her behind him.

"Please, no—it is Coman." Gabina rushed to the door, one hand on the knob, a palm aimed at Range. Eyes pleading. "My husband."

Kasra was in front of him, her eyes wide and outraged. "Put it away."

"Not happening."

She leaned in. "This is my friend's home. With children. Put. It. Away."

"So, children's innocence matters to you now?"

The door opened, ushering in a man. A broad smile split his dark beard as he greeted his wife, but vanished when he lit on Range and the gun he had been too slow in returning to its holster. "What—"

"Sh–sh." Catching her husband's shoulder, Gabina shut the door. "Peace, please. He helped Kasra."

"By holding us hostage?" the man balked, clearly affronted.

Range held the man's gaze, unrepentant. "No hostages," he

said in Pashto. "Just readiness. You came home rather fast in the middle of the day."

Displeasure apparent, Coman cleared his throat as he narrowed dark eyes on Range. "Word came to me that strangers had entered our home. Now what am I to wonder when I find an unknown man in my home with *a gun?*"

"Please." Kasra went to the man. "I know this is terrible, and I will leave if you insist. I came for help. Your help, Coman."

Coman frowned, heard one of the kids laugh. "Children. In the bedroom. Now."

With pouts but no complaints, the two shuffled into the other room.

Gabina closed the door and turned back to them. The man swallowed, and there was a stiff, silent conversation happening between the two. "What kind of help?"

"Supplies," Kasra said. "Food, clothes. A car would be good."

"What is this, Kasra?" Coman demanded in Pashto. "Word is all over the city about the compound—there was a raid. That Americans"—the man's eyes stabbed Range—"took all the girls."

"They did not"—she flinched—"take them all. I …" She touched her forehead. "It is a long story to tell with you so angry."

"It's a longer story than we have time for," Range put in, his Pashto not perfect but pretty close.

Coman eyed him speculatively. "Then we will talk—man to man—while the women get what is needed." He looked to his wife. "And maybe some dinner."

With a smile, Gabina gave him a nod.

It surprised Range that the man so wholly trusted the madam. That he'd accept her word and not be angry about the stranger in his home, though—by that suspicious, narrowing gaze—had figured out Range wasn't from around here. Then he'd offer supplies without further discussion and insisted they talk. Did this man know who Kasra really was? What she did for a living? And he didn't have a problem with it?

Well, he *had* mentioned the girls …

"American, come. Sit, talk." In the living area, Coman folded himself onto a cushion and eyed Range as he crossed the room. "You seem comfortable in my country and with my language."

Still speaking Pashto. To test him? Probably to keep him on his guard.

Range sat with one leg tucked under his bent knee. Easier to spring into action. "Comfortable is a stretch …" He was distracted for a moment, watching Kasra in the kitchen with Gabina, cooking up something that quickly filled the apartment with a spicy aroma. Definitely smelled curry, which made his stomach grumble.

Coman's cheek twitched. "It is not an easy language."

That was an understatement. Pashto was a Tier Two language right below the toughest, Mandarin and Russian.

The little boy came rushing in, showing his father a toy, which he complained it wasn't working. With a speculative look at Range, Coman pulled his son into his lap. Helped him worked though troubleshooting the problem. The sister hurried into the kitchen … surprisingly hugging the legs of not her mom, but Kasra, who laughed and bent down. Brushed the girl's hair from her face, said something, then kissed her cheek as she handed her a piece of fruit.

It was something so … domestic, so … weird.

"She is not what you expect, yes?" Coman said quietly as the boy scuttled off to the back room with his now-working toy.

Range dropped his gaze to the carpeted floor.

"I see on your face that you know what happens at Roud. How did you come to be with Kasra?"

The way the man said that somehow made Range feel guilty. And how exactly was he supposed to answer that?

"You arrest her?" Coman ask, his eyebrows lifted in amusement.

Range eyed the man, not feeling at liberty to discuss his operations.

"Now, you see in her a home and laughing, hugging children, just as any woman would do, and your military mind, it explodes." Coman nodded and chuckled.

Soon, the women placed platters of food before Coman and Range, then slipped into the back room. Should he be worried that she was out of sight? But then he saw her reflection in a mirror as she packed some items in a tapestry bag. Still, he wondered if she'd use her friends to betray him. Were they setting him up while even more men came as he sat here, stuffing himself?

Arm hooked over his leg, Coman took a piece of bread, but his gaze settled on Range for a long moment. "Where are the girls?"

Direct, to the point. Range respected that. In his periphery, he noticed Kasra move into the kitchen again. She had her back to him and had gone still. Listening, no doubt, for his answer. "We did not take them … all."

"Then the ones you did take." The man's chewed slowly.

"Safe." He hoped. With all that had gone south, he had no definitive answers.

Coman bent over the steaming food and scooped up rice and chicken with a piece of torn bread. "Where?"

Eating for a moment, he wouldn't give away vital intel. Couldn't risk this man being some leader of a local militia or something. "Can't answer that yet," he eyed Kasra, hoping she heard, reminding her she owed him a name.

The two women worked at a table in the kitchen.

"You do not trust me," Coman said.

"I don't know you." Which was rude. "You already proved

how fast word gets around this city. That's dangerous—to me and her. Her escape complicated things."

"Escape?" His dark eyes flicked to the madam. "Kasra, this is true? You did this?"

Jerking her gaze to the floor, she gave a faint bob of her head. "You said it was too dangerous."

"It is—was! They have shot at us, hunted us. If they learn where I am … It is why I must get supplies and leave the city as quickly as possible. I do not mean to bring trouble to you, Gabina, or the children."

After considering her for a long second, Coman nodded. Drew in a breath that lifted his jaw, which he jutted to his wife. "Give her the pottery money."

"No!" Kasra gasped. "No, Coman. It is too much. We only need—"

"Enough!" Coman said gruffly, silencing her.

Range frowned. Pottery money? Is that what the man did for a living?

"Work quickly and be gone." Coman refocused on eating.

Why was this man willing to help her escape? There was no familial resemblance, but that did not necessarily mean anything in a place where a man might have more than one wife. But here in a Muslim country, Range expected a more strident reaction to Kasra because of her profession. Their hardline approach to morality didn't sit well with most Westerners.

"You are confused."

Not a question, so technically nothing to answer.

"Most only see one side to her—the sinful side." Coman sipped from a small round cup. "Do you know her story?"

The man had his attention. his confusion, he nodded. "Some."

"Sadly, her story is not for me to tell, and as she is not family, it is not for me to defend her. However, I take very personally what happens to her."

A warning? Range squinted at him. "Why?"

"Two years ago, my Gabina and her sister were taken right off the street in Kabul and ended up ... at Roud."

Oh man ... Range wiped a hand over his mouth.

"Yes," Coman said gravely. "I searched and searched for her. When it was suggested that this evil thing was done to my wife, I went to Roud."

"That went over well, I bet."

"The guards beat me and left me on the side of the road to die."

Not surprising.

"But a week later, in the darkest art of the night, I hear a knock on my door." He let out a laugh-cry. "It is Gabina! She is free, and her sister."

Range shifted. "How did they get free? Did they run away?"

"No. No one can run away from that place."

Except Kasra. With all the girls ...

"Kasra did it." Coman nodded. "She returned my wife and her sister."

His earlier confusion had nothing on the ricochet in his head right now. "I don't ..." Range started to shake his head. Why would she send girls *back*? "How ... Why?"

"Ask her." Coman slapped his hands together, ending the meal—and apparently the conversation. "You take her, so you ask."

Wait. What? Head spinning, Range frowned. "No, she's in my custody. I'm"—hold up ... if these people were friends with her, it might not work in his favor to mention he was just detaining her until he could turn her over; that they'd made a deal—"getting her to safety."

"Yes, see? You a good man."

If he only knew ...

"I'm just doing my job."

"See?" He leaned forward conspiratorially. "Since she help

with my Gabina, I ask Allah to help Kasra find freedom." He thrust his jaw at him. "I see many American soldier in Roud. But they did not protect her like you. They do bad things ..." He nodded. "Understand?"

More than he wanted to admit.

"And you help but not worry about *her* job." He studied Range. "I think I know what you are."

Range frowned.

"You are a Christian, yes?" His voice had quieted, speaking something that could get them all killed now that the Taliban once again controlled with an iron fist.

Barking up the wrong end of that Bible, buddy.

"I think only a Christian could see past her job. Allah help you do that."

Her *job*? "She *sold kids* ... That's not a job, that's ..." Range clenched his teeth. Reminded himself he was a guest in this man's house. "Hard to overlook."

Coman arched an eyebrow and took another sip of his tea. "I see you avoid my question."

Range had nothing to prove here. Last thing he needed was a lecture about his abandoned beliefs. Well, maybe not abandoned, but stuffed in the attic with yearbooks and high school soccer trophies. "We should get going."

On his feet, Coman seemed alarmed. "I offend. My apologies, friend. Please, stay."

Range cocked his head. "We've been here too long."

"No, no. Too *soon*." The man held a hand out to Range, then indicated to the streets. "Too busy. Wait till late night." He touched his wife's shoulder. "Gabina, make *sheer pira*. Yes? Delicious."

"Of course," she said, emerging from the back room.

"No. No more food." Range remembered the last time someone conned him into eating *that* desert.

Kasra slipped around the couple and came to him. "You are

being rude," she hissed. The green kurta she now wore set off her eyes and accented her light olive complexion.

"I'm not here to make friends," he bit back.

"We leave now and we will be seen," she growled. "Night is safer. You cannot argue that."

"Being here puts your friends in danger." He angled closer. "Or do you just care about yourself? Again?"

Nostrils flaring, she seethed. Tightened her lips. "We should go," she quietly said to her friends, giving Range one last glare before turning to their hosts. "I do not want you hurt because of me."

"Baba, bad men are coming," one of the kids called.

Loud thuds came from below. Then shouts.

Range reached for his weapon.

"This way," Coman said, leading them to the back room. A tapestry hung on the wall and he nudged it aside to reveal a small door. He clenched it open. "Down the passage, to the left. It will take you to the back alley."

Banging came from the front room.

"Hurry!"

Range directed her into the space first, and though she gave him a dark look, she hugged the satchel and tucked through the small opening. He offered his hand to the man. "Manana."

Coman rested a hand on his back. "Ask, and protect her. Allah has put her in your care. Be careful how you handle that responsibility, brother."

Irritated with the instruction, Range folded himself through the tight space and crouched there a second to let his gaze adjust. Behind him the door clunked shut and then he heard Coman calling to the visitors.

CHAPTER TEN

Kandahar Province, Afghanistan

"I DO NOT NEED you to take care of me."

"Done."

Kasra's heart lurched into her throat when he turned away from her and banked down a side alley. She faltered, half stunned that he would leave her, half angry that he was so ready to be rid of her. She had a good mind to let him go.

Shots from behind whipped her around. She stared at the second-story flat. *Please ... no ...* Saw movements. Even as she reached for the small phone Gabina had secreted to her, she saw both Coman and Gabina moving there.

Oh, thank Allah!

When she turned back, she saw Rage had reached the end of the street and went to the left. Only as she rounded the corner and slammed straight into him, dropping the satchel, did she realize how panicked she had felt.

He flipped her around and pinned her to the wall. "Are you done with your games?" he growled in her ear. "Yes or no, *Madam*. Because if not, then go back. I can't worry about whether you're going to do something stupid and put me in danger."

She shoved him back. "Get off me." Wrested away from his touch and anger.

"Yes or no?"

Furious, she stared at him. Wanted to argue. Punch that smug look off his face. "Yes, only if—"

"No." He was in her face again. "No conditions. Either yes or no. You say no—realize your decision affects the other girls' lives."

"For a man who is self-righteous and claims to care about the welfare of others, you threaten their lives easily."

"Not me, Madam. *You*. Your answer affects them." He lifted his eyebrows and nodded in the direction they'd just come. "They're already looking for you, so decide fast."

"I just want information to underst—"

He strode away.

Kasra caught his arm. Anticipated him shoving or pinning her, and hopped aside. Felt a jolt of exultation at deflecting him. But saw the storm move into his eyes again. "I am sorry." She held up her palms. "I ... It is not easy for me to trust a man." Why on earth had she said *that*?

"We have a deal. I'll keep it. And considering things, that's saying a lot."

"Things."

Irritation made his jaw muscle jounce.

"I see." She saw revulsion so clear. Feeling defeated, lost, hopeless, she shifted aside and inclined her head in surrender.

When his hand moved to her, she cringed, expecting to be struck.

"For the love of—" He growled in frustration. Took her bag. Slung it over his shoulder. "Stay close." He crossed the road, streaming along parked cars.

What was happening in her life that she was following a

man? No, not just a man, but an *American*. As a young girl, she had admired the soldiers who came through with their weapons, candy, and the way things had changed. Thought them strong and handsome—heroes. But as a young woman, she came to know they were just as bad as Afghani men. Some were worse, far from home and feeling invulnerable to punishment.

She noticed almost too late that Rage had slowed, stepped back. "Wha—"

He opened a car door. Nodded her to the other side. "Get in."

She stood there mute, confused. "We would *steal*—"

He tossed the pack in the back, then sat behind the wheel, and reached beneath the dash. By the time she hustled inside and closed the passenger door, he had started the engine. They pulled away. At every crossroad, she felt the breath catch in her throat as they were forced to stop … then start again. Before long, they were out of the city. They whipped back to the village and retrieved the gear he'd stowed. In minutes they were racing southward, night quickly catching them.

Her thoughts were heavy as they drove, and her eyes all the heavier. But, worrying too much that they'd end up in some prison or something, she forbade herself from sleeping. Worried about the girls. About Razam and Fatina, Iamar. Were they okay? Rage said the other place had been compromised. How? He had mentioned Taweel. But what about the captain? It could not be a coincidence that he showed up at the safehouse, then it was attacked.

Somehow, she fell asleep as they barreled along Ring Road, waking only to jarring bouncing as they slowed suddenly on a dirt road. "What is wrong? What are we doing?"

He angled the car into some scrub and glanced around before jamming the gear into Park. "Sleep. Two hours. We'll head out on foot."

They were completely hidden from the road. "On foot? Why? The car—"

"Is almost out of gas."

"Then we *buy* gas," she said slowly, wondering why he did not plan that. "Why—"

"*Rest*," he growled, then reached down between the driver's door and the seat. Laid it back. Arms folded, he closed his eyes.

Just like that.

She grunted. Just like that he decides to sleep. And does. Irritated, she secretly envied his ability to sleep at will. Then again, he had not slept last night. He deserved it. Maybe she should stay awake. Keep a watchful eye for trouble.

Shifting on the seat, she felt something in the seat poke her hip. She adjusted again, an ache permeating her lower back and neck. Turning sideways, she tried to find a better position and let her seat back as far as it would go.

"*What* are you doing?" he barked.

"The car is old."

He scowled. "Are you kidding me?"

"Maybe steal a more comfortable car next time."

"Nothing ever pleases you, does it?"

"Not in a long time," she spat back, hurt piercing her heart.

Though it was dark and the engine lights were off, somehow light found his pale eyes as he stared at her. Question in his expression. Something … uncertain.

Feeling strangely exposed and vulnerable, she stuffed her hijab under her head and tried to look like she'd fallen asleep. Heard him sigh and get comfortable again. When she peeked, she was amused to see he had his ballcap on again and had pulled it down over his eyes. It was such an American thing.

His lips parted and a soft snore drifted into the confined space. Amazing how quickly he slipped into a deep sleep, his well-muscled chest rising and falling steadily. Long ago, she learned to sleep in expectation of being … interrupted. The other night, had she really dreamed, called out 'Atia?' She had not dreamed—not like that—in ages. She must have been very tired to do that. Still, to sleep so soundly in such a situation was very unlike her. She could not even sleep without her favorite pillow.

What had made it possible to sleep so soundly that she dreamed …? Her gaze slid again to this American, who put off a lot of rage like his name. Yet she saw a side of him that hinted at compassion—his anger about the children, the girls.

Coman had asked him about being a Christian, but she hadn't heard his answer. It would explain a lot of things … and in a way, it matched what she had read in that small book still tucked close to her chest.

"*Yes or no,*" he'd demanded back in the city.

She believed his world was very black and white. For him, there was only right and wrong. No gray area. No explanations or justifications. Which meant he would never understand her world. Her life. Her.

Just let it go. She closed her eyes, decided it did not matter. *He* did not matter. Yet, she had a feeling she would find out how untrue that was.

He grunted.

Kasra started, looking to him again. She couldn't see his eyes beneath the hat. Was he asleep, dreaming?

Another grunt. "No …" he mumbled.

What tormented his dreams? What had happened in his life that it invaded his sleep? She thought to touch his arm. But if he startled awake, he could read it wrong.

"No!" He snapped up, snatching off his hat. Roughed a hand over his face. Huffed. Slumped back down, his gaze briefly skating her way—clearly embarrassed about jolting awake. In a matter of minutes, he was asleep again.

Apparently they were both tormented.

Using the burqa into a pillow, she rested her head. Watching him. Wondering about him. Wondering if she could trust him to set aside Roud and help her. Protect her. It would take a very special man who could do that. She was not convinced it was him.

Aches wove through her neck, and Kasra blinked open her eyes, realizing she had somehow fallen asleep. With a groan, she lifted her head, only then realizing her forehead was against something firm. A bolt shot through her belly when she realized that something firm was Rage's bicep. Mortified, she pulled upright and faced the front.

Wiping his face, he eased his seat up.

Mercies, he had been awake! Knew she fell asleep on his arm. "I am sorry."

He started the car without a word.

"I thought … the car—we were to go to foot."

"Town's nearby."

Silently, he negotiated the car back onto the road, and they got up to speed. Less than ten minutes later, they pulled into a good-sized town with a market. He parked among a jostle of cars. "You have that money Coman gave you?"

Kasra eyed him.

"Buy some water. Maybe some falafel," he said with a shrug. "Meet me near that mosque"—he pointed up through the windshield to the blue mosque towering over the dilapidated structures—"in twenty minutes."

Surprised at his plan, she paused. "You trust me—to split up?"

Even though bloodshot, his eyes were startling blue in the morning light. "If you have better options, take them."

"Do you really hate me so very much?"

He traded the baseball cap for the turban again and grabbed the door handle. "Twenty minutes. The mosque." He nodded. "Go."

Nervous, she climbed out. Tucked the satchel over her

shoulder and headed toward the stands. She used the flip-phone Gabina had given her and texted her: SAFE. THANK YOU AGAIN. Pocketing the phone, she bought two bottled waters. Then mangos.

As she put them in her satchel, she spotted a falafel vendor. Though sure he was joking about the falafel, she thought a peace offering could not hurt and bought a small box. As she finished paying, the vendor's wife said a pretty hijab matched Kasra's eyes. The fuss she made was so odd—she was used to everyone avoiding her. Treating like she was a contagion. Feeling awkward as the woman draped it over the one Kasra already wore, raving about how wonderful it looked, Kasra cringed at the attention.

Embarrassed over the woman's loud, jovial demeanor, she glanced around, worried others were watching. She froze when she spotted Rage, two stalls down, talking on a phone. His eyes were piercing yet ... appreciative.

No, not from him.

The woman fussed and laughed. Clapped.

Desperate to be free of the woman, Kasra bought the hijab and scurried away. As she crossed the street, heading toward Rage, she noticed the green truck with lights. Afghan police.

Sucking in a breath, she adjusted her hijab. Tucked her chin. Hurried in the direction of the mosque, which—thank Allah—was the other way. She tucked the box in her satchel, and hurried down the street, keeping her head down and face covered.

She made it to the mosque without issue, though she did note two men scowling at her from a small shop across the street. Nerves rattling, she scanned for Rage. Up one street, down another. Where was he? She looked at the phone's clock. Okay, she was early. He would be here, right?

Her heart jarred in her chest. What if he had left her here? On her own?

To punish her because he hated her. Hated what she had done.

No. He would not do that. He had character. Honor. Even Coman saw it. So, he would come.

A third man joined the first two at the shop, all watching her.

She should not stay in one place too long. Kasra turned and walked around the fenced perimeter, praying Rage would think to look on all sides. Rounding one side, she found shade. Slowed, glad for the reprieve from the heat and the men's disapproving looks. She turned right, along the back side of the mosque, and faltered when an Afghan truck glided past.

Was it the same one? Heart in her throat, she searched for a place to hide—wait. Twenty minutes. She checked her phone. And stilled. It'd been twenty-two minutes. He was late.

He left me.

No. No no no. He would not. He wanted the name.

She had not proven her worth. Convinced him of the benefit in keeping her alive.

It was too late now.

No. No, it was not. He would come.

No man will ever come for you except in that *way.*

Rage would. He was not like the others.

No, he was worse.

You're being irrational.

She heard a strange whine of a car engine and realized she'd stopped walking. Saw at the end of the block the tail of the police truck backing up into view again.

Kasra scrambled around the corner. Plastered herself against the wall that hemmed in the mosque. Listened over the drumming of her heart. Heard the car shift gears. Tires crunched over rocks, drawing closer.

A car leapt the corner. She felt it lurch toward her.

She fought the urge to run. Shifted aside, head down. She

kept her gaze at an angle that allowed her to see to the road. It was clear straight ahead, if she had to run.

The door flung open. "Get in!" a voice commanded in Pashto.

His voice.

She stared in disbelief at the vehicle. A black Toyota SUV. Then his face. She strangled a cry of relief and jumped in. Shut the door even as it surged forward. Took everything in her not to drop her face into her hands and cry. Instead, she shuddered a breath and reached with trembling fingers to the belt.

"What were you doing?" he snapped. "Making me call out put us at risk. Why were you—"

"You were *late!*"

"Yeah, I had to disable the tracking first—wasn't easy to do."

Her panic was bottoming out, leaving her weak. "Why did you even steal another? Why not just buy gas for first one?"

"Someone berated me for stealing a car with lumpy seats."

Kasra started, considered him. Had he really …?

He hooked his arm over the steering wheel. "The engine in the other was about to die. Ditched it before we got in trouble."

So the new vehicle had nothing to do with her. It surprised how much that disappointed her.

His gaze skidded to hers and then back to the road as he navigated them back to Ring Road. Saw regret.

She must divert his attention. "The Afghan police—"

"Yeah."

"I had to pace the mosque and men saw me and gave me terrible looks. Then I saw the police, and I worried but kept moving. Then they circled back and. I …"

"Hey." His tone grabbed her attention. "Easy. It's okay. We're good." He nodded, his expression earnest beneath that baseball hat. "You did good."

She eyed him warily. In her world, praise always came with a catch. But none came. Saying thanks now seemed too late …

and awkward. Though she knew it was adrenaline, she still felt shaky. Still felt relieved—grateful that he had showed up, saved her.

There was a time she would have been angry at the thought of being *saved*. She had never relied on a man for saving. Kasra glanced down, then saw her satchel. Remembered the food. Glad she had a way to thank him without *thanking* him, she tugged it onto her lap and pulled out the box ... which was crushed on one side. Groaning, she realized there was grease all over her hand. And in her bag, too.

Rage glance at it and frowned.

With care, she opened the box and angled it to him. "Falafel."

His eyebrows lifted. "Seriously?" And he smiled.

The first she had seen since they'd left the safehouse and it warmed her heart. A lot more than it should. "It is probably cold. And squished." She held it out so he could take some.

"Doesn't change how it tastes." He plucked a deep-fried chickpea ball from the box and popped it into his mouth.

"I am not responsible for its ... after-effects," she teased, pulling water from her bag and setting it in the cupholder.

He said nothing, and she accepted the ensuing silence. At least he wasn't yelling at her. She ate and tried to put aside the intense experience, thinking he'd abandoned her. It should not affect her after all these years ...

There were more important matters. Should she push into this silence? She must. Knowledge was power. "Am I allowed to know where we are going?"

He pointed through the windshield. "South."

Of course he would not tell her. Just because he smiled at her and ate the falafel, did not mean he—

"There's an airstrip we'll hit by nightfall," came his gruff addendum. "Foamy Zebra was a code for this location."

She laughed. "I had wondered ..." Her gaze hit his, and she felt something twist in her stomach. "Thank you."

Arm on the ledge of the driver's side door window, he kept his gaze on the road now. "And I don't know anything about the others. Intel has been brief."

A thought—a fear—stole into her mood. "Then how do you know it can be trusted? That we are not going all this way for nothing?"

"Because I know the man who supplied it."

She understood that. Settling, her nerves no longer vibrating, she retrieved a mango, which made her mouth water. Only ... she had no knife. No way to cut or peel it. With a huff, she sagged. Bent back to the bag to—

A tap on her arm drew her gaze to the side.

Rage held out a knife to her, flipped it, hilt-side extended. "And I trust you'll clean it after you're done and not drive it into my heart."

"You have one?"

Irritation tightened the smooth planes of his face. "Many would say I don't."

She had witnessed his compassion and concern. "Then they are fools. I have seen your kindness."

"I think you said 'cruelty' wrong."

It made her sad that he thought of himself like that. "I have known enough cruelty to recognize its many forms, and you, Rage, do not have it."

Giving her the side-eye, he reflected that sadness. "I'm sorry you know it so well."

"See?" Kasra gave a half smile. "Kindness."

"That's not kindness. That's"—he negotiated around a lumbering truck—"acknowledgement."

"But many would not even acknowledge it." She cut the mango, pulling her dirty hijab to catch the juice. "There are times even I do not want to acknowledge it ... Wish I could wake up as if it were all a terrible dream …" Why was she babbling on?

Silence chased them once more into the lengthening day. As night fell, Rage turned onto a two-lane road that was not as busy or as well-paved. She did thank Allah for the more comfortable car—not just for the better-cushioned seats, but for the way it handled the rough roads.

After a couple of hours on the pot-hole laden road, he slowed and stopped at another station for gas and to use the amenities. She had expected, since he filled up the tank, that they would be driving for many more hours, but twenty minutes later, he banked onto what seemed a foot path and killed the lights.

He stopped and unbuckled, pulling out his weapon and checking it.

Kasra tensed, suddenly alert. "What's wrong?"

"Stay." He moved to the back of the vehicle, soon came the sound of breaking glass, and he returned, tucking a dagger into a sheath at his waist band. They were lumbering again, guided only by moonlight.

"What is going on?" He had said they were going to an airstrip, not an empty field!

A quarter of a mile later, he steered into the tall brush. "Grab your pack. Let's go."

"Where?" They were in the middle of nowhere! When he didn't answer, she hopped out and stomped around back. "What are we doing?"

"Not killing you, if that's what you think."

"Then what?"

His gaze sharpened, and he pointed behind her. "There."

She peered out and saw nothing. "I don't …" But then she did. A subtle glow and blinking lights blended with a steady whine. An airplane!

CHAPTER
ELEVEN

KANDAHAR PROVINCE, AFGHANISTAN

DANGER HAD a certain smell to it, and tonight, that odor was a lot like the fumes rolling off the blacked-out cargo plane idling at the end of the small airstrip. He'd texted Pike at the gas station they were running behind. Had hoped Omen would wait. Relief chugged at the sight of the chief. He'd soon be rid of her and back on familiar soil. She'd be out of business, and he could hit the next name on the list.

Shouldering into his ruck, he caught something in his periphery. Instinct had him palming her head and pushing her toward the ground. "Down!"

Red and white splashed across the brush as the distant wail of a siren rose.

What the heck? In a crouch, Sig Sauer in hand, he swiveled to find the source. Saw a stream of green trucks and SUVs. And cursed at the shadowed figures with rifles riding in truck beds.

"The police!" Kasra cried.

"Go!" Range barked, pitching her toward the field. "Run!" Even as he sprinted, he easily passed her. He slowed and caught her arm.

Heard the plane's engines whining louder.

No!

Grip tight, he nearly dragged her. Saw a handful of uniformed men disemboweled from the back of the plane. Pike. Had to be Pike. Maybe Luther.

Range grabbed his SureFire and aimed the beam at the airstrip. Pressed it twice, signaling their arrival and location. They still had a fence to clear and least another quarter klick to traverse.

The ALP sirens screamed closer and closer. Barreling on a parallel course to his nine ... straight at the airstrip. The plane.

They weren't going to make it.

No. They had to.

They rushed to the fence. "Up." He went to a knee and patted it, indicating for her to step up and climb over.

Toe on his knee, she pushed up. Caught the chain links.

Crack! Pop-pop-pop!

With a shout, Kasra pitched backward. Landed with a hard thud. On the ground, she held her arm where a dark stain bloomed across her sleeve.

What ...? Range eyed the plane. Felt a hollowing of awareness ... what he saw ... it was wrong. That ... He drew out his nocs. Four black-clad operators were moving across the tarmac in their general direction, M4s at the ready.

What!? He lowered himself as much as he could without losing visibility. Scanned the foursome. That wasn't Pike. Or Luther.

Shouts carried over the din of the revving engines. The four men backed toward the plane, still scanning, as the ALP closed in on them.

One word hit Range's brain: compromised.

The guy on the right sent a spray of bullets in their direction—suppressive fire, a last-ditch effort before he sprinted to the already rising ramp, wheels rolling as the plane started down the runway.

"Why are they leaving us?" Kasra balked. "We must run."

Ticked, stunned, Range stared at the ground. They were seriously out of luck here. That hadn't been a rescue effort, as he'd expected from Pike. That'd been an attempt to silence them. Kill them.

Gunfire peppered the night, ALP firing at the fleeing plane.

The engagement snapped Range out of his stupor. "C'mon." He launched up from the grass, shoving himself back toward the 4Runner he'd stolen.

Kasra didn't argue or hesitate.

Pitching his phone aside, he threw himself in the SUV. He started it even as her door closed.

Bullets pinged on the hood and roof.

"Down!" Gunning it, he drove backwards until he'd put enough distance between them and the ALP, then ripped it around and headed back to the main road. They hit the two-lane road with violence, the vehicle bucking and hopping. He smoothed it out and nailed the gas.

Headlights struck the rearview mirror.

He cursed.

Kasra held her seatbelt and glance back. "What do we do? They saw us."

Range tugged out his GPS to find another road out of here. Not a main one. With no taillights and headlamps off, he could ghost them in the darkness, but not on a main road. He also didn't want to wind up on a dead-end road.

They whipped around slow-moving vehicles and barreled around corners at dangerous speeds, but anything less would be lethal. They roared over a bridge.

"Where are you going? We have to get somewhere—"

Range nailed the brakes, glad he'd broken the taillights, and cranked it hard left. Into the oncoming lane, narrowly avoiding a vehicle, which elicited a scream from Kasra. He aimed them down the embankment. Gunned it. Prayed the plumes of dust weren't visible in the night. He yanked the wheel left and dived into the underpass. Hit the brakes, the 4Runner skidded on dirt.

With a yelp, Kasra braced against the sudden stop.

Rolling down the window, Range listened to the vehicles rushing across the small bridge above. He also heard her frantic breathing. Waited ... and waited ...

"We're clear."

And screwed. Betrayed.

Ticked, he pounded the steering wheel. Punched the dash. Again. Again and again. Skin crawling, needing to hurt someone, he shoved out of the SUV. Threw a punch at the sky. Kicked the vehicle. Cursed.

Hooked his hands over his head. Blowing out a thick breath, he swiped a hand over his face. Noticed movement to the side. The madam. She stood there, saying nothing. All the better. He'd probably just light into her if she spoke. What in the name of creation were they supposed to do now?

"Why did your friends shoot at us?"

"Wasn't my team." Which didn't make a lick of sense.

"Do you think the police scared them? They made a mistake, thinking we were ... bad?"

"It *wasn't* my team!"

She was reaching for justification. But there wasn't any. It might not have been Omen, but those had been American operators targeting them.

They'd been burned. Set up.

But Pike told him to come here. Right?

The madam still stood there, silent. Hugging herself.

No, idiot. Not hugging herself—holding her wounded arm. He turned to her. Saw the dark streaks down her sleeve. It took everything in him to speak with a civil tongue. "Your arm ..."

She glanced down, sheepish. "A graze."

That was a lot of blood for a graze. "Let me see." Tucking aside his anger, he moved toward her. Saw her kurta was bloodied too. "You eat two?"

"Eat two what?" Lifting her hand from the wound, she wobbled.

"Easy." Range caught her by the shoulders. "In the back. Lie down." He guided her to the back of the SUV. Once she lay down, he hiked in next to her and grabbed his field kit. "Entry and exit wounds—that's good. Soft part of your arm, so it'll be tender, but at least it missed the main artery." He made quick work of cleaning and packing the wound, then bandaged it. Gave her some ibuprofen. "If you want something stronger—"

"No." She gulped the pills down and grimaced.

He slumped down and stared into the distance. That was a complete cluster … Pike hadn't come. Which meant communications with Omen were compromised. Might as well consider all communications compromised.

So, no support. No freaking way out of this mess or this country.

Feeling her gaze, the pressure of her presence, he hopped out of the truck. Wandered to the berm of the bridge and sat. Put his back to the dirt.

Who had been waiting at the airstrip to take them out? What was going on? What was he supposed to do now?

Okay, he didn't have those answers. And they couldn't stay here. He had no money or ID. ALP was looking for them. Likely knew the make and model of this SUV. They'd have to ditch it. Hoof it for a while. Would she be okay with that wound?

She was still in the back of the truck, lying down. Had she fallen asleep? He had no idea how long he'd been sitting here going through options, but they should get out of here. Drive for a while in the dark, then ditch the SUV. At least he'd been smart enough to kill the GPS before boosting it.

Range stood and dusted his pants as he moved to the SUV.

Palmed the bumper, and only then did he noticed her eyes shift to him. "You're awake."

"Hard to sleep right now …" She shifted upright and propped herself against the interior hull. "Is there a plan, a new one?"

Staring at nothing in particular, he realized as much he couldn't stand her, they were in this together. God had a *sick* sense of humor. "We need to drive a while farther—not on open roads. We'll have to ditch the truck eventually and hoof it until I can secure another vehicle."

"And where are we going?" Her voice was quiet, but her fear wasn't.

He shifted around and leaned back against the SUV. Huffed. "I have no idea. I tossed my phone so they can't track us."

The 4Runner shifted as she moved to perch on the bumper next to him. "If those weren't your friends with the plane, then how did they know you would come?"

"I don't know. Those men had one mission: kill us. I don't know why or who they were. The chief told me to come here, and either he's compromised—which I refuse to believe—or they were monitoring the phone. Which is why I got rid of it." He scratched the side of his face. "Have no idea where to go or how to get to safe ground with everything compromised."

If he weren't stuck with her, if he could get to an embassy or consulate, he could get out of country. But her … With Hellqvist hunting them, Omen compromised …

"I … I have a friend who lives on the southern border. I think it is only a few hours from here. He would help us."

A few hours by car. A day on foot, since they'd have to travel at night to stay hidden.

"Anywhere we go could put others in danger."

Silence hung in the thick night air.

"Is it that bad?" she asked. "Why are they trying to kill us?"

Her, she was the reason someone had sent a team after

them. But blaming her didn't do them any good. And it'd only make him angrier.

"Rage?"

He sniffed. "That's not my name."

More silence.

"It's Range. Like gun range." Though his mom had teased him that it was all about "home on the range."

"That is ... unusual."

He sniffed again, folding his arms. "It's a family thing. We're all named after earthy things—Stone, Brooke, Canyon, Willow, Leif."

"*Leaf?*" she wrinkled her nose. "It would be like naming your child Dirt or Mud."

He breathed a laugh. "Pretty sure I said that very thing to my parents. They did not appreciate my humor."

What would Canyon think about this situation? He would no doubt tell Range he deserved it, then laugh his fool head off.

"We should get going. I want to find a place to hide out before sunrise."

"Hide?"

"Too visible in daylight. Hike at night, sleep during daylight." He straightened and looked at her arm. "How's that doing?"

She shrugged. "It will heal."

When he noticed the blood on her shirt, he indicated to it. "You should change clothes."

Kasra glanced at the stain. "Oh, yes ..."

He nodded to the vehicle. "I'll stand guard so you can change, then we'll get underway." While she did that, he grabbed two MREs out of his ruck then positioned his ruck between the seats.

She climbed into the passenger side and frowned at his pack.

"For now, keep your arm elevated." When she seemed to accept this, he tore open the MRE and handed it to her. "Not a gourmet meal, but it will keep your energy going. And constipate you."

She frowned at him.

"It's mostly protein," he said with a shrug and started the truck.

They drove on hardpacked roads and even made their own roads in a few places over the next three hours. He found an abandoned lean-to and parked the SUV. He wiped it down and grabbed their gear, shouldering both packs so she didn't stress her injury. Then as dawn began to push back the veil of darkness, they trekked over a rocky slope.

It took a while, but he finally located a small cave just large enough for them to stretch out and sleep. He laid out waterproof canvas to protect them from the damp earth. "Go ahead and get some rest."

"You need rest, too. You have slept little the last two days."

Surprised she had noticed or cared, he nodded. "Just need to rig a covering." On a camouflage net, he threaded local vegetation into it, then used metal spikes to drape it over the opening.

Exhaustion tugging at him, he sat on his half of the canvas and couldn't believe this irony. Arm beneath his head, he laid back, sliding his Sig to his chest, palm over it, ready to defend. He'd gone into Roud to bring this woman down ... and now what? A team had been sent to neutralize them? Why? What did they think she knew?

The name.

She hadn't given it up yet. Would she ever?

Did it matter now?

Abso-freakin-lutely. He wasn't going to be shot at and run all over this godforsaken country for nothing. She would cough it up. Even if he had to force it out of her. Wouldn't be the first time he'd had to use advanced interview methods to get a subject to cooperate.

"I have seen your kindness."

She really hadn't. Because he hadn't shown it. That wasn't him anymore.

She shifted onto her side next to him and her breath hitched. A hand went to her injury.

"Would a sling help?" he offered.

"What …?"

Range sat up and fumbled for his ruck. Morning sun filtering through the slots of the net, he grabbed the sling from his medkit. Shifted and sat in front of her. Slipped it under her forearm. As soon as he drew the ends toward the back of her neck, she stilled. Lowered her gaze, and Range felt this weird tremoring in his veins. She lifted her hair, so he could Velcro it.

Ignoring the awareness, the silkiness of her hair, he grunted. "Stabilizing it will help it heal and avoid tearing it. When we get to your friend's place, I should look at it again, see if it needs stitches." He adjusted the sling so it didn't pinch her neck. "There. I think …"

Her eyes came to his, and even with the dimness of the cave, Range could see those gold flecks. Felt her breath hitch.

Realized that in another life where she wasn't actually a madam, this might be where he thought about how pretty she was. What those sultry eyes seemed to offer—a kiss.

Heck no.

He laid back. Stretched out.

"Ask her …" Coman's words haunted the cave. *"It is not my story to tell … Ask her."*

Range cleared his throat. Shifted, palming the Sig again. Told his brain to shut up and go to sleep. Kasra had been right—he hadn't slept in two days. Had to be why he'd totally missed the signals that something was off at the airstrip. He'd been so focused on passing her onto the others. Getting that name.

Lying there, he heard a noise … glanced to the side and saw her shivering. Hard. Stealthily so he didn't disturb her, he shifted the gear to the other side of her, then angled a little closer. Her shivering slowed.

He rolled his head to the side. Wondered how she could live with herself, selling people ... It was obvious why she'd ended up in this business ... with those full lips and oval face. Dark lashes that dusted her cheeks. Her hair lay askew, a dark complement to her olive complexion. She seemed ... familiar. As if he'd seen her before.

His gut clenched, realizing how much she looked like Dani ...

Range rolled his gaze to the ceiling and exhaled. God forgive him, but nobody would compare to her. It's why he left home. Left the family. Never forgave Canyon.

Grunts and pain pulled her from a deep sleep.

A master at waking stealthily so as not to disturb whoever lay in her bed, Kasra pried herself from Slumber's torment and found herself staring at the strong, handsome face of Rag—*Range*.

He had told her his name. Let her peek into the soul of the man who had been trapped in this nightmare with her. The way he had gotten them away from the police, delivered them to safety, tended her injury. Not once had he sneered at her, though she sensed he blamed her for this mess.

As he probably should. Taweel had powerful connections but even more, the German did. And the captain ... his pockets were full of their money and investments in his career. If they wanted her found, they would find her. She had aroused the beast, and by it, she would be slain.

At least Range had not been shot last night.

He grunted again. Twitched. His face contorted.

Instinct had Kasra place her hand on his arm. Felt the

constriction of his bicep when she did. But he still dreamt, grunted. Muttered. She moved her hand to his chest. Sculpted. Firm. Heart thundering.

What tormented him?

"Shh," she whispered, telling herself not to focus on the firmness of the muscles beneath her fingers. The way his chest rose and fell.

He was a good man.

She could not recall the last good man she had known. Coman was close, but he was more a brother than …

Range's hand slapped onto hers.

Sucking in a breath, she lifted her head. Opened her mouth to apologize.

But he did not throw off her touch or hurt her. He simply … held it, sort of. And his pulse slowed.

Unlike hers. Pounding like a drum. As it had when he'd put the sling on her. He had been so close, his moves practiced and experienced as he helped her. His eyes so blue and pretty. He had felt it, too, she was sure. He'd hesitated.

Don't be a fool. He despises you.

Her wound pinched at holding it in this position for so long, but she feared to move and wake him. Honestly, she did not want to move. She appreciated the warmth of his hand and chest. Appreciated that it had calmed him in his sleep.

Oh, Allah. I like him. He is such a good man … Though he spews his rage, I see beneath it. As if I know him, understand him.

She closed her eyes, let herself live the fantasy that his fingers actually threaded with hers. That he wanted her close, wanted her touch.

It would never happen. To a man like him, she was filth. Were he awake, he would throw off her touch. Yell at her.

But … what if he saw her …? The *real* her … the one buried beneath years of … Roud? What if …

She imagined his touch. His kiss ... He would be ardent, but gentle. Passionate yet not demanding like—

No. That could never happen. It was a physical impossibility with the way he recoiled from her, snarled at her ... curled his lip.

Kasra drew her hand back and rested it on her hip to keep it elevated. She should sleep but there were ... others there, in her dreams. Others from her past. And she did not want to let them into her thoughts. To violate her.

Needing a distraction and confident he slept, she reached into the satchel and drew out the phone Gabina had given her. Shielding the light from him, she powered it up and opened it. Saw a text from her friend, asking how she was.

I AM HERE. THINGS WENT BADLY. PRAY ALLAH WILL HELP US.

A moment later, a text came in and she found comfort that her friend was there, thinking of her, talking to her across the distance. She was not alone. MEN TOOK COMAN, BUT HE IS HOME NOW. THEY ASKED WHERE YOU ARE. HE DID NOT TELL THEM. BE SAFE.

How her heart hurt that her friend had trouble because of her. And she imagined they had released him in the hopes he would lead them to Kasra. I AM SORRY.

IS MR. BLUE EYES BEING NICE TO YOU?

A LEOPARD CANNOT CHANGE HIS SPOTS. BUT AT LEAST I AM ALIVE.

I'NSH ALLAH.

"No."

The half grumble, half groan startled her. She shoved the phone back into her satchel and looked up at him, saw him rotating his head. A grunt. Another "no." More dreams. Tentatively, she slid her hand back over to him. Touched his arm.

Another grunt. Blond brows knotted. His bicep twitched. He was still immersed in whatever was distressing him. But if he called out ...

She slid her hand over his abdomen, to where he held the gun. "It's okay ..." she whispered.

Though it made no sense, he again calmed. Heart rate slowed. His pursed lips slackened, parting as he slipped free of whatever tormented him. What did torment someone like him? He had a family—several siblings, talked about his mom.

"Augh," he suddenly grunted. His hand clamped onto hers and he jerked her toward him.

Kasra cried out, her wounds pinching sharply.

Range's eyes struck hers. "What're you doing?" Throat hoarse, he glowered. "I help and protect you, and you go for my gun?"

"What?" She withdrew. "No! I—you were dreaming. *Loud*. I was just ..." The pain in her wound made tears prick. It felt warm now. She held the spot and tried to shift away, but cracked her head on the cave ceiling.

Accusation speared his expression as he hiked himself upright, something she could not do for the way the cave sloped. "I would be a fool with my arm injured to even try to overtake you."

"As if you could."

Defiance flashed through her. "Maybe you should rethink sleeping so close to me and so deeply next time."

Blue eyes met hers, probing that threat she had just thrown out. "You really do not want me as your enemy."

"I think we are entirely past that." Heart thundering, she regretted the words as soon as they stung her lips. She did not think of him as an enemy, but that was how he saw her. Doubtful it could ever be any other way.

"Your survival depends on me, so I'd be careful—"

"I don't need your advice! I've survived men like you for the last ten years." She had learned to be what men needed, what they wanted—the only way to survive. She might not have a soul left, but she was alive.

Now those blue eyes danced with surprise. Perhaps even a tinge of regret. But it did not last long. This one liked to brood, feast on his wounds and anger, so she would make sure he was distracted with his selfishness so that he did not see her own brand of anger. And that started with Zaki.

CHAPTER
TWELVE

K*andahar* P*rovince,* A*fghanistan*

"I DON'T NEED *your advice! I've survived men like you for the last ten years.*"

Men like him. Those words had concertina wire wrapped around them, shredding his pride. Exactly what had that meant? He'd gotten her away from the compound, taken her to friends for supplies, endured a lecture by a man who knew nothing about him. Stole a different car—because she complained about comfort. Had nothing to do with the engine—it'd been fine. He thought it'd amuse her. Instead, it'd embarrassed him when she grumbled about it. Then, he'd saved her life last night, stitched up her arm. Gotten her to safety. Instead of trying to take his gun, she should be thankful.

For treating her with disdain and ridicule the whole time? It was something Willow would slap him with, if she were here.

He was stuck with her. No—it was worse than that: he was now responsible for her. And if he focused on her trade, he'd never get past it. And it'd be a miserable freaking week, if not longer.

"Tread carefully, little brother." Canyon's words haunted him as the sun nestled into the horizon.

Just like always—family ganging up on him. Couldn't do anything right.

Ready to get moving once light faded, he packed up the canvas, netting, and ruck. "Where is your friend who can help us?"

Mouth tight, holding her arm—blood was seeping through the bandage—she would not meet his gaze.

On his knees, Range hung his head. Got a whiff of himself and struggled not to cringe. "Look." He ran a hand down the back of his neck. "You ... startled me awake. Never a good scenario in a situation like this."

Her gaze skipped around the darkening cave.

Play nice. She's wounded. "I need to know where he lives so I can plot our course. Figure out if there's somewhere to get another vehicle."

"You mean *steal* another one." More accusation.

He shirked it off. "*Borrow* a comfortable one."

A furtive glance came with a twitch at her lips. A near smile. "You are very good with words, saying what you do not mean."

Do not react. Do not react. "Your friend ...?"

She stared at him for a long minute, then sighed. "Zaki lives in Wesh."

"*Wesh*? As in Spin Buldak District?"

She stared at him blankly.

"On the border of not-so-friendly Pakistan." He dropped onto his backside and bit down on another curse.

She shrugged. "By car, I could make the trip in a couple of hours."

"From Kandahar."

She nodded, and then her eyes widened in understanding.

Yeah, exactly. Wesh was about a twenty-four hour journey on foot from Kandahar. But they had gone west for a full day to hook-up with Omen, only to get burned. They'd headed back and made up some of that distance, but not enough for this to be a quick trip. It put them a full three days on foot to Wesh.

"And you're sure he's a safe place to go?"

Her gaze darted around, then she shrugged. "He is my only friend I trust."

"Wesh it is." Range dug into his pack and grabbed one of the last three MREs. He handed her one. "Eat. We set out within the hour."

She took it, flinching in pain—her arm.

Range grabbed his medkit. "Here. Let me look at that."

"No. I am okay."

"Bullspit. It's seeping. If I don't clean it, infection could set in."

She lifted her jaw. Said nothing but angled around so her arm was nearer.

Range removed the bandage and eyed the entry wound. "The liquid stitches didn't work."

"Because you nearly yanked my arm off."

He owned that. His fault but she shouldn't be touching him—but he wasn't opening that can of worms. Instead, he took out a needle and thread.

She drew in a quick breath. "Can you not just use more of the—"

"Can't risk it tearing open again." He propped his ruck and angled her arm over it. "Just relax."

"Do not take too much pleasure in making me hurt again, yes?"

Range bounced his gaze to hers, feeling the sharpness of her words. Knowing it was his own fault. He applied a topical anesthetic and began stitching, knowing this stung like heck. Yet she only tightened her lips more. Fisted her hand. She was tough, he'd give her that.

Ten years … ten years enduring men like him, she'd said. A

decade. That was a long time. Almost as old as his nephew, Owen.

"How do you know this Zaki guy?" he asked, as he worked.

"Family"—she grunted and grimaced—"friend."

Not surprised, again, at her vague answer, he tied off the stitches and snipped the thread. Added an antibacterial and bandaged it. Handed her some ibuprofen.

Once nighttime overpowered daylight, they set out eastward, guided by a good old-fashioned compass. Crossed a small creek, and skirted around mud-plastered cluster of homes. No market. No shops.

"Are you going to *borrow* another car?" she asked wearily as they kept moving, stopping only a few times for bio breaks.

"If the opportunity presents itself."

"What is the plan, once we got documents?"

"Cross the border into Pakistan as soon as we can. Probably head to the UAE."

"Yes," she said with more than a little excitement. "That is near Saudi."

Hiking, Range slowed, glanced over his shoulder at her. "What's in Saudi Arabia?"

She drew up, but then averted her gaze. "Friends."

The way she said, that certain pique to her voice … "You have friends in the strangest places."

Kasra looked startled. "They have helped me in hard times."

"What were you doing in Saudi Arabia?"

"I was not there," she said quietly. "A friend here in Afghanistan married and moved there."

"Most people would move to a location with a possibility of a career and providing for a family."

"They went there three years ago," she said, "to help be a part of the provisional transition and help implement the Constitutional Declaration."

He grunted. "And they stayed after its collapse? And all the refugees …"

"True, it did not go as planned or hoped, but Tahir says they are safe. Happy." She sounded like she was trying to convince herself. "For me, it is too much like Afghanistan."

He slid her a look, the moonlight tracing her features, her full lips held tight as she continued on. Should he mention she would be on a fast-track trip to the States to face justice for her crimes? Nah, confrontation wouldn't foster cooperation and this adventure had been fun enough already.

"I want to go as far as I can from this place." She gave a breathy laugh as they climbed a small hill. "Maybe Alaska."

Range snorted. "Too cold. It digs into your bones."

She shuffled to catch up. "You have been there?"

He nodded. "Juneau. For a year. Terrific scenery, but the cold and fifteen, sixteen hours of daylight got to me. But being on the water …" He bobbed his head. "That worked for me."

"Why were you on the water?"

"I served in the Coast Guard for nine years. Preferred patrolling the southern hemisphere where it was warmer."

"So … you know how to swim?"

Range gave her a look at the way she said that, the longing in her words. "You don't?"

She shook her head. "We have mountains and deserts, but no oceans. A few lakes, but I never lived near them. When I saw movies I wondered what it would be like to be on the ocean. It seemed so wonderful and open."

"The ocean can be a temperamental goddess, jealous when you dare tread her waters. I've seen squalls rise out of seemingly nowhere and thrash fishing trawlers." He shook his head, remembering the effort to pull drowned children from one such vessel.

"I think you have fought this jealous goddess many times and she has won."

"Why's that?"

"Your expression has turned very grave."

Watery grave, that's why. "Many of the rescue calls quickly turned into recovery missions." He shook his head. "Not pleasant. And yet ... I still love being on a boat. Nothing like it. Looking out and seeing clear blue to the horizon. It's like I can finally ... breathe."

"I would like to breathe," she said softly.

"Well, you'll likely get the chance."

She startled. "What?"

"To get to the UAE, we'll probably take a boat across the gulf."

"Why not a plane?" She negotiated some boulders and avoided a smelly creek. "We will have documents."

"Flights require passports—"

"Which we will have—"

"—and our names would be run through watch-lists."

"Ah."

"We should put more distance between us and Kandahar before we risk flights. I plan to hitch a ride on a cargo ship or fishing trawler to get across the gulf." And even as he said it, he realized while that was all true, traveling via boat meant *days* at sea. He'd be stuck with her for at least another week. Dang, if that didn't make him mad all over again.

He had to figure out what was going on. Not that he could really do that out here. "That name you're harboring," Range said, "How dangerous is it?" One of his dumber questions, but he had to get her to talk.

"I can tell by how you asked, that you already know the answer."

He huffed. "I do. Just thinking if that name—that person is so important, why didn't they kill you before now?"

Kasra slowed until she came to a stop. Then she looked to the south. Sighed. "I learned very quickly to be what they needed me to be. The men who bought an hour with me. The men who controlled my every move. If they wanted me to be compliant, I was compliant."

Range cocked his head. "Why? You know how to fight."

She stared at him for a weighted second, then stumbled on. "It was … safer."

Not *safe*. Safer. His mind went a dozen different directions with that. Seeing she needed a rest, he indicated her toward a slope where there they could rest and be hidden. "How so?"

"Let them think they had power and they were nicer, less prone to beat or abuse the girls."

Or me. He had no idea how he heard that in what she left unsaid, but it was there, gaping between them. "That's … sick."

"Indeed, but it was also effective. Feigning compliance fostered their complacency. They did not see me as a threat."

"And they were wrong."

She lifted her eyebrows and shrugged.

He sat, knees bent, arms hooked over them. Eventually grabbed a protein bar. Only one left now. He snapped it in half and handed one to her. "The longer I am an operator, the more I think the depravity of men cannot surprise me."

She drew out some jerky from her satchel and gave him some. "Some are truly horrific. Thankfully, Taweel was very severe on anyone who hurt the girls. Roud earned a … reputation."

"How can you be thankful for that?"

"Very easily when you have been beaten to unconsciousness or worse." She lowered her gaze, turning a piece of dried jerky. "It was my job to protect the girls, to make sure …"

Even in the darkness, he could see the emotion writhing through her pretty face.

She cleared her throat. Squinted. "So." She bit into the jerky. "Will we sleep beneath the stars tonight?"

Aware of a rawness to her words, to a vulnerability he had

only seen in the safehouse—when she'd seen the captain—he chose to draw down the questions. He retrieved his nocs and scanned the terrain. Saw ... more of the same. Couple klicks out, there was a small structure. A stand of some kind, maybe a farmer selling his wares had built it. "There might be shelter."

"I do not mind sleeping here," she said, rubbing her legs. Likely exhausted.

"You will—the temps will drop and we won't have any wind cover. You'll be shivering worse than you were last night."

She startled. "What?"

He smirked. "Your chattering teeth kept me awake."

Eyebrows lifted, she sniffed a laugh. "I ... I cannot believe I did not wake myself. I usually sleep so light, I hear *everything*. Like *your* grunts."

Range froze. Had some ... impression of holding her hand ... which rested on his chest. No, that was just a blurring from when she'd tried to wake him. "It's been a rough trip for both of us. We're exhausted."

"Yes," she agreed too heartily and peered to the sky. "The air is thickening—rain."

"Yeah, noticed that, too. Let's get to that stand before it hits. Otherwise, we're going to be mud rats."

They trudged on, but about halfway there, the sky cracked open its fountain and sent a deluge, drenching them almost instantly. "C'mon!" he shouted in frustration. Could they not catch a break. He angled to her and they hustled for a solid ten minutes, the ground slicking beneath their feet as they struggled through the wind and rain.

The stand door was padlocked. He shouldered into it, not wanting to break the hinges but trusting the old wood would yield. It surrendered and they rushed inside, laughing. The interior was no more than four feet deep and five feet wide. But it had a roof, though a leaky one, and the ground was mostly dry.

Kasra laughed, water running off her hair and dripping. Forming a mud puddle.

"You get to sit there," Range teased.

She laughed harder. "That was … glorious!" But even as she said that, tremors rippled through her drenched form. She glanced around the confined space. "Will we stay here during the day?"

"Hope to be long gone by daylight. Hoping this is just a flash flood."

Creak … creak …

They both looked up at the ceiling that seemed to be struggling beneath the weight of the water pooling there.

"Oh no," Kasra said.

Whoosh! The far side of the roof dropped.

At the same time Range reached to pull her away, Kasra leapt away from the falling roof—colliding with him. Water shoved into the stand, effectively cutting their shelter in half.

Kasra gave a nervous laugh. "At least the whole thing didn't collapse." She looked up into his eyes … and stilled.

So did he, entirely too aware of her slumped against him, eyes alight with the absurd hilarity of it all. Dark hair plastered to her face, he brushed it back. Felt the electrical reaction of that touch.

She straightened, her gaze bouncing around his face as he thumbed a splotch of mud from her cheek, which was wet, but not cold. At all. Warmth pulsed from her. Or was that the fire in his gut he felt?

Crack! Boom!

Light exploded, stabbing shards of brilliance into the stand.

Snapping Range out of the idiotic stupor. He set her—and himself—straight, in more ways than one. "Sounds like it's already slowing." It wasn't. But he needed air. Needed her out of his arms. He set her back. Looked out the slats that provided shelter.

Felt more than saw her tuck her hair back.

"I love storms," she whispered.

"I don't." Why did he feel so irritable now?

"Why? They're cleansing."

He scoffed. "That's an interesting way to look at them."

"How do you see them?"

"Destructive. I once airlifted a woman from a boat during a storm."

"What happened to her?"

He heard the awe in her voice. "I lost her." Then he thought of the little girl who died … "I lost another one in a storm, too." He watched the downpour, willing it to slow so they could be on their way. So they weren't stuck together. So close together.

"Storms are merely a delivery system," she said quietly, shivering and staring out at the storm as well.

Wind whipped up a frenzy. Rain, thrashing and dancing in a dozen different directions. Reminded him of hurricane personality. Something struck the side of the stand at the same time the roof seemed to press in on them more.

"Oh!" Kasra yelped, stumbling backward into him.

His hand found her waist. Steadied her. "Keep still." He gritted his teeth, no idea where to put his hand, so he dropped it to his side, feeling awkward and entirely too aware. The space was so ridiculously confined now, they might as well be in a phone booth—which likely had more room.

"Sorry." She shifted forward, all but pressed to the dripping wall. Rested her head there. Sighed.

Somehow, his hand found her hip again. He cursed himself. "Watch out." He rolled around her. "I'll be back." And he struck out across the plain, no idea what he was doing. Just had to get out of there. Breathe. Think. Find a bigger shelter. Find a phone. Find out what the heck happened to Pike, how he could hang him out to dry. Deliver this woman for justice.

"Range!"

Furious, he turned, disbelieving that she'd followed. That she didn't stay put. "Get back—"

"Look!" she shouted, pointing back in the direction from which they'd come.

Lightning crackled along the sky and ground.

But what crawled the ground in the midst of the torrents … that wasn't lighting.

Headlamps!

He cursed. Shoved himself forward, boots sliding in the now-muddy field. How had they found them? For a half-second he entertained the thought it wasn't an enemy vehicle. But they were coming too fast and too direct.

Doing his best to fight the elements and get back, he quickly saw he wouldn't make it. The vehicle would get there first. "Back! Inside!" he shouted as he struggled toward her.

She faltered, expression wild with panic beneath the driving rain and incoming threat.

Thank God they weren't shooting at her, but he more than felt the bullets streaking past him. The one that seared his side. Felt his ear burn. Didn't care. He wasn't stopping.

The Toyota pick-up slid to a stop between him and Kasra, three yards away. Men rushed her.

Her scream seared his heart.

Only it wasn't her scream. She wasn't the type to do that. In fact, the men who moved on her found themselves in a fierce fight.

Range surged at the vehicle, only then able to see it clearly. Not ANP. And no uniforms. Mercs or black ops.

The driver aimed a gun out the window at him. Range threw himself at the arm, drove it back until he felt the sickening crunch of bones. Heard the man's feral screams as his hand went limp. The weapon plunked to the ground.

AK-47 snatched up, Range whipped around. Slammed it into the driver's temple.

Slowed but not disabled, the guard lifted a handgun.

Range fired a burst into the cab, and the driver went as limp as his arm. Verifying he was dead—didn't want bullets in his back—Range grabbed the gun from him, too. Holstered it at the small of his back. Pivoted, saw a guard on the ground. The other had Kasra pinned to the wall, gun at her head.

Advancing, coming up on the guy's left, Range squeezed off two rounds. When the guy froze Kasra flipped the guy's weapon and fired it into his chest.

The thug crumpled.

Kasra shuddered her breaths, staring in disbelief at the body at her feet.

He saw it—the terror of what she'd done.

Range edged into her personal space. Caught her face. "Hey." Wild eyes met him. "You did what you had to." He nodded, waited for her to do the same. "We have to get out of here. Grab our packs and get them to the truck. Okay?"

"Ye—" Her throat convulsed. She nodded.

"Do it." After nudging her toward the shelter and their packs, he dragged the nearest body into the stand. When she hurried past him with the gear, he grabbed the boots of the driver, then noticing a phone on the floorboard. Took it. Turned, surprised to see Kasra moving the third guy into the shelter. The woman impressed again. He placed the driver in front of the door and tugged his shirt as he eased out, so his weight would keep it shut. No accidental discoveries.

Turning, he found her close. Had to roll around her to avoid a collision. "Get in." He hopped into the idling truck and swiped a hand over his face. Felt weird.

Clothes and hair drenched, Kasra shivered in her seat. "You're shot!"

Range glanced to where she pointed and remembered feeling a sting there. He grunted. Palmed it. Felt the hole. No exit wound. Not good. "Just a graze," he lied. She was traumatized enough. It was one thing to endure sexual abuse for years. Another to take a life.

They had to put distance between them and the bodies. Phone in hand, he pulled up GPS. Got a bead on their location. "Few hours to Wesh."

"A–are we going to keep the truck the whole time?"

"Probably." He put the truck in DRIVE and headed toward a main road. "We'll dump the phones a few klicks up and then book it to Wesh." Eying the gas gauge told him they'd need to gas up.

"H–how did they find us?" she balked, her eyes watering like the rest of her.

"No idea." He huffed, the *swump-swump-swump* of the windshield wipers grating on his nerves. "Figure we've got a couple of hours before someone notices them missing. Thankfully, this truck is old enough not to have GPS. Ditching the phone we found—"

Kasra sucked in a hard breath. Grabbed her satchel. She pulled something out, her eyes as huge as MRAP wheels, held it out to him. A flip phone sat in her hand.

His eyes widened. "Are you *trying* to get us killed?"

"I … I forgot about it. When you were dreaming and I tried to steady you, I just tossed it aside. Did not turn it off." She looked pale. "It was a throw-away phone. I didn't think—"

"The point of a throw-away is that you use it and *Throw. It. Away!*" He growled. "Destroy the SIM. We'll throw the phones out at the river."

She made quick work of removing the sim and breaking the phone. Then sat there, silent, hugging herself. "I am sorry."

"That was a deadly mistake."

"I know." Her voice was small, and she seemed to shrink.

In the distance, he saw a glimmer. The river. As they crossed the bridge, he slowed and handed her the driver's. "Throw them into the water."

Kasra rolled down her window and pitched them over the side of the bridge.

"Any other phones or devices you're hiding?"

"No."

"I don't want to get shot again."

She dropped her face into her hands burst into tears.

Range huffed. It was just adrenaline making her cry. An adrenaline dump. Emotions skyrocket then hit rock bottom, making the person emotional. Nothing to say here. Nothing to do.

But it bugged him. He'd never seen her weep. Never seen her *weak*.

Elbow on the ledge of the window, he rubbed his temple as they blazed down the bumpy road, heading southeasterly. How were they going to get documents to get out of the country? What if they tried to cross somewhere that didn't require documents? Less chance to get tracked down.

American military. Those local fighters they'd taken out ... the operators at the airfield. Hellqvist, who'd seen Range with Kasra at the safehouse, had been to Roud. That meant the captain likely knew the name that Kasra harbored. Probably had a vested interest in that name *not* coming out.

Which made Range wonder—did this name connect some pretty important dots? Implicate some higher-ups in either JSOC or SOCOM. Or was it something else?

Who was the person that had so many people protecting them?

Man, his side was aching. Pressing his palm there, he felt the squish and a spike of pain. Winced. Probably should've taken time to pack it.

"Are you o—"

"Fine."

She gave him a sorrowful expression. "I am truly sorry about the phone. I ..."

Though he wanted to be angrier about it, he couldn't. Even he hadn't anticipated the local mercs coming after them. "We all make mistakes."

"Why are you being nice to me? Do not be nice. It … scares me."

"Not my anger?" he scoffed.

She kept her injured arm elevated. "Your anger has never frightened me. I … understand. It makes sense. It's an armor around you, shielding wounds you nurse, ones you think make you stronger."

"Don't hold back. Tell me what you really think."

"I do not mean to offend—I just … see through it," she said, using her fingers to comb through her hair. "Somehow, it helps me understand you. I've been there. Felt it. Lived it."

Range side-eyed her. "But not niceness?"

"People are only nice when they want something."

Dang. "It sucks that you see the world like that."

"The world *is* like that. Especially now."

Feeling some current run through his gut, he thought of his sister. "My sister, Willow, would disagree. She's like this Pollyanna who doesn't know how to be mean. She's a lot like our mom." He looked across the seat at her. Saw something he had no idea how to process. Could almost hear her say, *"You're being a nice again."*

And he was. No idea why. Maybe he'd just had enough of this running-for-his-life thing. Maybe seeing that merc with the gun to her head had done something to him.

Had to change the topic. Distract. "It stopped raining." *The weather? Seriously, genius?*

A red light on the instrument board drew his gaze. Engine light.

"Crap!"

"What?"

"Engine light." He scanned the dusky sky, still moody from

the earlier storm. "We are either going to need to take another vehicle or walk."

"I suddenly do not mind stealing …"

He huffed a smile, then noticing in the distance that a dull glow was invading the growing darkness. "Looks like a village up ahead somewhere. If we can get another car, should make your friend's by nightfall."

"Maybe there I could make a call, warn him we are coming."

"No calls. Can't risk it."

"Right." She seemed to wilt. "I am no good at this …"

The car died.

Range fought the urge to curse as he let the car drift off the road. Still had a klick or two to go. Grabbing the gear, he saw Kasra slipped on her hijab. And it ticked him off. She had no need to hide her beauty. No woman should. If men couldn't control themselves, maybe they should be the ones hiding. Or castrated. He was all for that with pedophiles.

As they hoofed it to the village, he struggled to hide the pain. How the bullet was pinching a nerve, possibly causing internal damage. And sadly, the selection of vehicles in this town proved paltry.

"This one," Kasra said, indicating a Corolla.

"Negative," he bit out and kept moving.

She skipped a step to catch up. "Why?"

Not good enough … And he wasn't thinking about himself.

Well, he wasn't thinking at all. Because why would he be so concerned about making *her* happy—*again*? Who cared what vehicle they got as long as it worked?

Yeah, but if he could buy some peace with a comfortable car, then wasn't that worth it?

Keep telling yourself that, Rage. His wound must be making him delirious.

At the far end of the road, he spotted a black Toyota. Newer model. High end, yet old enough not to have tracking. "There."

They hurried up the street and climbed into the SUV. They pulled away and headed out of town. The trip to her friend's took just shy of two hours. They wound down a crowded street that ended in what he would loosely describe as a residential neighborhood. He eased to the curb across the street from the home.

"Let me go in," she said, unbuckling. "He might shoot you."

"Should I be worried about this guy?"

"He is one of the nicest people I know."

He frowned. "You said nice people can't be trusted."

"Who do you think inspired that?" She threw him a smile and climbed out.

Wait … *what*? What was he supposed to make of that? He watched her vanish through a door in the compound wall and his gut tightened. Waiting, no idea how long this would take, he wished he had a phone. Wanted to call Dani.

Still hadn't figured out how to broach that subject with her, but if anyone could help him know how to deal with Kasra, it'd be Dani. But if this friend of Jazani's worked out—

The compound's big gate was lumbering open.

Range swung into the drive and gaped at what he saw. "What the …?" Stunned, he eased under a carport that bridged two of the three-story structures. Good, at least SATINT wouldn't be able to spot it easily. But this place … unreal. Couldn't tell from the outside how lush this place was, but palatial came to mine. Instead of a dirt driveway, concrete pavers laid out in an intricate design formed the drive. A fountain hogged the center. Gilded gates over doors. Corinthian columns.

Who was this friend of hers?

He killed the engine. Grunted at the pinch in his side, took a moment to brace himself.

Kasra opened the passenger door and bent inside, her brown-green eyes vibrant. "He was not happy I did not call."

Who was this man that put color in her cheeks again? He grimace-smiled.

With a half smile, she grabbed her satchel and bag. "Come."

He swiveled his legs out of the car, told himself to go slow. The bullet ... But even as he stood, he felt the world object. Or maybe that was his head. Or his whole body. Heard Kasra's breath. Quick steps.

Hands caught and steadied him. "Zaki, help!"

The world was going upside-down. "Whoa." He clenched his eyes. Shook his head sharp. His ears were hollowing, his vision ghosting.

"Merciful God!" came a thickly accented voice. "Inside, inside!"

"Kas ..." Range breathed as the world blurred into vague shapes. Darkness swooped in.

CHAPTER
THIRTEEN

WESH, KANDAHAR PROVINCE, AFGHANISTAN

"WHO IS HE?"

Kasra hugged herself, watching Zaki set gauze on the abdomen wound on which he had performed surgery. Shifted her gaze up his muscled chest to the slack, pale face of Range who lay unconscious. How had she not noticed how bad his injury was? This brave, honorable man had done so much for her, and she had nearly let him die.

A scar on his shoulder warned this was not the first time he had been shot. She recalled that moment in the hut when the roof had fallen and she had stumbled into him. Her hand on his chest. He had brushed her hair from her face and she felt as if fire had spread through her belly.

"Kasra!" Zaki hissed, coming toward her. "Stop staring at him unclothed. It is not proper." He wagged a hand. "Come. Out."

Startled out of her musings and inventory of Range, she turned away. "Do not be ridiculous." Though Range was only missing his shirt—cut off by Zaki so he could tend the wound—she averted her gaze. Followed him out of the bedroom and down the hall, where he washed his hands at the kitchen sink. Worry held her hostage as she sat at the table.

Here, Zaki had many of the Western comforts that most Afghan homes went without. He had spent too much time doing work in England and France and brought his love of certain amenities back to Wesh.

"Who is he, Kasra?" Zaki hissed. "That was a bullet wound!"

"An American soldier." Feeling the weariness of being on the run for the past several days and needing to do something not to feel strangely guilty, she made tea. "He ..." She sniffed. "He captured me. Arrested me."

Zaki jerked around, water splashing as he pierced her with those near-black eyes. "I should have put poison in that wound!"

"Again, you are being ridiculous." She lifted a shoulder in a lazy shrug as she cradled the mug in her hand. If Range had not captured her, he would not have come into her life. And she was growing very glad for that.

After he finished sanitizing his hands and drying them, Zaki pulled meat and cheese from the fridge, then joined her at the table. "From start to finish. Tell me how you have come to be with this man."

She gave a laugh she did not feel. "You have always been a gossip."

"And you have always had the best stories." He snagged his phone from a counter. "First, I must tell—"

"No!" Kasra slapped the device from his hand. "Tell no one that I am here. And *never* mention him. Ever."

Surprise creased his eyes into a greedy smile. "You care about this American."

"No! Of course not." Her racing heart argued. "But the last time I used a phone, he was shot."

Zaki's thick black eyebrows lifted. "I must know *everything*!"

So Kasra launched into the story, keeping no secret from the man who had been her best friend since they were children. Told about the escape, then seeing the Americans, then being captured, pretending to be Fatina, then being discovered, escaping and everything going wrong.

"There you have it," she said, tucking cheese into her mouth. "It has been only a week, but it feels a month. And truly, I am more exhausted than I have ever been."

Shaking his head, Zaki smiled. "That story is both amazing and terrible." He arched one of those thick eyebrows. "But why come to me, Kasra? You vowed—"

"We need documents …"

He gaped. "Doc—" Shoving back, he wagged his head. "No! You know it is illegal. If I am caught, I risk everything."

"And if you do not help us, you risk our lives!"

"That is not fair to put that on me."

"I know, Zaki, but …" She lowered her face to her hands and rubbed hard. As if she could rub away the sleep, guilt, and blame. "You know what—*who* else is in jeopardy."

Distress pinched his normally smooth features. "Fakes are too dangerous."

"Zaki, we have to get out of the country. Taweel took every piece of identification I have, so I could not escape." She cradled her mug of tea in her hands. "If you do this for me, you will give me a new life. And I know how much you want to help do that after …" It was unfair—cruel even—for her to ply his guilt against him. "I beg you—help us."

He looked down. After a long sigh, he looked up, his dark eyes probing. "You are sure, Kasra? With *this* man, you are sure? He is *American*."

"It is the only way. He is as desperate as I am to get somewhere safe. I have to take this chance, this opportunity."

"But him? This American—"

"What about me?"

At Range's irritated voice, Kasra came out of her seat and

turned toward him. Was glad for those blue eyes to see her again but he looked so very pale. "What are you doing? You should be resting! That wound—"

"*What* about me?" he demanded. Arm on the wall, he watched them, sweat beading on his brow and upper lip.

Kasra drew him around, surprised when he let her. "We were only talking about the documents. Zaki is surprised I am willing to help you. That is all." She led him back to the room.

He dropped heavily onto the edge of the mattress. "Why do I feel ... whacked?"

"The bullet angered the organs around it, and your kidney was especially angry, so, I operated." Zaki said from the door. "You need rest and antibiotics to fight off the infection."

Range scowled at him. "You a doctor?"

"YouTube," Zaki said, all too happily. "You can learn anything with Google."

Range struggled off the bed. "Are you kidding me?"

"It is a *bad* joke." Kasra nudged him back down. "He is a fool that way." She sat beside him. "Zaki's dad was a doctor. Together, they treated a lot of the villagers."

"Until one of those villagers killed him," Zaki said, perturbed. "Everyone always killing everyone else." He clucked his tongue and wandered back down the hall toward the kitchen.

"Zaki is ... unusual but a good man," Kasra said softly.

He tried to reach for a backpack, but froze and grimaced. Irritation scratched into his face as he lifted his arm, studying the gauze that hugged his abdomen.

"You were unconscious for quite a while. Zaki said infection set in pretty quickly."

"Gut wounds are tricky." He went to the mirror and started unwinding the bandage.

"No, leave it." Kasra hurried to his side and bent, bracing him. Took the end of the gauze he'd managed to undo and rewrapped it. "Let it heal." Only then, only as his hand lowered to her shoulder, sending a jolt of that electricity through her, did she realize what she was doing. That his shirt was still off. That he wasn't moving. Or speaking. She forbade herself from looking into his blue eyes. "Sleep. You need rest to get better."

"You're bossy ..." he muttered. His hand came to her face. "Like my sisters ..."

Was that a good thing? Instinct told her to stop him. Step back. But curiosity, admiration of this soldier who had saved her life and fought to keep her alive, made her stay those reactions.

He touched her cheek then his hand slipped around the back of her neck.

Breath staggered through her lungs, surprised at the intention digging into his handsome face as he drew her gently closer.

She finally brought her gaze up even as a feathery sweep of his thumb across her lower lip teased her. Felt a stirring she had not felt in ... ever. An inability to breathe or move as blue eyes homed in on her mouth.

Kasra lifted her head slightly, angling nearer, not sure he wanted this. Not sure *she* wanted it. Yet scared not to know that answer. What if she did? A man like him ... it was more than she could hope for.

His breath skated across her cheek.

She did not dare move, decided he would regret this later. When he felt better, was in a clearer frame of mind. "You should ..."

He tilted his mouth toward hers. A tingling taunt of a touch that made her stiffen.

No ... not stiffen. *Still*. Afraid to burst this bubble. *I am so confused*. What if he kissed her, then realized it had been a mistake? He would blame her. Say she was trying to seduce him.

Unable to bear that, she shifted aside. "You should rest."

His breathing went ragged as he followed her around—and

his gaze went unfocused. He swayed backward. Then forward. Dropped hard onto the bed. With a groan, he collapsed, unconscious.

She expelled the breath she held. Shuddered. Realized how uncomfortable he looked. Then lifted his legs onto the bed and shifted him over. Covered him. Smoothed her fingers over his mussed blond hair. The stubble that was becoming a beard. "You are a beautiful man." She sighed. "Far too good for me."

He almost kissed her.

Range might have been out of his gourd from the bullet wound and drugs her friend had given him, but he wasn't *that* out of it. He remembered her eyes, the way she'd frozen, not moving away but also not encouraging him. She seemed as conflicted as he had been when his brain told him to veer off.

But her lips ... her beauty ... *Her*.

He growled at his idiocy, at himself. He'd told her she was bossy ... like his sisters. Who were strong. Assertive. Beautiful. So similar to Willow and Brooke. And Mom. He wouldn't want her any other way.

And dang, he *did* want her. Didn't he?

No. It was the exhaustion and injury talking. She was a prostitute. Slept with men. *Many* men. Wasn't sure he could ever get past that, past her selling her body for sex. And not just hers, but others' ... children ...

Definitely couldn't get past it.

Core muscles screaming from the wound, he peeled himself off the mattress. Sat on the edge. Gritting through the pain, he pushed to his feet. Grabbed his toiletries and found a bathroom. He shed his clothes, and removed the bandage. Winced at the red welt and stitches. Yeah, definitely angry, as her friend had said.

He showered, protecting the wound from the water, then considered shaving. Stared at himself in the foggy mirror. They were going to hike through Pakistan. Maybe he'd keep the beard—it hid the shape of his face. But he hated the thing. It itched.

Cleaned and dressed, he stepped out. Nearly collided with Kasra. Jerked back, tensing in pain.

"How are you?" She wouldn't meet his gaze, and he knew why. "You slept nearly a whole day."

"Dang." That long? It'd felt like a blink. "Can't believe that wound put me out of commission so fast."

"I'm glad we were able to come here so Zaki could help."

"Same."

She smiled, tucking her chin as she tried to move around him, a nervous energy in the confined space.

Because of that near-kiss. "Hey." He touched her arm. "I'm … sorry about …" When her gaze hit his lips, he knew she tracked what his apology was about. And he also felt a stupid swarm in his gut at the same time. Then saw her uncertainty and fear. He had to majorly veer off—she'd been mistreated by men and didn't need to add his name to that list. "Yeah, *that*. You shouldn't ever have to worry about me trying to …" He couldn't even say it. "I wouldn't. Ever."

"No," she said, surprised. "I do not think you would."

Wait. Did that mean she didn't think he'd try to take favors from her? Or that she wasn't interested in him?

Why was he even asking the latter?

"I was coming to find you," she said, folding her arms. "Breakfast is ready."

"Lead the way." As he followed her down the hall, he chucked his toiletries in the room. "Where's Zookie?" He planted himself in one of the wood chairs at the kitchen table.

She laughed as she carried a big pan over and set it on a stone trivet. "*Zaki* is in his office on the other side of the compound." She passed him a plate. "Hope you don't mind spices."

He eyed the pan. "Sweet! *Tokhme banjanromi.*"

"Ah, you know it?" Her expression said she approved. "It is my favorite."

Poached eggs nestled in a bed of tomatoes, onion, chili, and— "You added potatoes."

"I did." She slid into a seat across from him.

Why did he feel so awkward around her suddenly? He nodded and took the first bite. Flavorful and delicious. "I approve." He eyed the drink in a mug. "Shir chai?"

Again she flashed surprised and poured him a cup of the warmed, sweetened milk as she squinted at him. "How do you know our traditions so well?"

"Immersion." Range thanked God for a good homecooked meal, which his body sorely needed and a conversation to divert their attention from the tension he'd created. "When I left the Coast Guard, I was thrown into the deep end, had to sink or swim."

She smiled and took a bite. "Again, you taunt me with swimming."

"Too bad Zookie doesn't have a pool."

Another laugh. "He has threatened to get one, but it would only give the imam more reason to chastise his gluttonous lifestyle."

He glanced around. "This is normal back home."

"I have heard so much about America," Kasra said as she scooped up some egg. "I hope to see it someday."

"I think you'd love it." Why did his heart pound out a cadence at that? "Couple years ago, my oldest brother bought a lodge up in the mountains—it has a pool. Pretty legit. The views are killer. And the snow—"

"I love snow."

He smirked. Knew she'd love it there.

"What about Texas? Does everyone wear cowboy boots and hats?"

"Not quite," he said. "America has some pretty amazing mountains like the Shenandoah, Blue Ridge, Rocky Mountains, but I don't think they compare to the rugged beauty of the Hindu Kush."

Kasra set down her fork and gaped at him. "Now that I did not expect to hear—an American saying Afghanistan has something more beautiful than America has."

Like you? Stretching his neck, Range shoved his gaze to his plate. "Don't get me wrong. I'm a die-hard patriot. I'll fight to my dying breath for the ideals on which America was founded."

"I think, if we are all honest, anyone could say the same of their country."

He felt more than saw the presence looming in the hall. "Would you agree, Zaki?"

The man emerged from the shadows. "I would—to a degree." His words were lathered in his southern accent. "But I do not smile upon those who would take the beauty from my country for their own gain."

That was about as overt a comment as one could make without blatantly stating the point—the man was jealous.

"Zaki," Kasra hissed, touching his arm. "We talked about this."

The man locked his gaze on Range. "Why would I help you leave this country when you are taking my Kasra away to give her to police? That is no life for her!"

"Zaki, *please*. I do not need you—"

"*Tss!*" He shook two fingers to silence her. "I will have his answer." He jutted his bearded chin at Range. "Why? Why should I help?"

"Zaki, stop!" She stood up, then looked at Range. "Ignore him. I will—"

"No, it's okay." Range felt the testosterone war and was unable to resist. "We can handle this like men."

She faltered, then hurried from the room.

Range trailed her with his gaze. Was she upset? Should he go after her? He rose.

"Give her some privacy after all you have caused her."

"After all *I* caused?" Jaw clenched, Range sat back down.

Zaki gave him a fierce look. "You arrested her."

"My team and I were tasked with bringing her in for questioning."

"You interrupted her plan to help free all the girls!" His voice sounded strained. "Why would I do anything for you? Now, the girls are in American custody somewhere—with my brother."

Why hadn't he seen it before? The eyes ... a dead giveaway. "Razam."

The man inclined his head. "My mother has been ill since his arrest was made known and Kasra captured."

Why would the man's mother be ill over Kasra's arrest? Okay, wait. This ... this ... "Kasra ... She's from *here* ...?"

As if he seemed to realize he'd given something away, Zaki gave a small, stiff nod.

Kasra was from this village. It explained why she knew so much. Knew this man so well. But what did that mean? There was something here, something he couldn't put his finger on ...

The man lifted his downcast eyes. Challenge added to the grim set of his jaw. "Do you care about her?"

Staring at the guy who seemed to be drowning in guilt about something, Range wasn't going to play this game. Or answer that question. Mostly because he couldn't figure out what to say.

"Kasra ask me to do this thing—and I could lose my job. My home. For her? Yes! I would help with my dying breath. But you?" He touched his temples, then flicked his hands outward in exasperation. "Pfft! I do not know why she would help you."

"You would sacrifice your livelihood, the means to providing for yourself and your mom ... for a woman who ran a brothel."

Daggers shot from Zaki's eyes. "You do not know what you speak of!"

"No, I really do. I was there. Where she lived. Selling girls, herself—"

"Augh!" Zaki pitched himself at Range. They tumbled to the stone floor as the man pounded at him.

Wound screaming from the impact, Range struggled to subdue the man. Flipped him onto his stomach. Put a knee in his back. Held his hand hooked up and behind. "Enough!"

The man began trembling. Sobbing. "It is my fault." He banged his head against the stone. "All my fault that she was sold to them!"

Stunned, Range shifted back. Holding his side, he found his chair. Dropped onto it in disbelief. "What do you mean?"

Dragging himself up against the wall, Zaki cried. "I wanted to marry her, but Razam asked our father for her. I was so angry and did not want my brother to have her. So, I told her brother, Dawud, he could solve their money problems if he sold her. I meant to me!" He beat his chest. *"To me!"* Sobs wracked the man's body. "I loved her, would have taken care of her. Provided for her. But Dawud heard of traders ... and Kasra was gone."

Sold. She had been *sold*. *She* had been sold. Like a used car. Cattle.

An RPG hit his chest at the revelation. Made it hard to think. Obliterated all his arguments about her. The news was a gamechanger. Shifted Kasra from the category of "monster" to ...

What exactly?

Sickened, Range pushed to his feet. Felt sorry for the guy who would have to live with that mistake for the rest of his life—yet he also wanted to pound him into the next life. "Does she know what you did?"

Regret clawed at the young, bearded face as he nodded. "And she never hated me for it." His lips trembled again.

Unfathomable—Kasra knew her childhood friend was the reason she had been sold and didn't hate him? "Never?"

"Not even the day they took her."

Range stood. Looked at a man he suddenly wanted nothing to do with. Wanted to lay into him. Instead, he pivoted and stalked down the hall. Felt like he could tear something to shreds. He heard soft steps coming down the front hall ahead. Did not want conversation. Or those green-brown eyes boring into his willpower. Needed time to unpack what he'd just learned.

He banked left and up a flight of stairs. Found his way onto a rooftop terrace that looked south toward Pakistan. The privacy was surprising in such a tightly packed town. But he was grateful for the solitude. Stood staring out into the distance. Could almost see the border crossing with its towering checkpoints and dust stirred by the busy site.

They would head more southwesterly. Maybe stay in Afghanistan another day, then veer off the beaten path across the border.

Who was he kidding? He couldn't focus on their plan. His thoughts were still in that kitchen. Still unpacking the betrayal perpetrated by a friend.

Her own brother sold her.

How had she risen to power over Roud then, if she'd been sold? All this time, he'd ... hated her. She had been betrayed by her closest friend and sold by her brother—and no hatred.

Range regretted that he'd never considered that she might've been sold into that life. That he'd treated her so poorly. Apparently like every other man in her life.

"It was a mistake to come here." Her voice was quiet as she joined him. "Zaki ... he is a good friend—"

"How can you say that?" He adjusted to face her, ignoring the tweak of pain in his side. "He is responsible for—"

"No!" Kasra strode to his side. "No, he is not. Even at fifteen I knew the fault of being sold rested with men who only knew how to hurt people." She sighed. "Zaki and I were dearest of friends all those years ago. When Razam asked for me … It was so terrible. Two brothers at war"—she motioned to herself—"over me. This! Can you imagine?"

"Yes!" Way too much.

Expression startled, she seemed to shrink away. "No, do not do that." Her words were taut, strained, then she looked to the distance again. "I told you not to be nice to me. It makes me not trust you."

He caught her arm, but she tried to tug away, her laugh empty and pained. "Kasra, look at me."

She tried to wrest free. "Why?" Writhing, she slipped into a fierce visage. Jerked free. Stepped back.

It was like an animal with its foot caught in a trap. Any attempt to help free it was met with frenzied panic. He made the mistake of tugging her back.

With a lightning strike to his face—which missed—she hopped away. Startled. Then laughed. "This is what we do best, yes? Spar."

"No. Kas …" He knew if he made a move, she would begin fighting. "Please—" He held out a hand, knowing if he protected his wound, he wouldn't be able to block her. "Let's—"

A jab. A strike. A knife-hand. A flurry of movements.

"Please—"

One of her so-called playful strikes nailed his wound. He doubled, groaning.

"Range!" She was at his side. "I am sorry. I did not—"

He wrapped her into his arms. "Listen."

She stiffened. "Let me go."

"Listen—"

"Let. Me. Go." Lips flat, she glowered. Eyes blazed. She looked ready to kill. Like that trapped animal, afraid a bigger predator had swooped in for the kill.

Shifting his hands to her shoulders, he nodded. "I'm not trying to hurt you."

"You are being nice. *Don't* be nice," she said, baring her teeth.

He lifted his palms. "Kas ..."

She flinched. Hurried away, heading to the door inside.

"Who's Atia?"

She stopped short. Hung her head. Then straightened. Turned. "I will tell you if you will tell me the nightmare that torments your sleep."

Hadn't seen that coming. But ... "Fair."

She faltered, as if she hadn't expected him to yield. "I ..." She looked away, clearly struggling with the secret she must now share.

"I would like to know," he said, feeling the need to extend an olive branch, "but you do not have to tell me. Even though we made an agreement."

"So, you think me a liar."

"No, I think you've been through a lot—"

She scoffed. "Zaki fills your head with things and suddenly you are my ally?"

He frowned. "Did you forget the last six days on the run together?"

"That was an alliance of self-preservation."

He saw it now. Saw the way she deflected every chance, every possibility of a connection. Excused it. Rationalized it. He had to come at this, at her, in a way she wouldn't expect. Not to trick her but to let her know he was serious. To his surprise, he found he did want to be allies.

Wasn't sure it was possible with all the stuff between them. "I owe you an apology."

"No!" she growled. "I said don't be nice."

He held up his hands. "It's long overdue." He edged nearer, holding his side. "I assumed the worst of you. Never even let it enter my thick skull that you might be anything other than a madam working kids."

"You and everyone else."

He angled his head. "But that … that's not who you are. Is it?"

"It is! *I* ran Roud. It was me!"

He stopped, considered her. Something about the way she said that warned there was a lot more to the story. "Why are you shouldering all the blame?"

"Because!" She drew in herself. "It was me."

"It was you," he said, agreeing, "who was betrayed by family. Taken from those you knew and loved. Abused for money." Sensing the tremor of anger at what she had been put through, he slowly erased the distance. "Betrayed by a boy you loved. Parents—"

"They were dead. It is why Dawud … sold me." A tear pushed free and slowly slid down her cheek, as if it too hesitated over the past.

"Kasra …"

"No!" she snapped. "Stop! *Stop* being nice." Her chin bounced as she fought tears. Shook her head. It seemed the rabbit was beginning to tire … or trust.

The scream of those last words drew him closer. "It was wrong. Horrible." Gently, he cupped her shoulders. "They were your family. They should have loved you—"

"You do not—"

"Protected you."

A sob choked from her. She tilted toward him, her body rigid as steel when her forehead met his chest. Another sob.

"You did not deserve it, Kasra."

Her fingers coiled into his shirt. Fists pulling.

He folded her into arms. "And I am going to make sure it never happens again."

What. The. Heck? He had no idea what he was saying, but her grievous sobs that broke free from the cage in which she held them told him he'd said the right thing. As he stood there, he slid a hand over her back in comfort and felt ... ridges ... Not a bra strap. But something worse, more detestable ... Scars.

She pushed into his hold, burying her face and hurts there. Drenched his shirt with her tears and her heartache. He held her. Didn't have the answer to the future. To looking past all the men who'd ripped out a piece of her soul.

But he did know he was supposed to be right here. In Wesh. Holding Kasra Jazani.

CHAPTER
FOURTEEN

Wesh, Kandahar Province, Afghanistan

SHE HAD FOUND HEAVEN on earth and it was in a man's arms. A miracle she never thought possible. Healing and hope sprouted as he held her close. Words ... Range had spoken words she wanted to hear for a very long time. They stood there on the terrace, staring out over the edge of Afghanistan with her afraid to move or speak. Afraid he would realize his mistake.

"I'm going to need a baseball bat."

She lifted her head and peered at him. "What?"

"Well, I just said I was going to protect you ..."

The broken, brittle pieces of her heart swelled beneath his words. "Zaki and I made our peace long ago."

"And the scars on your back?"

Kasra faltered. Well, he knew everything else ... "Taweel punished me a few times in the beginning. Made an example of me."

"Skip the baseball bat. Give me an M4." He stared down at her with a raw intensity. The same desire that had his breath mingling with hers in the bedroom last night was here again. He understood more about her now and probably, more than ever, wanted nothing like that from her. She doubted he would ever be the one to cross that line. Should *she* kiss him? Let him know it was okay …?

But was it?

She did not know. In truth, she was not even sure if what she felt was okay, if it was right. Perhaps she was just infatuated with this man who had saved her life. Repeatedly. What did love look like? Was this it? Would she ever recognize it? Embrace it? She had vowed long ago to never give a man that kind of control over her again.

His hands slid away and he stepped back. A near smile touched his lips beneath that thickening stubble. His hand rand down the back of his neck "I'm going to head in, clean the weapons. See about—"

"No." Kasra startled herself with the answer, surprised at how much she did not want him to leave. "Stop being nice." She feinted toward him, fighting hands up.

"Kas …" Range cocked his head in warning. "No more. My wound … I'm not doing this again."

If he would not spar … She tiptoed up and caught the back of his neck. Pulled his face to hers. Set her mouth on his.

Range tensed.

Please do not reject me. Please don't. She shuttered her eyes closed, not wanting to see the rejection parked on his face. Instead, she focused on her heart stampeding across the distance her brokenness created. The way everything felt right and perfect here with him. In his arms. How her entire being seemed to melt into his and find … *home.*

He lifted his head. Blue eyes probed hers and she begged him not to think about her past. To just live here … He cupped her face and returned the kiss.

Electricity shot through her veins at his moan as he deepened the kiss. Strong hands found her waist. Tugged her to himself and groaned.

Enlivened, she hooked her arms around his shoulders, fell into an unimaginable well of warmth and passion. Felt his mouth trail along her jaw and nuzzling her ear, then back to her mouth for a deep, lingering kiss.

And then he was gone. Backing up. A chill in his expression as he expelled a thick, heavy breath and considered her.

Face flushed, every nerve alive, she stared back. Shocked. When had she ever experienced *that*?

"This … This is trouble," he said, his voice husky.

She swallowed, covering her mouth. Still living that kiss. Smiled.

He shook his head. "I need air."

She snorted. "We're on the roof."

But he went inside. Left her there.

Left her.

Alone.

Like everyone else.

After all she'd just offered. Not intimacy, though she had never kissed or been kissed like that—a shared passion. But … herself. The real her.

What in Sam Hill had he been thinking?

Range paced his bedroom, hands clasped behind his thick skull. That kiss had pulled out all the stops in their relationship. He'd never felt anything like that. Ever. It was like getting caught in a riptide. Yanked out to sea, drowning. Drowning in passion and a … deepness. A connection.

"No, no," he gritted out, turning toward the window and closing his eyes. There was only one place a kiss like that led. And it couldn't. Wouldn't. Ever.

Yet he had weeks more to spend with her to get her out of the country, through Pakistan, down to the gulf. Should he risk them catching a flight in Pakistan instead? Speed things up in getting back?

Heck yes.

No, that was panic, desperation talking. No need to pile mistakes on top of mistakes. How had he'd gotten so far from "she's a monster" to ... *this*? They needed to get moving. Idle hands made for trouble. He stalked out of the room and found Zaki. The man did not look up.

"Where are we on the documents?"

"I told you tomorrow," Zaki said, words and mouth tight.

Range hesitated. Was something wrong? Eh, didn't care. Time to get back to business. "Is there somewhere I can pick up supplies and disposable phones?"

Zaki gave him a furtive glance. "What supplies?"

The guy was upset about something, but Range was done playing nice. "Standard—protein bars, medkit, thermal blankets. I'd like some ammunition, but that might be a stre—"

"Caliber?"

Seriously?

"Come." Zaki motioned him to follow. They wound out of the house and across the carport into the second structure, which held another complete house with a greasy, spicy smell. "*Moor*, just coming through," he shouted to his mother as they wound to the left, ducked through a door and down a set of stairs.

Light erupted below, tempting him deeper into this hidden madness. Cursing himself for leaving his Sig, he snagged his KA-BAR and held the blade along his wrist and forearm.

He heard a beeping—was that a detonation timer or a security pad? Then a buzz from somewhere that sounded ... distant.

Feet shuffled back to him and Zaki peered around the corner. "Come, come."

Range joined him and found a stone wall with a reinforced steel door partially ajar. Unsettled at this new aspect to the seemingly innocuous man who had betrayed his childhood sweetheart, Range slipped through the opening.

And stopped short. "What the …?" He sheathed the dagger. It was like something out of a James Bond movie—almost. Not quite as sophisticated, but he half expected Q to come out and start explaining how things worked.

Zaki held his hands toward the space the size of a small warehouse. "Supplies."

"No kidding." Racks of handguns, rifles, and knives lined the wall. Phones hung in plastic packaging that was likely more tamperproof than a vault. Backpacks and crates littered the floor with supplies that … shouldn't be here.

"What exactly do you do for the Ministry of Health?" Range moved to the wall where an M4 peered down at him. "This is American—military grade." He eyed the guy, not appreciating the likelihood of how he'd come into possession of all this. "How d'you end up with this?"

Zaki nodded around. "The same I did with the others. They were either left or … borrowed. And there are certain soldiers who, in exchange for information, look the other way when weapons go missing."

"You're spying on your own people?" Range balked, half tempted to turn the weapon on the guy.

"Not me." He shook a finger as if that was beneath him. "But I do not feel it safe for certain people to possess weapons such as these."

"But it's safe with you," Range said, the sarcasm dripping from his words.

"As you see. All safe."

"Your collection has grown." Kasra's soft voice reached through the room and tried to lure him to look at her.

"How did you get in?" Zaki balked. "It was secured."

"You still use my birthday for the code." Kasra laughed.

Not in the mood for flirting, Range glanced around and spotted a tactical pack. He grabbed it and stuffed in some flares and flashbangs. From the wall, he took the Glock and M4, hating the way his ears tracked her movement as she came near.

Kasra joined him at the workbench where he picked up seven 30-round mags for the M4. She retrieved a knife and drew off the sheath.

He eyed the blade. The way she handled it. Knew she had the skills to put it to good use.

She shifted around him and lifted a black ruck from a corner.

"Pack light," he gruffed, crouching and scanning the lower shelf. "We have to walk with whatever we bring." He spotted a compass and night-vision goggles. Rolled up a couple of shirts. Socks. MREs, though it was probably a kindness if he ate dirt instead.

An hour later, they were back in their rooms. Range dumped his ruck and the new ruck out on the floor and knelt—using kneepads he'd taken from Zaki's Weapons SuperMart—and started organizing.

"You are avoiding me."

"Not avoiding," he lied. "Prepping to leave." He rolled the shirts, pants, and socks. Set them aside. Things went silent and he wondered if she'd left. But then she set the first-aid kit near the clothes in his periphery. "You should pack."

"I will never pack the way you do. How do you make it all so small and ... tight?"

He kept working because she wasn't looking for answers. This was small talk, and he didn't do small talk.

"You know—"

Range pushed to his haunches and straightened. Moved past her.

But she caught his arm.

Anticipating another sparring session, he jerked free. Winced in pain as he lifted his hands. Tried to level as much warning into his expression as he could. "No more."

"So that's it?" Her words were strangely thick. "You decide I'm a problem and throw ice between us?"

"Not what I said." That wasn't what he'd said. But he didn't trust himself to talk. Or even to be here right now. "I have to find Zaki." He stepped into the hall.

"He went into town."

Range stopped.

"We're adults. Let's talk—"

"Talk is cheap."

"Agreed!" she snapped. "But it's better than the cold shoulder."

"This isn't a cold shoulder. This is my job. You are—" Man, he just couldn't say it.

"Your prisoner? A whore?"

Hands on his belt, he clenched his jaw. "We had a deal—"

"Yes, and where are the others?"

"How would I know? I've been too busy saving your freakin' life!"

"And kissing me."

He huffed. Closed his eyes.

"What? You figured I'd been with so many men that adding you wouldn't matter?"

Assaulted by her accusation, he straightened. "I *never* treated you like that," he said in a low, fierce tone.

"You just did! You took what you wanted and walked away. Only difference is you didn't leave money."

He was going to be sick. Wanted to argue. Fight. But Canyon's warning to tread carefully hammered him. "You're …" He huffed. "You are right. It will not happen again."

She recoiled and he had no idea why.

"The fear you've lived in for the last ten years? What

happened between you and all those men? Never worry that will happen between us."

"*Between?*" she scoffed. "You don't understand, do you? Nothing happened *between* me and any of the men who ..." She shoved her hair from her face. "Never mind." She stormed from the room.

And he let her go, suddenly so lost and out of his depth even a sonar ping couldn't help him find his way.

CHAPTER
FIFTEEN

Wesh, Kandahar Province, Afghanistan

SCREWED IT UP AGAIN, *genius*.

Later that night, Range tossed the ruck against the wall next to the door. Wouldn't Canyon love to rub this in his face? Went for the wrong girl. Again.

But ... was she wrong?

Madam.

Definitely wrong.

Yet there was this gut instinct that told him it went way deeper. When was the last time he'd kissed someone? What he'd felt had far exceeded anything he had felt before. It stripped him of his excuses regarding her so-called profession. It had been her *existence*. She'd been sold into it—

Didn't excuse what she'd done. The children ...

She'd been sold. Sold into that life.

Dang, this was so muffed. Which way was up? He sat on the edge of the bed, scrubbing the back of his neck. He seriously needed to talk to someone. Find out—

Shouts echoed through the house.

When no answer met the shouts, Range snatched up the M4

and swung back from the door, weapon trained on it as feet slapped the stone floor.

"American? American!" someone bellowed in alarm. Panic. The door flung open and a boy of maybe fifteen saw the weapon and leapt back. "No shoot! No shoot."

What the heck? Range angled it down. "Who are you? What—"

"Altair." He patted his chest, eyes wide. "Hurry! Hurry. They take her," he said in Pashto. "Zaki said to find you. They take Kasra."

The words would not process. "What? Who?"

"Men. Many men!"

Always one to verify intel—especially when it came from a kid he didn't know from Adam—he rushed down the hall. "Zaki! Kasra!" When no answer came, he started gearing up and looked at the teen. "How many?"

"Ten, twelve." Altair shrugged.

Sliding on a tac vest, he snagged his Sig. Tucked it at the small of his back. Clipped the M4 to the vest.

"Please hurry. They kill her because imam say she is harlot."

Heart in his throat, Range rounded on the teen. "Where? Show me."

They hurried into the dark night, the kid running and Range doing his best to keep up but also move tactically. Pay attention to corners, clear them, watched second levels and rooftops.Around another corner he spotted the mosque. They entered via a main door, then banked right instead of heading through the intricately carved lattice that separated the front from the sacred area of worship.

The teen was about to bust open a door.

Range caught his shirt. Dragged him back. "Is there another door to this room?"

Altair shook his head frantically. "Hurry, please. They kill her—the imam said so."

Not wanting this kid to get hurt, Range motioned him back. "Go. Out." He waited until the kid shuffled away. Stretched his neck. Wished he had a team, especially when he didn't know what was on the other side of the door.

God ... help me.

Cries and yelps came from within, followed by meaty thuds.

He cursed himself for not grabbing a flash-bang. With a flick of his wrist, he opened the door and slid into the room. Windows on the far side. Floor-to-ceiling wooden divider screens to his three.

Men shouted at him, barking about defiling their mosque with violence and bloodshed.

Promises, promises ...

In Pashto, he ordered them to get on the ground, his gaze sweeping, taking in the small room that had a dais at the front. Four men stood there, watching him with keen interest, their attention bouncing to the floor—Kasra. Curled in a fetal position. Hands and face bloodied.

A man kicked her in the side.

Ticked and ready for blood, Range stalked forward. "Touch her again and it'll be the last time you touch anyone." As he swept toward the front, half the men backed up. "Kasra." Two meters separated them. "Kasra, can you get up?"

"Yes," she groaned, rolling onto all fours.

"No!" A man with a turban and nice clothes produced a handgun and brought it to bear.

In response to the threat, Range fired a short burst.

Shouts went up as the body dropped to the carpeted floor, the remaining three Muslims huddling. One shoved another man forward to secure Kasra and slid behind him. Two human shields.

"That was foolish," the coward said.

"What was foolish was pulling a gun," Range said. "If I see another, I won't hesitate to drop everyone in here." Staring down the sights of his M4, Range adjusted position so nobody could come up behind him. Sensed the men who'd scattered regrouping on his three. Sidestepping, he worked his way closer to Kasra.

Even as Range negotiated around, the threesome holding her swung like the hands of a clock, making it impossible to get a clear shot on the last guy, who had a weapon thrust past middleman to Kasra's back. Clever.

"Let her go, and we can talk." Understanding the man's determination, he angled his M4 to the floor.

"Talk?" The man balked. "There will be no talk. She will be put to death for her adultery and sin!"

Clearly this man did not keep a strict adherence to their religious edicts, at least pertaining to violence in his mosque.

"The Quran demands 100 lashes, not death," came a voice from his ten—Zaki.

Range eyed Kasra, ticked at the violence done to her. Fury coursing, he forced himself to think. Reason.

"Imam Butrus," Zaki said, coming forward, "where is the man with which you accuse her in this fornication? Does the Quran not condemn the men *and* women who fornicate? If she is guilty as you have charged, then where is the man?"

"Are we to bring ten years of men to this hall?" the imam scoffed. "We must rid this village of her filth before she can pollute it any more."

"Ten years," Range said, inching closer. "Where did you get that number? That you know it's been ten years tells me you knew when she was sold and taken from here. Forced into it. Not her choice."

"She could have escaped, *refused*. Even killing herself would have been better than to live in such sin!"

Kill herself? This sick p—

"But no, she took men's honor, destroyed women and

children. She is not only a whore but an abomination!" He stabbed a finger in the air. "She must be punished."

Another seemingly pious man came forward. "Imam Butrus is right. The Quran say *'The woman and the man guilty of fornication, flog each one of them with a hundred stripes—and let not any pity for them restrain you in regard to a matter prescribed by Allah, if you believe in Allah and the Last Day, and let some of the believers witness the punishment inflicted on them.'*"

"As Zaki said—lashes, not death," Range stated.

"You are American," Butrus said, "I do not expect such an immoral man to understand our laws. Neither do you have a say in it. She will die—"

"Your own religion says no violence in the mosque, yet here we are," Range barked, taking two steps forward, weapon ready again. "Touch her—"

"Why do you care so much for this whore, American?"

He was going to kill this guy if he called her that one more time. Or if he lifted that gun. "She's my prisoner. I'm taking her in."

The imam scowled at Zaki. "Is this true?"

"He has said that, but she has not been in cuffs since they forced their way into my home."

Forced our way ... What the fluff was going on ? Range wanted to punch the guy ... but swiftly realized Zaki needed to say that—he had to live in this village and not have his throat slit in the night for harboring a prostitute and American. "We were trying to leave when you took my prisoner." Not a whole truth, but close enough.

"And how often do you *kiss* your prisoner?" Zaki challenged, his eyes blazing with legit outrage.

So, he'd seen them ...

The guy turned to the imam. "I saw them in a very passionate kiss just a few hours ago."

"Zaki," Kasra hissed, earning another kick from the second man.

Range snapped his weapon and fired a short burst, the deafening barrage left a ringing in his ears. Bullets skimmed the man's tunic, earning a shout and angry retort. *"Don't* touch her."

"Does a soldier try to kill an imam and his caliph over a prisoner?" Zaki laughed. "I think not! It is much more than a captor and his prisoner."

"What're you doing?" Range glowered.

"Since Yusuf is filming," Zaki went on, "Imam Butrus, why do you not make an example of them? Force the American to marry the harlot—let him buy her freedom by making her his wife!"

A sick gleam hit the imam's eyes that shifted to Range. "Would you do this? Buy her life with marriage?"

"Is this a joke?" Range couldn't believe his ears. I'm detaining her, not marrying her!" How did that even make sense to them? "She's my *prisoner*—I'll take her off your hands, out of your village."

Butrus peered over the shoulder of his caliph. "That does nothing but condone what she has done, the lives she destroyed running that brothel."

"You seem to know a lot about her," Range said, trying to find a better line of sight. Could he just double-tap these men—Zaki included—then grab her and run?

Anger slid through the imam's face. "Marry her or she dies."

What the freakin' fluff? This was the most ludicrous—"What's the point of that? How would that change anything?" Range demanded, frustration tightening his grip on the M4. His gaze slid to Kasra whose expression was a mural of pain, fear, grief, and hopelessness.

"It does not change her at all. But it would appease me for Afghanistan to humiliate an American soldier—who should no longer be in my country—by forcing you to marry an adulteress!"

Head swinging back and forth mournfully, silent tears slipping down her swollen, bloodied face, Kasra seemed to be telling him not to do this.

Zaki was at his side. He lowered his chin, looking behind them to the door. "Butrus's sister was abused by American soldiers years ago and he threw her out. She ended up at Roud ... she reappeared here last year, broken. Very broken. He killed her." His gaze held hers. "What I do is for Kasra. Because he will *not* stop till you are humiliated and Kasra is dead. It is why they are videoing it."

Range then noticed the camera in the corner and sneered at Zaki. "You're a piece of—"

"I am sorry you think that, but *this*"—he bobbed his head to where Butrus held Kasra—"is the only way she lives. The power is in your hands to save her life."

Staring at the coward again, Range knew one thing without a doubt. "I'm not an idiot. You'll kill us both."

"Unlike you Americans, I am a man of my word," Abdullah High and Mighty announced. "Marry her and she is your stain to live with."

"Range, I am not worth it. Do not—" Kasra was hauled backward, hand clamped over her mouth by the caliph, but she struggled, doing her best to shake her head and tell him not to do this.

"What is your answer, American?"

Range tightened his jaw. This made no freakin' sense. Did it matter as long as Kasra could walk out of here?

Fake it till you make it ... out of the country.

Which was a problem. This imam wasn't going to let them walk out of here, no matter what dance they performed for him. But it'd buy time to figure out their path to freedom. "Fine," he finally said, motioning Kasra to come to him, hand bracing the M4. "We get married. Then walk."

"Do you think us so weak and foolish, American?" Butrus stretched his chin at him. "Put down the weapon."

"Not happening."

Butrus stepped closer to his caliph, his arm again reaching toward Kasra's head with that gun.

Ticked, Range bit back a curse—no clear line of sight. If he fired, he'd hit Kasra, too. No options here. "Okay!" Glowering at the imam, he removed the magazine from the rifle, then ejected the round from the chamber. Downloaded the magazine, removing the rounds and slipping them into his pocket. He then dropped the useless weapon on the ground. Kicked it to his nine, farthest from anyone here. If he couldn't use it, no one would.

When one of the villagers rushed toward it, Range coldcocked him, appreciated the release of anger. Rolled his shoulders. "Now, are we doing this or not?"

"Where is your Walwar?" the imam asked.

At the ridiculous demand for a bride price, Kasra stilled, saw the confusion on Range's face. Hated herself for this mess. It seemed no matter what she did, how hard she tried to extricate herself from this life, her terrible past haunted every step toward freedom and dragged her back into its dark depths.

"It means head-money," Zaki whispered to Range. "You pay an agreed-upon price—"

"I didn't agree on any money," Range growled.

Butrus seemed far too pleased with himself. "You must pay for her."

Hands out to his sides, Range arched an eyebrow. "I don't have money."

"Then your weapon."

Range's lips thinned. His nostrils flared. Staring at Butrus with a look that said he would readily kill the imam, he kicked over the M4 and nodded. "Reach for it before we're married and I will drop you."

"Threatening the man who holds this woman's life in his hands is not very smart." The caliph clucked his tongue. Sounded like a chicken. "You and your ego, American." His grip on her arm nearly cut off the circulation, but she would not give him the pleasure of hearing her cry out. With a grunt, he thrust her forward.

Shocked that he had released her, that this entire scheme was happening, Kasra stumbled into Range, who steadied her. "I am sorry," she whispered.

He kept his attention trained on the imam and shifted her behind him. Protecting her.

She peered up at him as he stood there, his shoulders broad, his jaw set firmly.

"As her Nikah Father," Zaki said, "I will give them provisions to leave the country."

Imam Butrus narrowed his eyes, then looked to Range. "Your name—and tell the truth" He looked to the caliph. "We will verify it."

"Range Metcalfe." He sounded so very angry.

They all watched the caliph, and after several long minutes, he nodded.

Who had verified his name?

Oh he would hate her for this. She hated *herself* for it. For rushing out of the house after their argument. She had just wanted to think. Walk. Distraught, she had not even seen the men stalking toward her.

"Range Metcalfe, Kasra Jazani," the imam began the ceremony. "Range Metcalfe, Kasra Jazani. Range Metcalfe, Kasra Jazani." Arrogance lifted his bearded face. "Do you, Range

Metcalfe, in the presence of these witnesses agree to take this whore as your wife?"

"No," Range growled.

She should have known. It was too much to ask. Too much to hope for, that he would—

"No," the word struggled from between his teeth, "I don't take a whore. But I do take Kasra Jazani as my wife."

Jolted at what he spoke, the way he rejected the cruel name, she drew back. Disbelief curled through her, constricting her breath. Stinging her eyes. He said words she never thought to hear from any man. She kept her gaze down as Imam Butrus then recited verses from the Holy Quran, which felt like a mockery since they were forcing them to marry.

"She is your wife now, American."

It was fake ... forced ... but it was done.

Still tense, rigid, Range caught her hand with his left as he backed away. Eyed the M4, clearly annoyed he had been conned out of it. "Now, I'll take my wife and leave." Challenge glinted in his blue eyes as he urged her out of the room. Then he nodded to her. "Go."

Vision half blocked by the swelling, she shifted. Stumbled and started for the door. Held her breath as she left the antechamber. Aimed for the side door. Shocked that she was still alive, that they had not done something far worse, Kasra glanced back at Range, only to find him right there, back to her as he aimed his weapon inside the hall and edged into the darkness.

A man appeared from the side.

"*Don't*," came Range's feral warning.

"I did not say *how* you would leave," Butrus said as he edged into view, nodding at someone. "Dead works for me."

Too late, Kasra saw the shadowy man aim a weapon at her.

"No!" Zaki shouted, diving in front of her.

A weight plowed into her back.

Pop! Pop!

The cracks echoed through the night.

Shots ricocheted as she hit the ground. "Next person that moves dies," Range barked. "Do it! Test me!"

Kasra's attention darted to Zaki, prone on the ground. Then saw him roll onto his back, clutching his chest. "Zaki!" She scrambled to his side. "Zaki!"

"Get him up," Range barked, weapon moving back and forth, holding the others at bay as she slipped her arm under her friend's and helped him stand. "Go," he instructed, his gaze still on the foul men of this village. "If you come after us, you will not live to see the dawn."

Hurrying Zaki to the street, she felt … numb. Could not process what happened. Worried her only childhood friend would die before they could get him help.

"Here," Range said, indicating to a small sedan, windows still rolled down and engine left running.

She helped Zaki into the back and sat down. Barely closed the door when they whipped away from the mosque. In minutes, they pulled into his courtyard. Parked. Helped Zaki into the house, where his mom flew into a frantic frenzy, shouting she would get the doctor and vanished.

"Can you patch him?" Range asked.

Kasra faltered. "What?"

"I need to pack our truck, so we can leave."

"Now?"

"Two minutes ago."

"No, he needs a doctor. We—"

"Go," Zaki said, his color very pale, a ghostly sheen. "I have had worse."

Range considered him for a second, then gave a grim nod and stalked off.

"You have not had worse," Kasra argued.

"I will be okay." He hissed a breath and slumped against the wall. He slid down.

"Zaki!" Kasra tried to help him. "Range, we need a doctor."

"Kasra," Zaki wheezed. "Please—I am at peace."

"You will be fine. Just wait. The doctor is coming."

Gear in hand, Range stalked down the hall. He squatted, his face still painted with that grim expression and some pain.

"I am sorry," Zaki whispered to him. "Take care of her ... yes?"

"Zaki, just hold on." She looked toward the door. "Where is the doctor?"

"Kas," Range said quietly. "We leave in two. Understood?"

"We can't leave him!"

"Be at peace." After touching Zaki's shoulder, Range went outside with the gear.

"Please," her friend said, "I do this ... maybe make a wrong right?"

Crying made her eyes and face hurt, but she could not stand this. "There is nothing to make right, Zaki."

"I am sorry for what I did ... to you." His hand flopped, reaching for hers, so she held it. "You are married ... good man ..." A strange whistle came from his throat and he wheezed his last. Head lolled to the side.

"*Noo!*" she wailed. "Please, please, Zaki." She shifted forward, hooked his head and hugged him. "You silly fool." She kissed his temple.

"Kas, they're coming down the street. We have to go."

CHAPTER SIXTEEN

BEXAR-WOLFE LODGE, NORTHERN VIRGINIA

"GO AHEAD, TAGGART. WE'RE HERE." Canyon stood with is hands tucked under his armpits and nodded at the video feeding into Stone's Smart TV in his living room.

"Stone," Cord Taggart greeted him. "Congrats to you and Brighton on the bun in the oven." He grinned. "Sure didn't waste time."

Smoothing a hand over his clean-shaven jaw, Stone nodded his thanks. "So ... what's happening?"

Cord's demeanor shifted to serious. More than ever for the guy. "Look, I'm not going to blow smoke up your skirts—Range is in trouble."

While their brother was notoriously hotheaded—especially toward Canyon—ironically, he had an amazing knack for *not* getting into trouble. He was a rule follower and self-righteous suck-up. And Canyon meant that in the best way possible. Which is why he shared a look with Stone.

"And by trouble," Cord continued, "I mean some serious muff. Give a watch."

"Thoughts?" Canyon asked his brother.

"It's not like him." The tautness in Stone's shoulders warned of his irritation as the screen went blank, then staticky. "He's always been able to handle what gets thrown at him."

"And by handle, you mean hold a grudge for ten years."

Stone met Canyon's gaze with a stern look. "You did the same."

"Me?"

"You had the power to make peace. Instead, you've thrown his grudge in his face every chance you get."

"Not—"

Crack! Crack!

Gunshots yanked their attention back to the screen where they saw their brother moving into a room with an M4 tucked into his shoulder. Couldn't tell who he'd just shot. *"I won't hesitate to drop everyone in here!"* Range moved toward the front where two men stood with a woman laid out on the floor. *"Let her go, and we can talk."*

"Talk?" The man balked, and though it was hard to tell, it seemed he might have drawn a gun. *"There will be no talk. She will be put to death for her adultery and sin!"*

"The Quran demands 100 lashes," came another voice, a man shifting into view from the side.

Range hadn't moved or spoken. Still had his gun trained the three.

"We must rid this village of her filth, before she can pollute it more." The main speaker shifted behind another man and the woman now on her feet.

"Coward," Canyon muttered, "hiding behind a woman."

"Ten years," Range said as he moved closer. *"It's been ten years when she left here. Her choice."*

"Wait," Stone said, indicating to something on the screen. "D'you see that?"

"I'm taking her."

The imam scowled at a fourth man. *"Is this true?"*

"They forced their way into my home. I saw them in a very passionate kiss just a few hours ago."

"There, again," Stone said.

That's when Canyon started connecting the dots, too. "It's edited."

"Heavily."

Range snapped his weapon and fired at a man, who shouted at him. But he was still alive. *"Don't touch her."*

"Does a soldier try to kill an imam and his caliph?" a man asked, incredulously.

The imam shifted to Range. *"Would you buy her life with marriage?"*

Range considered the offer. *"I'll take her."*

The man peered over the shoulder of his caliph. *"That does nothing but condone what she has done, the lives she destroyed running that brothel. The one you helped her run."*

Canyon barked a laugh. "Okay, calling it—this is bull."

"You seem to know a lot." Range adjusted as if trying to get a better line of sight.

The imam looked furious. *"Marry her or she dies. It would appease Afghanistan to humiliate an American soldier—who should no longer be in my country—to marry an adulteress!"*

Another man talked to Range, who seemed to be hedging. *"I'm not an idiot—you'll kill us both."*

"Unlike you Americans, I am a man of my word," the imam said. *"Marry her and she is yours."*

"Range, I am not worth it. Do not—" The woman was hauled backward.

"What is your answer, American?"

"Fine," Range said, motioning to the woman. *"We get married. Then walk."*

"Do you think us so weak and foolish, American?" the imam said. *"Put down the weapon."*

Range disassembled the weapon and dropped it on the floor. "Are we doing this or not?"

"Where is your Walwar?" the imam asked.

Range held his hands out. "I don't have money."

"Then your weapon."

Range kicked over the M4 and nodded. "Marry us or I will drop you."

"Threatening the man who holds this woman's life in his hands …?" a second man said.

The imam pushed her toward Range. "Your name?"

"Range Metcalfe."

Holy crud … On camera …

"Range Metcalfe, Kasra Jazani. Range Metcalfe, Kasra Jazani. Range Metcalfe, Kasra Jazani." The imam eyed them. "Do you, Range Metcalfe, in the presence of these witnesses agree to take this whore as your wife?"

"I do."

"She is your wife now, American."

Range took the girl's hand and moved backward. "Now, I'll leave." He nodded to her. "Go."

Light flooded the camera, blinding the screen.

Pop! Pop!

A moment later, the lens flare cleared and the camera scanned bodies. Then a car speeding away.

The screen blanked.

Stone huffed and turned away, running a hand down the back of his neck.

Cord reappeared in the feed. "So … crapstorm."

"It was heavily edited," Canyon argued, "and there were spots where it wasn't Range's voice doing the talking."

"You know that," Cord said, "I know that, but the world doesn't. Deep Fake is nothing new, but this is some serious damage. Your brother now has a very big target on his head. He's in country without ID, without support, purportedly without authorization—which Pike is arguing up and down the Potomac since he was forced stateside." He sighed and shook his head. "Add to that this supposed marriage—"

"Who's the woman?" Stone asked.

"Kasra Jazani, the Madam who ran the Roud Compound."

"A *madam*?" Stone drew back.

Nodding, Cord went on. "Range had been tasked with securing her in a joint operation to take down the Trench—the region of the trafficking pipeline we've been working to dismantle. We get those names—huge dent."

"Which explains why they've painted a target on his head," Canyon muttered.

"I don't get it," Stone said, "why didn't that imam just kill her there?"

"As you said—that video was pretty heavily edited. Our analysts have been all over it and believe they *did* try to kill her. What you hear afterward, outside? It wasn't just Range shooting. My guess? They were threatening to kill her and to humiliate him, forced him to marry her, but that imam couldn't let a prostitute walk out of a mosque seemingly redeemed."

"And we're sure Range is still alive?"

"Definitively. Too many mobilized locals for a dead guy," Cord said. "Also, the walled home we believed he took shelter in with the madam? SATINT showed three vehicles in the compound two days ago. Now, only two."

"Any idea where they went?" Canyon pulled up a map.

"My guess? South via Pakistan."

"The gulf," he agreed. "Yeah, water is his territory."

"That's what we're hoping. Trying to get some assets in place to assist, but with the maelstrom surrounding this now—an American soldier verified operating within Afghanistan has every officer and enlisted blacklisting him. Which is why I called. Think you can get some guys spun up and headed that way? He needs help, but he's not going to get it through official channels, especially with his name and face all over the world after shooting an imam—which is not verified—and taking Jazani."

"*Marrying*," Stone gruffed. "Is that ... was it real? Are they ...?"

Cord looked grim. "From what that video showed, it is in accordance with Afghani law, so by all accounts, the marriage is legit. In a mosque, officiated by an imam, he agreed to take her, paid a bride price by the ..."

"He'd *never* marry her," Canyon said. "He was there to take her in."

"Right now, that's the least of our worries or his. He has to keep moving to stay alive."

"I'll make some calls."

"Good copy." Cord seemed to hesitate. "Either of you hear from Brooke lately?"

Stone cocked his head. "Why?"

"Haven't you heard, brother?" Canyon taunted, grinning at the screen. "Taggart has the hots for our sister."

With a groan, Cord shook his bald head. "That's not—" He looked aside and huffed. "I'm worried about her. Concerned that I haven't heard from her in a few weeks and she won't return my calls."

"Never were one take a hint," Stone said.

Canyon nodded. "Brooke's as cold as they come. Never seen anyone who knew how to ghost people the way she does."

"I think this is different."

"Because it's you?" His protective brother instincts kicked in.

"The *point*"—Cord's voice sounded strained—"is that she'd been communicating with me, asking questions about MiLE and trafficking. A lot of questions. *Knowledgeable* ones."

"Her company does charity work."

"It's more than that. Like I told you, she showed up in Nigeria for no reason."

"Willow is there."

"You really aren't this dense, Midas."

"It's not about being dense," Stone said. "This is normal for Brooke. She vanishes for weeks, months at a time. Nobody hears from her. Then she's back. All sweet and honey. That's her M.O. Wasn't good for her marriage or her girls."

Canyon felt bad for the guy. "Look, we don't want you to get burned, and we're not blowing you off, but this is Classic Brooke." He shifted and edged nearer. "And hey, we know this probably dredges up a lot of memories about your sister—"

"*Don't* go there. This is totally different from Fallon ..." Considering them, lips pursed, he finally nodded. "As for Brooke, I think you're wrong. Have a bad feeling she's in trouble. She asked about MiLE's work in Thailand. That's specific. Too specific," Cord said evenly, then grunted. Shook his head in annoyance. "I need to go. But get that team spun up. Plan to head east and I'll see what I can coordinate on this side."

"I'll reach out to Leif. He's might be over there now."

Cord nodded and disconnected.

Chewing all that intel, Canyon lowered himself to the leather sofa in the living room. "Range called Dani."

Pivoting, Stone scowled. "What?"

He sniffed. "Yeah, surprised me, too. She found a voicemail on her phone and wasn't sure if she should return the call. Encouraged her to do it, but Range just cut her off. Said to never mind, so I called him."

"I think I might need to sit down."

Canyon smirked. "Couldn't believe he answered. Asked him about the Nigerian girls who vanished when he and Omen interdicted in the Canary Islands." He remembered that call, Range's voice. "He bit my head off, but ... something was eating at him."

"Why are you telling me this?" Stone asked, lowering himself to the recliner and smoothing a hand over his big Malinois, Grief.

"The old Range, the one who hugged grudges tighter than his M4? He wouldn't have answered my call. Hadn't in the last ten years. Not since Dani and I returned from the Philippines." He had to own a lot of the strife between himself and Range. "Anyway, I think he somehow knew on that call that he was in over his head." He cracked his knuckles. "He's changed ... Never could've imagined seeing him in a situation like that, taking on a half-dozen men. Being willing to risk humiliation and marriage to keep his package alive."

"And I never imagined Brooke calling someone like Taggart." Canyon sniffed. "Copy that."

"Think we should be concerned about her?"

Although he wanted to shrug it off—Brooke had always given them the snotty end of her nose—she was a Metcalfe. "We do all seem to be attracting trouble lately." He shrugged. "A call wouldn't hurt ... much."

"Agreed. I think we both should put in a call." Stone pursed his lips, blue eyes weighted with concern. "A lot sure has changed in our family in the last year," he said. "And it seems we have a new sister-in-law."

CHAPTER
SEVENTEEN

Kandahar Province, Afghanistan

THEY COULDN'T RISK the border into Pakistan. Not after the mosque. So Range had headed east as the imam and his men expected, but banked sharply south a half-klick out. Took a road that was more hole than pot, which wreaked havoc on his wound. Miserable ride, especially since he wasn't taking it slow. Couldn't afford to. But at least it muffled her crying. A sound that somehow carved a hard line through in his chest as he aimed them into Pakistan.

He finally found a partially paved road and nailed the gas. It had a ton of road noise which made chitchat impossible. Suited him fine. No idea what to say. There was obviously the whole "married" thing hanging between them like some concrete barrier. Was the marriage real? As in *legit*-real. Recognizable by authorities? Clearly Kasra thought it was, or she wouldn't have gone silent.

Could be that her best friend just sacrificed himself for her, idiot.

He had to work up the courage to speak. "Sorry about Zaki."

Kasra shifted, her gaze bouncing in his direction but not quite finding him.

A little disappointed that she didn't say anything, he decided to keep his trap shut. Had no idea what she thought of him. Of their ... situation.

They hadn't signed any documents, so the marriage wasn't real. Right?

Did it matter? He wasn't sure, because when he'd uttered those words—*"I do take Kasra Jazani as my wife"*—some gear, some definitive life marker, thudded into place. He had literally felt it hit his chest. His heart. Changed him. How? He didn't know. Just ... did. Changed his mind. Changed what he ...

Thought of her? Was that possible? Maybe his view had been transforming over the last ten days. The more he learned about her, her past, what'd happened to her ...

What if I'm here for a reason. For her.

He snorted. Right. God sent him to Afghanistan to find and marry a notorious madam who traded in sex.

He seemed to recall a story in the Bible where that'd happened with some prophet.

He was no prophet.

What the freak am I supposed to do?

Shut up and drive. What happened in the mosque had no bearing on what needed to happen, the mission to carry out. Still had to get through Pakistan. Still had to find passage across the gulf to the UAE. Find a flight home.

With my wife.

Internally, he groaned. Veered his gaze in her direction. Saw her hand limp in her lap. Peered at her face. She'd finally fallen asleep. Gave him a chance to flick his gazes between the road and the assault she'd endured. Bruised. Split lip. Both eyes swollen. Cut above the left one that likely needed a butterfly stitch.

Never wanted to kill someone so much in all his life. She didn't deserve that. Nobody did.

The farther he drove, the more he wanted to call Canyon, but he didn't need to be mocked or lectured. But his brother was the only one with enough field experience to know what that ceremony meant legally. What to do. Ideas on getting stateside.

Kasra jolted awake with a cry.

"Easy," he said quietly.

Looking around the terrain, she touched her face and stiffened. "Where are we?"

"Halfway to the sea."

She sighed and slumped back in the seat. "Before ... you said we had to hide in the daylight. Not now?"

"No choice. That video exposed us. We have to get ahead of it. Put as much distance as possible between us and them while we can."

She said nothing, just stared out the window.

Which was better.

"His name was Calvin Hellqvist," she said out of the blue. "He was an Army captain."

He knew this. What was her point?

"The first time he came to the compound, Taweel was there, too. The two of them came to an arrangement ... that Americans would look the other way and the captain could have his pick of the girls. After a while, I became his favorite. And it was better this way because he was not kind. At first, I thought he was very nice, handsome, but the more he came, the more his darkness came, too. He was manipulative, controlling ... psychotic."

Why the heck was she telling him this? He already wanted to kill the guy.

"Three years ago, he had just visited Roud then went back to America for a year. When he left, a girl discovered she was pregnant with his baby."

"Not to be insensitive, but how did she know—"

"Because he bargained with Taweel that certain girls were only for him."

"Son of a witch."

"Yes." She managed a smile—then winced at the pain of that facial expression. "In most brothels, the girls have abortions when things like this happen. But I had seen a girl die from one, so I provided every measure I could to ensure unexpected pregnancies did not happen. When they did, we would help the girl disappear. This girl, however, had no home, no family outside of Roud. We hid the pregnancy—it was such a miracle. Taweel had been traveling to see the Viper and things were quiet at Roud."

Range tightened his grip on the steering wheel.

"The baby was born—a girl, Atia—and I hid her."

"That's the name you called out in your dreams."

She gave a slow nod. "It is. Nobody has spoken of the baby or the pregnancy since … but he somehow found out this last time he was back in America. Sent me all sorts of crazy texts demanding his child. To know what happened to the baby, what sex."

There had to be a point, and he would wait for it.

Kasra shuddered. "Knowing his evil nature, I could never let him get her. That's when I put the escape into play. Knew when he returned, he would hound us." She drew her feet up onto the dash and hugged her legs, which made her look so very small. "I want to go to Saudi Arabia. That is where I hid her."

Range jerked. "Saudi? Do you have any idea how far—"

"Only a little farther than the UAE." She tucked her chin. "Take me to the child so I can be sure she is safe, and—"

"That wasn't the deal. What? Now you're withholding the name of the Number Two guy until this girl?"

"I am sorry for all that has happened," she said, her voice barely audible. "The … mosque … but our deal was always that you would prove the girls were safe and I would give you the name. I have not altered anything."

The anger he usually clung to, the grudges that bolstered his attitude seemed to wash away like sugar in water. "Except my entire life."

She cast him a furtive glance. "I … told you not to do it. I'm not worth—"

"And *what?*" he barked. "Stand there and watch them put you down like a dog? Is that what you think of me?"

"No," she said, her words pitching. "You came … You could have just walked out of Zaki's house and left when you knew they'd taken me. But … you came."

The emotion in her words, the way her eyes seemed to puddle undid him. The last tether on his reserve strength. "Remember what you said to me about being nice?" He nodded at her. "Goes both ways."

She swallowed. "You told Butrus I was your prisoner. Is that the real reason you came to the mosque?"

Vulnerability skated through her expression warning him to be careful what words he spoke next. In truth, when the teen had come, Range hadn't given a thought to her being his prisoner. "No." He'd just charged right into the night. And though he didn't look at her just now, he felt the sorrow she wafted at that thought. He hated it, though he could not say why. "It never even crossed my mind."

Her gaze darted to his, then away. She sat there, hands on her knees, feet on the dash. Sitting up, she set her feet on the floorboard. "Are you hungry?"

He just admitted he hadn't thought about her being his prisoner—a gamechanger for him—and she asks about eating? "No." His stomach contradicted him—loudly.

"Just grumpy then."

He gave her a look and found a wry smile cutting through all the bruises and swollen eyes as she dug into the satchel and pulled out a protein bar. She tore the wrapper and handed it to him.

He couldn't voice his thanks because this was too ... domestic. Weird.

Why? It wasn't any different than the way they'd traveled before.

Before, they hadn't been married. Or whatever this was.

Man, he didn't want her being nice. Didn't want comfortableness between them. Because he didn't know what to do with it. Or her.

GWADAR PORT, PAKISTAN

By nightfall, she could smell the sea. At first, she had not recognized the smell but the thickening air and the salty tinge finally made her wonder. "Are we near the water?"

Range smirked and navigated around a bend—and there, splayed before them, glittering beneath the full moon was a great expanse of water.

Kasra gasped. "It is massive!"

"You've never seen it?" He veered around another corner.

"Never," she said, unable to hide her awe, but then it was sliding out of sight. "Oh, wait wait—I can't see it." She strained to peer from the back window.

Range sniggered.

"Stop! Please, just for a moment." When he ignored her, she slumped in the seat, defeated. "What could a few moments hurt?"

"In the open? Plenty."

Used to disappointment, Kasra settled. He said they would be on a boat, so she would see it eventually. They negotiated a series of turns and rises, then he did a U-turn, pulling in behind a house. With an embankment on the left and the two-story building on the right, the car was hidden. That was a good thing, even if she could not see the water. Yet, to be so close and not see it …

"Grab the gear." Range climbed out of the vehicle.

Kasra stilled, then did as instructed. She joined him, feeling very conspicuous with her battered face, though it was the dead of night. "What are we doing?" she whispered, donning a hijab.

He led her down the street a bit and then around a building. A dozen paces more and lights glittered in the distance.

Kasra drew in a breath, slowing. Saw massive cranes and ships sitting in the water. "What is this?"

"*Bandar gāh Gwadar*," he said. "Gwadar port. Hopefully, we find a ride out of here. Stand guard." He took the gear and bags from her, then stuffed them beneath some stairs up into a building, the shadows concealing it well. "Okay, c'mon."

She marveled at the expanse of the water. "It's so dark."

"The color depends on the light we see it in." He kept moving, their feet sinking into the sandy stretch.

But it took everything in Kasra to not stop and gape at the sea. What was it like in daylight? She could only imagine … They made their way to where giant ships were berthed, their decks covered with enormous steel containers. Light glared at them, but did not help her see the water better.

"Back," Range hissed.

Backing up, Kasra felt her heart hitch, wondering what he saw. Her gaze wandered down the long, seemingly thin dock that had ships berthed on each side. Strolling languidly, an armed guard was coming this way. She drew in a breath.

Range turned, took her hand, and led her off the dock. To the steps. Crouched there, watching up the dock as the guard came closer … closer.

He hadn't expected Pakistani Naval personnel to be guarding the port. Armed guards complicated this. Hunkered out of the sight on the steps to the beach, he set Kasra behind him. Felt her hand on his spine. He checked the guard. Two meters and they'd be discovered.

Yet if they left this spot, they'd be in the open. He scanned the beach. Thought about the guard's line of sight, the way he was sweeping back and forth. When he went to the far side, they might make it to that first boat.

Was the guard—

Light struck his eyes from across the way. Range jerked his attention back to that spot. Where had that light come from? It seemed left of center on the far side.

"Is he gone?" Kasra whispered.

His gaze probed the other side where trawlers and merchant ships were docked. The light came again from the left. His gaze bounced between a reefer and a trawler. Which one—

A flash. There and gone. *What ...?*

Range diverted his attention right as the light blipped again. Watched and saw a pattern to the blipping. S-O-S. From the reefer.

A dozen thoughts hit his brain at once—someone was signaling him. Which made no sense. How would they know to signal him? Was it for someone else? What were the odds ...?

"What is wrong?" Kasra whispered, hunkering closer and glancing over her shoulder in the direction he looked.

Could he trust the source of the signal? That question held the most potential for danger. Clearly they had eyes on him, even if he couldn't see who was sending the morse code.

And he'd be stupid not to check it out. He slunk down the steps. "This way."

"I thought ..." Her voice trailed off but she stayed with him as they darted to a fishing boat waiting in the night for its crew.

They scurried from boat to boat along the shore, making

their way to the far side where there were berthed tankers and product ships. Squinting up, the glitter of ships' lights in the darkness pinching his vision, he eyed the source of the SOS.

"What are we doing?" Kasra asked, kneeling beside him.

"The white reefer," he said with a nod, "someone was signaling from it."

"The—are you sure? Wait, you know someone here?"

He shook his head, scanning the multistoried tower with the bridge and accommodations. "Stay here. I'm going to—"

"No." Kasra grabbed his arm. Eyes wide, she looked at him in terror. "I go with you."

Range took a knee. "I don't know if it's a trap. I can't take you up there—"

"I am *not* staying behind. Anything could happen …"

It seemed too great a risk but they didn't have time to argue. "Fine. Keep your hand on my back. Stay close and low."

They made it up to the dock. Halfway down the platform, a guard had his back to them, smoking and chatting up someone. Hurrying forward in a crouch, Range stuck to the shadows as much as he could. He found the reefer's gangway. A dozen paces up the roped plank, he saw a shadow move. Snapped up his Sig and aimed.

"Prefer Glocks myself," a man said in English.

"I prefer whatever works." He jutted his jaw. "Who are you?"

Feet thudded toward them, the man still fully in shadow.

Range's veins iced. He'd made a mistake. This wasn't help. It was an ambush. "Back," he hissed to Kasra, forcing her to retreat.

"Canyon asked us to watch for you."

The name stilled Range. Staring down his sights at the faceless shadow, he knew that a little research could tell anyone that Canyon was his brother. Weapon still trained on the shadow, he stood there, indecision screaming.

Voices came from the dock—a flurry of Urdu.

"Wire won't be able to distract that guard indefinitely," the man said quietly and turned. "Going topside. If you want a ride, follow me." He moved onto the ship's deck.

"They're coming," Kasra hissed.

Range started up the gangway, edging around the corner with his weapon. Nosing out. Then pulled Kasra from the gangway. On the open deck, lights from the dock and the ship itself bathed them and the upper refrigerated units in a stiff glow. Too much. They needed to get out of sight.

Kasra held a tentative hand on his back.

He spotted their welcomer hiking up the stairs to the tower. "C'mon."

She stopped him. "You trust him?"

"No," Range breathed. "But what alternatives do we have?" He listened for the guard below and heard him still talking. "Wait till he heads the other way, then we—"

Thuds sounded on the ramp. Two voices—one seemingly nervous, frustrated.

"On me!" Range bolted to the side. Dove between a line of refrigerated containers and sprinted toward the tower. Darted to the stairs and raced up.

"Here!" The voice belonged to their welcomer who now stood in an open door.

Range didn't falter—they had no choice, but he wasn't letting his guard down—and slid through the opening, circling around, and drew Kasra to his side.

"This way." Welcomer hustled through narrow passage, then grabbed the stair rail, hiked his boots on and slid down to the next level. "Guard's coming topside."

Tempted to do the same and slide down, Range stayed with Kasra. When they had descended two more levels, voices from the ramp echoed above.

"Wire sucks at subterfuge," the guy said quietly. "Probably made the guard nervous."

"What's with the armed patrols?" Range asked, careful to keep his voice low.

"Pakistani ports have seen a big increase in criminal activity. So much that China gave Pakistan two gunships to ramp up patrols. Ports are now only open to commercial traffic, so we worked a deal with Jaeger to operate out of his reefer."

On the third level, the guy banked away from the stairs and trudged down the passage. He pointed to one door. "Galley is there." Two more doors on the right, he flicked open the next one. "It's all we have left. Only twelve cabins and we're running hot with a dozen."

Range eyed the cabin—a bed, head and shower, table with chairs. Wanting her safe, he guided Kasra inside then angled between her and the guy. "Who are you?"

"Spike Renner. Onetime 5th Group."

A SEAL. "And now?"

Renner lifted a shoulder. "Little of this, little of that."

"How d'you know Cannon?"

Renner's gray eyes hit his. He sniffed. "I get that you feel the need to test me. After that video hit the dark web, I'm guessing you've had some heat on you. Heard some chatter about you catching a rogue prostitute who killed the girls in her brothel."

Kasra gasped. "I did not—"

Gaze on Renner, Range silenced her. "Guess I'm not the only one testing people."

"I know Canyon through Max Jacobs, but I don't know you."

"Likewise."

Renner sucked his cheek. "Fun times, Blue Eyes." He rapped on the hull. "Help yourself to the galley, if you're hungry."

"I stowed some gear at a building—"

"Saw that," Renner nodded. "Wire will retrieve it later and bring it aboard." He scanned Range head to toe. "We wear the ship's uniforms while onboard to avoid hiccups with port authority if they run random inspections. I'll check with Jaeger and see if he can spare a couple uniforms for you and"—his gaze slid to Kasra, then back to Range with a smirk—"the, uh ... missus." His chuckle trailed him down the passage.

Missus. The guy was well informed. Range stepped out and eyed his back. "Renner."

Hand on the bulkhead to the stairs, the SEAL glanced back.

"What port are we headed to?"

"Does it matter?"

Range held his gaze, irritated at the inference that, with the manhunt on for them, beggars couldn't be choosy. But they needed that intel in order to plan and prepare.

"Zayed Port."

"Emirates?" Surprise squirreled through his veins. What were the chances ...? "Hey." He shifted more into the passage, not wanting Kasra to hear. "That dark-web video you mentioned ...?"

Renner nodded.

"Later, I'd like to see that."

"Bet you do." Renner cocked his head. "They've painted you to look like a rogue operator with a vendetta."

"Not far from the truth."

CHAPTER
EIGHTEEN

Pakistani Reefer, Gwadar Port, Pakistan

AFTER SHOWERING and changing into the provided overalls, Kasra frowned at herself in the old, dingy mirror in the bathroom. The bruises were yellowing, most of the swelling had gone down, but she still looked terrible. Tired. Dark circles beneath her eyes that had nothing to do with the imam's ordered beating. It had not been the first time she had endured a man's fury. Likely not the last.

Men just did not understand. Nobody did. And it made her doubt herself all over again. Could she have escaped before a week ago? Sure. And if she had been caught, more marks would have been burned into her back. Into her mind. Or he would have killed Fatina. Or one of the younger girls.

"I do take Kasra Jazani as my wife."

Her stomach swam, remembering Range's words. His resolute response and his fierce visage. So angry. Did this mean she was now his wife? Legally?

It did not matter, since it was not what he really wanted. Since they had fled, he had been cold, withdrawn. What few words he had spoken were sharp and direct. Nothing less, nothing more. No conversation, no smiles. Because of the truth: he was trapped.

She must assure him that she would not hold him to the coerced vows.

He would leave—have the marriage annulled. She shoved aside how that thought hurt. The point was, at least she was out of Afghanistan and—Allah willing—soon out of Pakistan. Freedom would be hers. The road ahead, eking out a life, would be hard. Difficult. But she had carved out a semblance of a life once before in the midst of darkness, she could do it again.

Yet … what would it be like to stay with him? What if he—by some miracle—said he was not leaving her? What if marriage vows were as sacred to him as they were to her? She had begged him not to agree to the imam's demand. He deserved a beautiful wife, untainted. *Not baggage like me.*

Even when he left, she would have something she never dreamed: the memory of his kiss. Not the hungry, demanding kind of most men. But an ardent, passionate one that had somehow been both tender and left her wanting more. His breath against her cheek. His hand slipping around her waist …

Thud! Thud!

She started at a knock. Drew up straight.

"Kasra?"

At Range's voice her heart jostled into a slower rhythm. "Yes?"

"Gear's here. And food."

Their bags. She glanced once more at her reflection, wished she'd had make-up to hide the bruises at little, but maybe it would be easier this way. The bruises would help him walk away. Tentatively, she stepped out.

His back to her, he was doing something at the table.

She saw her bag on the bed and went to it. Dug in it and considered putting on a hijab, feeling a little underdressed—and in her periphery noticed his gear on the floor with a blanket and pillow. He intended to sleep there …?

"Food's probably sludge like all galley food," he said, coming round—and stopped short. His gaze slid over her from head to toe, then back up, blue eyes pinning her. He swung back to the food. Ran a hand down the back of his neck. "It … um … looks like mush." He huffed a laugh. "Maybe they should let you cook for us next time."

Had she missed a snap or zipper? Kasra glanced at the uniform, checked the closures—all done. "It cannot be that bad."

He folded himself into one of the chairs. "Suggest we chow down quickly."

"Are we not going to stay on the ship?" She took the seat opposite him and considered the food. Wrinkled her nose. "What is it?"

Range smirked. "Told you," he said with a shrug. "We'll be aboard for a couple of days, but who knows what could happen. If anyone saw us sneak on, authorities could board us. If that happens, we should be prepared to take to the water."

"Take to the water? You mean jump … in?" Instinctively, she pulled away from him.

Gaze never quite meeting hers as he ate, he bobbed his head. "Ship could lose dock privileges, which would cripple the business—"

"But I told you—I cannot swim!"

His blue eyes finally met hers, seemingly confused by her fear. "I'll be there." His gaze hit her uniform again, then darted down. "I won't let anything happen to you."

Was there something wrong with the way she had put on the uniform? But then his words filtered into her brain and made her pulse thump crazily. *Stop being a fool. He just meant he will not let you drown.* Which should be a comfort …

"We should stick to the cabin as much as possible."

"Why?"

"The crew is all-male."

She paused, realizing his meaning. Was he worried about her, or about the men …? Regardless … "I am not in the mood to entertain anyone, especially men."

His gaze hit the table with a grim expression.

Understanding how her words likely sounded, she covered her mouth. Then leaned forward. "I did not—I only meant—"

"Relax." He went back to eating. "I know what you meant, Kas."

Scooting the food around on the metal tray, she remembered her friend. Her now-dead friend. "Zaki called me that," she said softly, then hurriedly took a bite so she did not have to think about him sacrificing himself. A terrible trade. Salt clogged her throat. She uncapped a bottled water and drank. "It is so salty!"

"Hides the lack of taste." His voice was dull. After several moments of silent brooding, he tossed down his fork. Rested both forearms on the table. "I think …" He swiped a hand over his thickening beard. "I need to hear your story."

Now her heart trounced for an entirely different reason. "My story …" Why did he need to hear it? To justify negating the marriage he had been forced into? To solidify his rejection of her?

He again studied the table, then sighed. "Zaki believed in you … a lot."

"He was a fool of a boy in love with a girl who could not return his love."

"I think there's more to it than that."

"What? You can read people?"

He squinted. "Seems that's your gift." He considered her for a long second. "Please."

Panic clawed at her hastily erected defenses.

"I want to understand." For a man with a temper and ability to wield violence, he was inordinately calm.

Which made her feel defensive. "Why?"

His frown wavered and he folded his arms. Seemed mad. "Because we're married?"

Those words stole her breath. "You know I will not hold you to that." Kasra eased forward to put emphasis behind her words. "I begged you not to do it!"

His blue eyes held her hostage. "So it's my fault."

"No!"

"What was I to do? Watch them execute you?" Shaking his head, he adjusted on the chair. "I may be a lot of things, but that wasn't something I could do."

"Why?" she gaped. "I am nothing to you. A whore who trafficked kids for sex. I heard you say that to Zaki!"

"I never called you that," he growled. "But trafficking women and children—that's why I need to hear your story. Because if what happened in that mosque is legal … no matter how I feel, I will be held accountable by God."

Surprise tilted her head. "You believe in God?"

Range winced. "Grew up going to church." He scratched his jaw. "Youth group, summer camp, winter camp … I was the rule follower, and that was one thing my mom raised us to adhere to."

Something had changed. She could not tell what it was … except nice and strange at the same time. And 'nice' was never good. "What happened?"

He groaned. "Not going easy on me, are you?"

"My brother. My theory is we were born too close together. He beat me out of everything all through life. He was bigger than life, just like our dad—heroic, handsome, and smooth. I was awkward, shy, uncertain. Always a day late and a dollar short compared to Canyon, who could convince an ice hauler he needed a refrigerator. When he'd enlisted, I thought life gave me a gift. But he came home on leave and stole my girl right out from under me before prom. Slept with her." He shook his head again, flicking the fork around his fingers. "Then he stole Dani. I rescued her from the sea and looked after her, fell head over heels. Things were fine, I thought. She went to the Coast Guard ball with me, then ... she ends up on a mission with Canyon, and he sweeps her off her feet and gets her pregnant. It was the last straw. I left them."

"This woman and your brother?"

His gaze struck her. "Everyone. My family—mom, sisters. Couldn't take it anymore. They always made excuses for him, and I always ended up with the short end of the stick."

"What do sticks have to do with it?"

Range smirked. "It's a phrase that means ... unlucky." He shrugged. "I'd had an engagement ring picked out for Dani. Was so convinced I was in love, and that while she wasn't delirious about me, she liked me. Thought we could make it work. Then they return and Canyon calls the family meeting. Tells us Dani's pregnant. The family just hugged her and welcomed her to the family." He swiped a hand over his mouth. "I left the house that night. Never went back. Separated from the Coast Guard a year later to do black ops with the DIA. Decided I was tired of playing the nice guy. Of not measuring up to their standards."

For her, he was the measuring stick by which she had begun comparing men. She could not fathom this family of his treating him so awfully when he had been nothing but heroic since they met. "Then I think I do not like this family of yours."

He grimaced. "Don't ... make that decision yet."

She frowned.

"They're good people." He flicked the fork around faster. "I went back a couple of years ago for my brother's campaign. Someone attacked the lodge, but we handled it. Anyway, I left feeling like I didn't fit in anymore. They were all happy, married, ... friends." He met her gaze again. "I wasn't."

"And that was their fault?" She felt bad for challenging him.

He stared her down, then cocked his head. "I own my part in

it. After Canyon and Dani, I dug into my anger. Threw everything I had at black ops."

"Coming after people like me."

Range stacked their trays and set them to the side. Folded his arms on the table. "Depends."

"On what?"

"Your side of the story."

If there were any more shifts in his world, he would fall through the cracks. He'd opened the dialogue about her past to get his mind off how much that jumpsuit hugged every curve she had. Way more curves than were apparent when she wore the kurta and pants. Her waist was tiny and her—

Not helping, genius.

Kasra faltered, then looked at the table. "That is a ... long story."

"Well," he said, trying to inject some levity, "start now. We have two days till we reach port."

Vulnerability tremored through her, and she decided to lay it all out. She could lose everything, but she would rather know now if he could handle it than to find out ... later.

"I have not told anyone what I will speak here." Even now she did not want to speak of it, but she was so very weary of the tension and anger, of hiding. *Just get it done. State the facts.* "Dawud was my half-brother. His father took a second wife—my mother—when Dawud was ten. She was young but more important, they took over my grandfather's fields. Both Dawud and his mother resented my mother and hated me from the time I was born."

What she should mention next? The chickens ... "When I was eight, I had been out collecting eggs from the chickens and saw blood near the coop. I ran to it—only to get knocked down by Dawud, who burst out of the shanty. I got up and went in ... and found her on the ground, dead." She hugged herself.

"You think he killed her?"

"I do," she said quietly. "He was not a good person. Ever. Years later, our father died in a freak accident during harvest, and Dawud, though a man, did not know how to take care of a family. It was not long before the field and house were going to be lost ..." She sighed and shook her head. "I know Zaki believed he gave Dawud the idea to sell me, but ..." She wet her lips and caught the lower one between her teeth, fighting memories that threatened to drown her. "Dawud had already ... paid some debts by trading ... me. The first time it happened, I was twelve."

"What a piece of work." Range propped his elbows on the table and rubbed his forehead.

After hearing all this, would he abandon her on this ship? It was too terrible, and if she had more time to think about it ... "I hated him so much, my naïve self was glad when he took the man's money and handed me over."

"To Taweel?"

She swallowed. Shook her head. "Not yet." She rubbed her palms. "I thought—if the worst they do is take what was already gone, so what? At least I would be free of their hatred." Her throat was raw and thick as she recalled the awful moments. "I had no idea how .... bad it could be. The things men did to a woman ..."

He fisted his hands, knuckles white beneath his apparent anger.

These secrets, these thoughts were from a vault in her heart she had long ago thought the key lost to. How had he managed to convince her to open it? She did not need to recite the gory details. It was awful enough in her own head, why put it in someone else's? "I was sold again"—she nodded—"this time to Taweel. He, uh ... he liked me."

"I'm going to need a laser-guided missile."

What did that mean? She better hurry or she would lose her courage. "He took me to Roud."

What came next ... he would not like. She did not like it. This, she believed, was what he truly wanted to know.

She cleared her throat. "I was ... favored. From the beginning. He said I was smart, pretty." She saw him nod and startled that he agreed. "He told Manal—she was the madam then—to tutor me. Teach me. I was given my own room. Clothes, jewels, shoes." She shrugged. "Whatever I wanted, really. Eventually, my own apartment and car. In a lot of ways, being one of his favored ones—Poppies, he called us—saved me. Of course, not completely. As a Poppy, I was also given to his VIPs: high-ranking officials, officers, dignitaries, soldiers. Whoever he wanted to impress. Because of that, I also became"—she eyed him—"the captain's favorite, too."

He violently bounced his legs, his blue eyes fierce with anger.

Did he think poorly of her—more than before? Hate her? Good men could not accept that she had been so ... used. So much. Readily she could admit to not wanting to see his anger, his rejection. Theirs was a marriage she desperately wanted to be real. But it was a fantasy. Had to be.

Range folded his arms over his chest. "I'm listening."

Kasra drew in a breath for courage. Thought of her friend. "Another Poppy was my good friend, Alzena. She was Manal's sister, so we were both protected from much. I should have been given to anyone high enough in the architecture of the ring, but Madam kept both Alzena and I busy with chores, errands, gave us extra things—which I always shared with the others. I saw how our treatment hurt and angered the other girls, and that hurt and angered me. I was not any better and I certainly did not deserve protection when they were abused so horribly." Her heart raced as it had each time she thought of all the things she had been unable to prevent and forced to do. "For a long time, I thought that Madam gave us this treatment because she liked us and she wanted us happy so Taweel would be happy."

Range narrowed his gaze. "It was for her."

She inclined her head. "She did want Taweel happy, but not for the reason I supposed. But because I discovered she was stealing from him. I was terrified he would learn of her treachery. Terrified she would be killed and then us, so I kept the secret. Kept my mouth closed."

"He found out."

"He always did." Kasra remembered that day as if it had just happened. "He killed her right in front of me and the other Poppies—beat her to death with a cudgel." She touched her cheek, remembering the blood that had splatted there. "And he walked over to me, his hands sticky with her blood, cupped my face, and said I had always been his favorite. That it was my turn."

His nostrils flared. "When was that?"

"Five years ago."

His dark blond brows furrowed as he angled in closer, resting his arms on the table. "Why did you stay? Why didn't you get out sooner? How could you run that place?"

"*Stay?*" she repeated, frowning. Maybe the question did not have disgust in it, but it did have judgment. "I did not *stay*—I was a hostage. A captive, as all the girls were! True, I had no cuffs on my arms or shackles on my legs, but there were bars around my mind. Terror caged my heart and courage."

"But you know how to fight. Why did you not—"

"Because!" she snapped, then drew in on herself. Withdrew the futile hope that he would ever understand or forgive her. No one who had not been abused or violated could ever really understand.

Especially men.

To them, it was simple. Black and white. Get away. Leave.

They did not know the paralyzing, immobilizing fear after watching a friend hacked to death. Or being raped so violently, you could not stand for days. "I saw what he did to others who tried to run. Manal was not the only one he beat to death or had his guards gang-rape. There were girls whose insides he burned out with acid. Each time I thought I had succeeded in overcoming his controlling nature, something would happen. Someone would die or vanish. Every day, I knew I could be next. Life at Roud was … terrifying. There were cameras everywhere. Our rooms, the kitchen, the office … My days were monitored. When I went into the market, he would send me texts, telling me what I did. Photos of me with mangos or talking to children. All to show me he knew *everything*. My every move. My thoughts!"

Range shifted to the side. Away from the table. Bent forward and pinched the bridge of his nose.

"I thought like you once, that I could just leave. Be smart, think like James Bond, plan an escape. So, I watched the people in the city, found someone that everyone seemed to trust and like. I reached out for help." She exhaled heavily. "Back at Roud that night, I learned he was Taweel's cousin." She felt her chin bouncing and fought to control the tears. "Taweel pulled me out into the courtyard where Alzena was tied to a stake. The guards raped her repeatedly in front of Allah and everyone. They then killed her, *dis*"—the word caught in her throat—"*membered* her … Sent a piece of her chopped-up body to other compounds as a warning." She struck her chest. "Because of me! Because I thought to escape."

The memory was too horrible, to atrocious to cry. She had sobbed and grieved her friend for a year.

"Kasra." He reached over. Touched her arm. "I'm sorry." He looked stricken. "What a mind-game."

"Truly. After that, every year on the anniversary of her death, I secreted one girl from the compound. It was my retribution.

Taweel did not care or notice as long as money came in and his *suppliers* brought more girls. But"—she made a claw-like gesture to her chest—"it ate at me, what he did to her. What I caused. What was done to all of us. I was so broken, so desperate for help, to find a way out ..." She wiped the tears that blurred her eyes. Tried not to focus on the way he had turned away from her. Stared at the steel floor. "After Alzena, I gave up. Decided it was better to sneak girls out one by one—though it meant others were not saved—than to dare escape and get another killed."

She shuddered a sigh, trying to ignore the way he pressed white knuckles to his lips. "Then the captain visited—one of the early times. His stays were often for a couple of days, so he would bring a pack like you have." She sniffled. "When he was in the shower, I saw his small book of Proverbs from the Christian Bible."

Range scowled.

"Ironic, is it not? Yet ... I think Allah did that for me. I hid it away and he did not miss it." A smile wavered on her lips as she shrugged. "Silly, I know."

"Not at all."

Unsure what do with that or that his blue gaze was so steady, she kept going. "In Afghanistan, I am not sure which is worse—being a Christian or a prostitute. But I read the Proverbs over and over." She almost smiled at him. "I have most of them memorized. The words helped me believe that Allah not only saw what was happening to us, He *hated* what was happening."

"Of course He does."

"It was those verses that gave me back my courage. There started my daring plan. I decided that even if I cannot save my soul, I would save as many girls as I could, even if it meant he killed me—that would be a relief. But I did not care. I hated that Taweel saw us as meat and profit, not people."

Range stood and paced the small space. Roughed his hands over his face.

Trembling from the vehemence of her words, the rumbling rage that had fueled her massive coup of Roud, Kasra watched him stand by the bed. Fingers steepled over his mouth and nose. Apparently, she just ruined what little had changed between them. Made the decision for him: the marriage was not real.

Her vision blurred again. Why was she crying? "I knew it would be too much …" Tears fell and she just did not care anymore. "You are too good for me, though I tried to tell myself different … that someone—that you—" She choked on the words.

The door to their cabin opened. "I'll be back." And closed.

She had just laid her heart bare before him and he … left? Shoving up from the table, she turned a circle. Felt a desperation she had not felt in a long time. Dropped onto the bed and sat there feeling an unholy rage, borne of grief … borne of … pain.

Then she threw herself at the door.

CHAPTER
NINETEEN

Pakistani Reefer, Gulf of Oman

GOD HELP him if he met this Taweel, he was going to kill him. Dismember the sick puke the way he had innocent girls. Range stalked down the passage, heading to the makeshift gym to work off some of this anger he felt. Maybe be able to—

"What was that?"

The enraged shout yanked him around. He found Kasra flying at him.

"I lay my heart and life at your feet and you *walk out*?"

A head poked out of the galley. Renner.

"Not here," Range said crowding her back to their cabin.

"Get off me!" Kasra shouted and hopped back, ready for a fight.

Palms up, he paused. Did his best to temper his own anger and cocked his head toward their room. But when she didn't budge, her green-brown gaze radiating fury, he thought to *make* her go inside.

Dang if he had any clue how to handle this. How to navigate the tricky waters of this woman's past. He heard steps thudding behind him and noted Kasra's gaze shift to the newcomer.

Straightening, she glowered at him once more then went into the cabin.

Son of a—

"Trouble in paradise, Honeymooners?"

Could he get no peace? He slid a scowl to the newcomer—he looked Pakistani. Wire?—then to Renner. Said nothing but stalked into the room after her. Shut the door.

Kasra paced the cabin, her face red. "I suddenly understand why your family wants nothing to do with you."

What the—

She stiffened and hugged herself. "Sorry. I … should not have said that. It was uncalled for." Her whole behavior seemed practiced, borne from years of placating men.

Man …

"Why did you leave?" she asked, wilting. In her gaze was anger, but not the kind he'd expected. This one was bathed in hurt. "I tell you *everything*—which I haven't done to another living soul—and you just walk out." Her voice cracked. Eyes glossed.

He lowered himself to the edge of the bed. "I'm sorry. I don't know … It reminds me of … a little girl we'd befriended on an op. Discovered she was being trafficked … When we made the call to interdict, someone warned the owners. They blew up the house. Killed her. I vowed after that incident that I would not stop until traffickers were run out of business or put down." He stood again. "I don't know what to do with this, Kasra. How to feel. How to unpack it. After hearing you, I want to kill someone."

Wariness crowded her beautiful-but-battered face. "Do you still blame me? Still feel disgusted with me?" Challenge hardened the edges of her words.

Tricky, tricky waters. He held her gaze. Wanted to say no. But if he were honest, disgust didn't just magically vanish. Change, yeah. But gone? He'd be lying if he said so. "I don't know …"

Her fair features twisted into grief. Sorrow. Hurt. She covered her face and turned away. Choked sobs.

He felt like a heel. "I'm not good with this stuff, Kasra. I ... I sink my teeth into a belief that something is wrong, and it's very hard to let it go." Case in point: his grudge toward Canyon still had razor-sharp teeth.

"You mean you *choose* to hold onto it."

"Back up there, chief."

"When you choose to harbor that grudge or wrong, to choose it over the person, you punish no one but yourself," she said. "You keep yourself in a prison of selfishness. Their lives go on, and you are left behind bars that keep your grudge safe and nursed."

Her words were like daggers pummeling his walls. Disbelieving and ticked, he stared at her. This woman who had done unpardonable things and yet she schooled *him*? And why the heck couldn't he figure out what to say?

Because there was no argument. No justification.

"You are right," he finally conceded.

She blinked, irritation smoothing from her brow. "And your hatred of me?"

This ... Man, he was tangled up. Mad. Yet ... "I can't say that I would've made the decisions you made," he said, holding out his hands in acknowledgement. "But I understand that you did what was necessary to survive. And ... against impossible situations and odds."

Lips parting, she stared up at him. Brow rolled. "Do you mock me?"

"No." He expelled a thick breath, ill at ease with this swift change. No idea what to say or do next. His gaze landed on the blanket by his ruck. "We should rest." He snagged it and dropped it on the floor. "You take the bed."

She stood there staring at him, then the bed, and the blanket. "That cannot be comfortable."

"Don't need comfort. Just sleep." He lowered himself to the deck and ran a hand over his face. Felt relief when she sat on the bed. Did his best not to look at her.

"You keep yourself in a prison of selfishness."

By her account, he had been in a prison for a decade. Hostage to that grudge between himself and Canyon. Who—as she so aptly pointed out—had gone on with his life. Had three kids with Dani.

He laid back against the pillow. Stared at the ceiling. Ten years. His thoughts landed on his nieces and nephews. Now Stone was going to be a dad again. Range hadn't even met his new supermodel wife. Or Willow's new husband. Dang—even Runt had family he hadn't met yet.

The Metcalfes were evolving. Without him. Those heavy thoughts dragged him into sleep.

Kasra bolted upright with a gasp, feeling as if the world was faltering beneath her.

"Easy," Range said from the table, where he sat with a cup of coffee, which smelled amazing.

"Wh …?" She had slept all night? Without nightmares? She shoved her hair from her face and glanced around, feeling a … wobbling. As if someone had put something in her tea. But she did not have tea.

"We set sail."

"Really?" Wavering, Kasra shoved off the bed and canted. Gasped as she braced herself against the wall, glancing around. "No windows."

He smirked. "Once you're ready, we can find a window and breakfast. Can't go out on deck yet because we're still too close to port."

She smiled, but then felt her stomach shift. Groaned at the swelling nausea. "Is it always like this?"

Range eyed her. "Seasickness is common. We might need to get you to a window sooner rather than later. Seeing the horizon will help. You want to freshen up?"

Indeed. Maybe get rid of this taste in her mouth. Quickly, Kasra brushed her teeth and hair, then remembered his promise to find a window so she could see the sea and experience a thrill of excitement … that merely rushed nausea up her esophagus. She groaned.

"Yep, let's go." Range opened the cabin door.

Kasra stepped out and let him lead. They headed up a level and then banked right, down a long passage, which seemed brighter than the others. At the far end, she saw a window. She quickened her pace, seeing the water. So blue! "It is unbelievable!"

The window was in a corner. To her right, another set of stairs. To her left, Range planted himself against the wall, arms folded as he eyed the water.

He nodded. "Once we're farther from port, we can go out on the deck. It'll be windy, since by then they'll be running at about eighteen or twenty knots."

"Is that fast?"

"For this size vessel, yes. But comparatively, no." He planted his hands on his belt and scanned the sea. "The Coast Guard has Fast Response Cutters that do twenty-eight knots and above. Defender Class boats, however, easily handle forty-six."

It sounded incredible, but she had no understanding of the speed. Instead, she focused on the water that stretched as far as she could see. Unfathomable. "I have been to lakes and even rivers, and there the water seemed incredible. But this …" She shook her head, taking it in. Impressed. In awe. "I did not imagine it to be so beautiful and … freeing. And yet, it seems so vast and terrifying."

Beside her, Range had something odd in his expression as they shared a glance. Sunlight reflecting off the waters made his eyes sparkle. "Most people see one side or the other, not both. 'The sea, once it casts its spell, holds one in its net of wonder forever.'"

"I am definitely in its spell," she said with a laugh. "Who said that?"

"Jacques Cousteau. Plato said the sea cures man of all ailments."

"Including yours?" she asked, feeling bold. Wanting to know him better.

Folding his arms, he scanned the glittering waves. "I'm not sure *all* ailments, but at least some. On the water—like you said—I feel free. Like I can breathe."

"Then why did you leave the Coast Guard?"

He smirked. "Sitting on a boat, interdicting drug runners or human trafficking, did little for the rage that I felt. I was recruited, told I could do more against smugglers by leaving. The opportunity presented itself, and I seized it." His brow furrowed in what appeared a moment of sadness.

Which did something odd to her heart, twisting it and clenching it. "I, for one, am glad you made the change."

He hesitated, then skirted her a glance.

"It brought you to … Afghanistan. To Roud."

This time he grinned. "You weren't happy the night we raided."

She laughed. "I was furious! For a year, I had worked to arrange that escape. For the girls to be free. It had taken months of preparation. Talking to the right people. Saving every afghani I could. Going without so there would be plenty to pay the *couriers* and Taweel."

Range shifted, putting his back to the wall as he cocked his head. "After ten years and all the people trafficked, you suddenly decided to try? Why?"

Defensiveness rose through her, and she angled back to the window, not wanting to tempt his disgust again. "I think I plotted it from the first day I stepped inside the brothel and met Taweel. Then Razam came and swiftly became someone I could depend on. He dared whisper that I did not belong there. Oh, I was furious the first time he spoke those words. I had worked so very hard to convince Taweel that Roud was under good management and feared his dangerous words would cause me to make a mistake."

"How did you do that, convince *Tarweed?*"

At the way he said the name, she nearly laughed. Made her want to tell him the truth of it. "Since I was in charge, I had an allowance. It mortified me at first to take the money, so I simply lived as the others and hid the money. Little by little, I secreted girls away. Used what I had saved to make up the difference in profits. One of the girls I helped escape later started a jewelry shop. She sent money every month to help free other girls."

His brow knotted. "You were helping girls escape?"

She had said that before, but apparently he had not understood. "So few, it seems insignificant, really."

"Not to the girls who got away."

It was kind of him to say so. "There were many I did not help. So many who had to endure being forced to have sex. Get raped. Beaten." Tears slipped down her cheeks, and she thought somehow they would blend with the ocean. "There was nothing I could do but train them to be smarter than the men. Teach them things to make their lives *less miserable*, yet not too brazen or repetitive that it would draw Taweel's attention and fury. One slip, one mistake, and someone died."

"Did he kill many?"

"Too many." Kasra took in the sea, its choppy blue-green waters ever reaching for the shore. "At least a dozen that I was aware of. There were girls who vanished, but I could not swear he or his guards were responsible." She sighed. "I blamed myself for each one. Thought if I had just trained her better, or done more …"

"That's how I felt patrolling with the Coast Guard. Too many bodies found adrift. Once, we found a floating container full of bodies—idiot smuggler didn't think through the heat of that thing in the baking sun. Turned it into an oven." He shook his head. "It's why I took a more active role in hunting those responsible for trafficking."

She met his gaze and held it. "Me."

Range considered her for a long moment, then slid his focus to the waters. "When I got word that we finally had clearance to hit Roud, I …" He shook his head. "I thirsted for vengeance against you."

It hurt, so terribly, knowing she was someone he had aimed his skills and anger at. "I hate that. That you … that I was your target."

He seemed chagrined.

"I had to live a double life. At Roud, I had to be the severe, mean madam in order to protect the girls from themselves, from the men, from the guards, from Taweel. Teach them to be shrewd. But when the doors were closed and the men gone, to the girls, I was …" She lifted a shoulder in a shrug. Straightened. "Some needed someone to hate for all the terrible things done to them. And I …" Her ears still burned from some of the curses thrown at her by the others. "I could be that."

Range wasn't sure he could stand to hear anymore. But she had lived and breathed it for ten years. The least he could do was listen and try to understand.

Since they were married and all.

Yet each word, each syllable she used to unveil her past drummed against the rhythm of his heart, his conscience.

Dismantled his arguments and left him standing—once again—on the shaky ground of his arrogance and self-righteous attitudes.

Wasn't pretty, admitting that. But he knew he had to own it. All his life, he'd felt like he didn't measure up. Always fell a little short. So he'd followed every rule. Lived every nuance of honor. Yet here stood a beautiful woman who had been through the unimaginable. And who was standing before her? Was it Canyon? Stone? Leif?

None of the above.

Hotheaded Range Metcalfe. *Yours truly.*

Though he had no idea how to help her, what to do with all this, he knew it started with ditching the anger. It seemed so simple all of a sudden. A blinding flash of the obvious that fed off her words from last night about him nursing the grudge.

Time to let go.

It struck him then that it really *was* that simple. All these years he had made the choice to nurse that anger against Canyon. Hold his toes to the fire. It hadn't been about making something right. It'd been about retaliation. Making them hurt.

The thought was a sucker punch that left a pool of shame in his gut. Definitely had a choice right here, about Canyon—and about his disgust toward the warrior in front of him: let go or hold on. The latter put the grudge and anger at the center of his focus, put him at the center. The former shifted focus to others. And hadn't Mom always said to prefer others above himself? He'd lived that for a long time.

Seemed trite. An easy answer. Too easy.

And really, maybe for her, he needed—wanted?—to do both, let go of her past, and hold onto her.

"You are deep in your thoughts."

Range blinked. Unfolded his arms. He shifted, suddenly feeling awkward. "Let's get something to eat." Extending a hand to let her go ahead of him, he felt like he'd been unmoored. Not himself.

Inaccurate. He felt like his old self, the Range of ten years ago.

Which was a bad ingredient to mix into a high-risk op like this.

They returned to the galley and he opened the fridge, staring into and seeing ... his past. Her past.

"Eggs and cheese are a good start," she said from next to him, then nudged him aside.

"What're you doing?"

"You said I should cook."

"It was a joke ..." Because he'd lost his ability to think when he saw her in that jumpsuit. Now he sounded like some kind of male domineering idiot. "I didn't mean for you to literally do it. I'm not—"

"Relax, Rage." Kasra smiled at him.

He stilled, eyeing her. Was she teasing him? Calling him Rage on purpose? A taunt? Why did it draw him like a moth to the flame?

Her black hair hung in a curtain over her shoulder as she moved to the counter with a handful of ingredients. "I like cooking. It calms me."

"Good." *Sit down, idiot, before you hurt yourself.* He planted his butt at the table and ... felt useless. And like a cad, sitting down, waiting for the little woman to feed him. The thought pushed him back to his feet. He joined her at the counter. "So ... what are you making?"

"Shakshuka." She side-eyed him as she let the onions and peppers sauté and sizzle while she went to a cabinet. "Assuming I can find canned tomatoes." Bent, she scanned the lower shelves. Then the upper. "Ah!" On her tiptoes, she reached for it.

The ship canted.

Kasra stumbled backward. "Whoa."

Steadying her with a hand, he snagged a can of diced tomatoes from the top shelf. Handed it to her. Didn't miss the coy look she shot him as she accepted it, then wheeled around him back to the counter. She added some spices. Slid the can to him. "Can you open that for me?"

"Ah, something I can do without burning down the ship."

She laughed. "You don't like to cook?"

"I like to protect the environment and its people—from me." He scrounged and located a can opener. Thing was about like trying to crank a rusted bolt loose. Success. He passed the opened can to her. "See, I stick to the skills I do have and everyone's better for it."

"I am better for your skills, thank you very much," she said quietly as she poured the tomatoes into the pan. She stirred it, let it rise to a boil, then lowered it to a simmer. Added salt and pepper. From a bottle she dumped some dried herbs into her palm, then shook them into the pan. "Range ..." Her voice was so soft it forced him closer to hear over the extractor on the stove and the sizzling shakshuka. Those green-brown eyes rose to him. "Please know that I do not think of you as misogynistic. Believe me, I have known those men." Her face seemed to pink as she stirred, then her gaze fluttered back to him. "You are not one of them."

Rip current. That's what her soft words and soft lips were. Somehow, his hand found the small of her back. "How do you know?" Because he had a powerful need to kiss her again but they hadn't clarified some things—like the marriage—yet.

She smiled at him. "Because I can tell you want to kiss me but will not."

That sounded like a challenge.

Or a warning.

"I don't want to be just another man lining up to taste your virtue."

"I do not think I have any of that left."

Range smirked. "Virtue also means a good or useful quality, and you have that in spades." Instead of taking that kiss, he brushed her hair from her shoulder. Appreciated how satiny it was. "You've had men take from you long enough, Kas."

Kasra returned her attention to the stove. Dropped eggs into the now-simmering mixture. "It's true," she said. "They have taken from me." Her wide, expressive eyes found his again. "But there is a man I would gladly give it all to."

Wait. What? Did she mean him? He searched her face as she turned to him.

"Yes, you, Rage."

His heart did the mamba. He moved his hand to the back of her neck. Diving in … Range caught her mouth with his. Felt that undertow of attraction that yanked his good sense from him. Knew that what he felt for her, thought of her, could tempt him to go places he'd vowed to never go.

"What smells so—Whoa-ho! Get it, Metcalfe!"

He broke off, automatically shifting to block her from Renner's sniggers and clapping. Scowled at the guy. "What do you want?"

Renner cocked his head. "Don't blame you, Pretty Boy. I'd go all alpha over her, too." He slapped Range's gut then moved to the stove and loudly inhaled the aroma. "About time we got a real cook up in here! Tell me you're making enough for me." He pressed his hands together. "I'll beg. I'm good at begging."

Kasra huffed a laugh, her cheeks pink.

"She's not your freakin' maid," Range growled, itching to rearrange his face.

Palms up, Renner acquiesced. "I hear you. I hear you."

"It is okay," Kasra said, hand on Range's abdomen. "It is the least I can do since they helped us leave Pakistan."

"You don't have to pay anyone for anything."

"No," Kasra agreed, "but if I can do this little thing as thanks, then why would it be wrong?"

Again, he threw a glower at him. "I don't want anyone on this ship thinking you owe them a thing."

"Except your life," Renner teased, arousing Range's anger, but he lifted his palms again. "Chill, dude. I get where you're coming from, but that was never my intention."

"Mr. Renner," Kasra said, touching Range's back. "You mentioned you saw a video on the dark web."

Range stood in a stiff standoff with the guy, who warily glanced at her.

"Yeah?"

"Could you show it to us? While you eat some shakshuka?"

A slow smile tugged into Renner's face and he wagged his eyebrows. "I like the way your missus thinks, Metcalfe."

Your missus ... The words stalled Range's brain and anger. He shifted his attention back to Kasra, felt the blaze of her touch against his delts. A fire that negated the one in his gut that wanted to throttle this guy.

Let go.

He had to admit, he liked the way Kasra thought, too. She was intelligent, shrewd. Stemmed the tide of his anger. Interdicted. "She's pretty amazing." Only when she parted her lips—still bright from their kiss—did he realize he'd said that out loud. Saw her surprise and appreciation.

Renner produced his phone, did some tapping and swiping, then handed it to Range. "It's about four minutes."

After turning off the heat on the stove, Kasra scooped shakshuka into three bowls, left some for another lucky intruder, then they went to one of the picnic-like tables.

Range sat beside her with the phone. Pressed Play. Knuckled his mouth as the video made them relive that moment. Only ... He frowned. "That ... that isn't what—"

Kas gasped. "You never said that." As the video continued,

she covered her mouth. "No … no that's not—" She caught his shoulder. "They made you look like a murderer, inciting violence."

Swallowing, he nodded. Watched it again. And again. "Deep fake."

All but licking his plate, Renner cocked his head in a nod. "Kinda figured. Most of us did. But I gotta be real. The type of people and money it took to create that"—he tapped his phone in Range's hand—"that's not remote village farmers and a small-town imam. That's Big Tech, big brother, or our own band of brothers breathing down your neck, Metcalfe."

Tell him what he didn't know. He eyed Kasra, recalling the captain who'd showed up at the safehouse, then squinted at Renner. "What do you know about a Captain Hellqvist?"

Renner's eyebrows lifted. "Hellion Hellqvist?" he balked. "He's a vindictive son of a"—his gaze bounced to Kasra then back—"biscuit."

"He showed up at the safehouse right after we'd taken her into custody."

Renner hesitated. "Hellqvist … he, uh … went to Roud?"

Gaze down, Kasra sighed. "I have no proof, but he worked for Taweel to make sure the Americans did not interrupt business at Roud." Her green-brown eyes rose to Range. "But you came—to Roud, to the mosque. I have been so worried about my own life, I never thought what they would do to you, for taking me. Saving me." Her expression crumpled. "I have been so selfish."

"You deserve to be, especially in this." Range instinctively slid an arm around her, appreciating how she drew closer.

"Okay, you two get a room." Renner took the phone and stood. "I would guess your missus has a point—not the selfish part, but you unwittingly dipped your M4 in their cauldron of fornication. And ticked some heavy hitters off." He went from nodding to shaking his head. "Well, now you've got trouble chomping at your heels. Now that she's out, free, with a voice and a hot-headed operator assisting her? It's sick as snot what men will do to hide their sexual exploits." He grunted a laugh, a dark one. "I'd keep your heads down until something drastically changes or this is forgotten."

"They will not forget," Kasra warned.

"Then stay frosty."

Great. The one thing he wasn't known for.

"And pray Jaeger doesn't find out, or you might be taking a long walk off a short plank."

CHAPTER TWENTY

Pakistani Reefer, Gulf of Oman

THE DEEP-FAKED VIDEO of himself slaughtering the imam and his caliph had put a huge bounty on their heads. With the anger he'd let fester, the reputation he'd developed ... nobody would believe he hadn't killed all those Muslims. Add to that the ticked-off, perverted sycophant who'd fathered a child and was now on a warpath because the only person who knew the girl's location was with Range, and he had no hope of a quiet exfil from this nightmare.

Once he heard Kasra brushing her teeth, Range dragged his shirt over his head. Huffed out a dozen push-ups. Used the bulkhead of the bed's berth for pull-ups. Worked off the frustration. Lowering himself to the deck, he had no idea what to do. They had documents but using them at any port or for flights would only put a laser bead on them. Little money. There were connections—that came with being black ops—but at this point in the game, with Hellqvist's position and power and whatever resources he was tapped into, they wouldn't be able to trust assets.

If he could get her to the States, maybe they could hide at

Stone's lodge. It was off-grid and safe. *First, get the kid. Then find a way home.*

How would they get past immigration?

This was so muffed up.

The door to the bathroom opened.

Range stood, suddenly realized he had his shirt off and hadn't finished his workout.

Kasra faltered, her gaze dancing across his chest, then to the deck. Back. Color flushed her cheeks, and he liked that he'd been the cause. "Your … the wound." She scratched her head. "Is it okay?"

Wound? Oh. He glanced at the stitches in his side. "Yeah. Healing. Hadn't thought about it."

"There is a lot on our minds," she said, moving to her satchel and storing her toiletry pack. "Do you really think the captain—" Her gaze again landed on his chest.

"Yeah. I do." Reading the situation, her attraction, remembering how very soft her lips were, Range knew he didn't need to distract them. He put his shirt back on and sat on the edge of the bed, lacing up his boots.

Hair loose and brushed, breath minty, she sat next to him. Which just made him aware—of her thigh touching his, how soft her lips had been, how willing …

He stretched his neck, took longer with tying his boots.

"What are we going to do once we reach the Emirates?"

With a heavy breath, he rested his forearms on his knees, his gaze on the deck. "No idea. Using the docs Zaki made would lead them straight to us." A hand on his leg, he angled to her. "Renner's right—we need to keep our heads down."

Concern danced in her irises. "Should we still go to Atia? I do not want her in danger."

She was really concerned about the captain's kid. "Good point." He scratched the beard, which made it burn and itch. "But I think securing her is a bigger priority."

She studied him. "Why?" It was a breathy question.

There was something unusual in the way she asked that. "DNA can prove she's Hellqvist's kid and that would connect him to Roud if we can get a sample from the mother. Can we?"

Her answer took a hot second. "Maybe."

Of course she was worried about the little girl should she be located by Hellqvist. "It'd help us take him down."

She pushed to her feet. Crossed the cabin to the table. Busied herself with a bottled water. "When I sent Atia away, it was to keep her safe. Make sure she could live. That he would not be able to touch or … ruin her." She tidied the table, but her movements slowed. "Using her against him—it would put her in danger, yes?"

Concern he understood, but this seemed like more. "Possibly."

She chewed her lower lip.

"Second thoughts?"

"No." With a groan, she sat sideways in a chair, her back against the wall and ran her hands over her face. "I do not know. I have not seen her since I left her in Saudi. But she is an innocent and does not know the monster who is her father. How she came into existence." Her eyes glossed. "But there, Atia is safe."

Which was a good thing. So why did she look ready to cry? Granted, safety was an illusion … "Nobody else knows where she is?"

Kas shrugged. "Only Razam. And Fatina, but they are safe with the chief." Her eyes held his, and she probably wanted to ask him to confirm that.

"After seeing him at the airstrip … I don't trust anything or anyone right now."

"Even the men on this boat?"

"Renner seems okay, but I don't know them."

The ship rode a swell, and the chair Kasra sat in started sliding—she yelped.

"Here," Range said, indicating behind him. "In the berth. Less chance of getting thrown around or hit by something." He reached out and she took his hand even as the deck canted in the opposite direction.

"What's wrong?" she asked, her words tight.

"Nothing, just the ocean being her normal, temperamental self." He shrugged as she slipped past him onto the bed. "Besides, reefers are notorious for rolling and pitching. It could get rough."

She climbed on the bed and laid flat, her toes against the wall, bracing herself. Which would be fine until the ship dipped toward the bow.

He sat on mattress, spine to the wall, legs stretched out.

"I really do not like this," she said nervously.

Kasra Jazani had weathered a lot. Endured terrible things. And she was afraid. It did something crazy to him. The ship pitched again.

Her feet thudded against the hull.

Then backward.

She flung out a hand to avoid falling into him. Laughed, nervously.

It bugged him that she was afraid. Made him want to protect her. He wrapped an arm around her. Drew her to himself.

Instantly, the tension seemed to leave her body. She huffed a laugh. "You must think me weak," she muttered as she burrowed into his chest.

Man, he liked this. Her in his arm. Looking to him for safety. "Reefers aren't the best seafaring crafts for your first sailing experience. I would've taken you on kayak or canoe on a still lake. Worked up from there. Maybe take you on a cruise—those are beasts built to handle pretty rugged waters. Although, there is no ship that could survive if Mother ocean decided to exert herself against it."

"That is not comforting," she gritted out.

He chuckled. "Fair." Holding onto each other, they endured the swells and pitches, bracing one way, then the next. Though Kasra murmured about feeling sick, the nausea did not progress. Thankfully, the seas didn't go full-on hull-breaker.

"When we were on the upper deck, looking out the window," Kasra said, her cheek against this chest, "you had this look on your face …"

"That's normally what a face does."

She set her chin on his ribs, peering up at him. "What were you thinking?"

He knew exactly he'd been thinking but didn't want to go there. "I don't recall."

She gave him a nudge. "You do. I see it in your eyes."

Frowning at her, he scoffed. "We've known each other three weeks. How can you—"

"I have been with you every minute of those three weeks." She laughed as she shifted ever closer, no propriety or gap left now. "But … I knew you even when we were at the safehouse. I could read your thoughts as if they were my own."

Needing to put space between them, Range shifted on his side. "Okay, then. Tell me what my thoughts were."

She rotated half on her side, half on her back, her hair cascading back against the white sheets as she peered up at him. The dull glow of the cabin lights caressed her face … then blinked off. Back on. She gasped.

"They should have a backup generator."

Her gaze darted around, then back to his.

"Not getting out of this one—what was I thinking?"

Eyes intent, features softening, she relaxed as she stared up at him. "It is impossible to know exactly what you were thinking—"

"Cheating." That lazy smile she gave him twisted his thoughts. "You seemed to come to a decision. A resolve. And it ..." She tracked her fingers over his beard. "It changed something in you. What decision was it?"

The reefer rose swiftly—Range thrust his hand against the low ceiling and braced, but Kasra slid down several inches, then was unceremoniously pitched back up, thrusting her into the gap he'd created.

When they collided, she gave a nervous laugh.

His hand settled on her waist to steady her. But it stirred desires. He told himself to veer off. Instead, he brushed raven hair from her face.

Her eyes brightened, went alert. Aware. Then she smiled and caught his hand. "Not going to distract me, Rage. Now, you owe me an answer."

"I hate when you call me that," he growled, then surrendered. "I was thinking"—*about kissing her* ... No, that's not what he'd been thinking ... Where did that thought go? He mentally walked himself back up to the deck, standing there, remembered—"that you were right."

Another slow smile slid across her lips. Like an invitation.

Accepting, he gently brushed her lips with his own. "About the grudge." A kiss at the corner of her mouth. "About letting go of my anger." He lingered on her mouth a little longer this time. "About you ..."

"Yeah ...?" She returned the kiss.

Nuzzled the spot where her jaw met her earlobe. Felt her respond, slid her hands up his chest and over his shoulders as he trailed kisses down her neck, burying his face there.

Easy, easy. Slow down.

Inhaling a floral scent that coiled around his brain and made it impossible to think. Taunted him as he walked kisses back up her neck to her earlobe.

But her hauled-in breath and soft moan scrambled that warning. He kissed her again, deepening it. Settling against her sent a jolt of desire through him. Passion roared as her hands slid up his back. She was sliding off his shirt. His hand found the sliver of space between her shirt and pants. Grazed flesh. Chased the shirt up to her—

Stand down!!

Range fought himself to veer off. Finally lifted his mouth from hers, though she pulled him back to her with a whimper.

With a growl, he yanked upward. Rolled to the side and sat on the edge of the bed, cradling his head. *What the heck are you doing?*

"Wh–what is wrong?" Her voice was husky and raw.

Danggit. "Nothing." Every nerve-ending was on fire. He wanted nothing more than to lie down again. Fall into the vat of passion. "Everything." On his feet, he stepped forward. "I've crossed a lot of lines in the last few years, but that … that's one I feel is … sacred."

She was at his side now, bare feet to the deck. "But … we are married."

He side-eyed her. "Are we? Who says it was legitimate?"

"You said you took me as your wife."

"I did, but you were held at gunpoint. Any judge would say that was an extenuating circumstance."

Her brow rippled as confusion, then hurt rolled across her pretty features. "So, even if it is real, you would want out." She jutted her jaw. "Because I am disgusting to you."

"*No.*"

"Do not lie to me." She pointed toward the berth. "You were ready to make love to me. Then you remembered I was the madam and—"

"No! That's not it."

She considered him for a second. "I do not believe you. What else would make you so heatedly passionate one second then cold and gone the next?"

"Me!" he barked. "Me—the pretty girls don't choose me!" Had he just said that? He scrambled for a better line. "If I justify that I want you with the pretty weak excuse of us being forced into marriage in a ceremony that was not of our choice, then I am no better than my brother or those men at Roud."

Her face contorted. "Your brother?"

Range sniffed. Couldn't believe he'd said that either. "Canyon ... he slept with Dani on that mission. I never let him live it down."

"So, again, this is about your grudge with your brother. About you—why did you say the beautiful women don't choose you? Haven't I?" She dropped onto the bed, her voice and lip trembling. "Didn't I?"

Somehow he was on a knee in front of her. "Look. What I am going to say, might hurt, but I want you to listen, hear me. Okay?"

She gave him a wary look ... filled with a whole lot of defiance.

"I think ... you said because of the passion shared on that bed, that you felt you chose me. Am I getting that right?"

Brow knotting, she shrug-nodded.

Canyon had warned him to tread carefully and he hadn't listened. But he was now. "Kasra, sex ..."

How did he say this? He couldn't say it and make her shoulder the whole thing. This was on him, too. "God created intimacy to be between a husband and wife. It's good. But that's not all that love is." What the heck? Never thought when he went into Roud that he'd be here three weeks later talking about love. "If you ever ... give yourself to me, I want it to be because you love me—really love me. Know me. Have chosen to be my wife."

Hold the heck up there, cowboy ...

She swallowed, staring at him.

"I don't want you to have sex with me just to say you like me." He nodded. "Understand?"

Uncertainty blanketed her pretty face and it broke his heart.

"You asked me what I was thinking on the upper deck ... it was about this very thing: about letting go of the grudge with Canyon. He and Dani got it backwards—sex first. Then he had to build a relationship with her." Peering into her brown-green eyes told him understanding was fighting its way past years of abuse. "I'm not making that mistake." His heart thundered around the next words he felt on his lips. Words that included 'falling in love.'

"I see."

Range drew back at the edge to her words. "I haven't finished—"

She pushed up, forcing him to leap backward. "You have said more than enough."

"Kasra, please let me finish—"

"Forget it."

Bang! Bang!

"Metcalfe!"

Range jerked and looked over his shoulder.

"Open up!"

Not now. He had to tell her. But it sounded like Renner was going to come through that hatch. He yanked the door open. "What?"

"You've got trouble."

He braced himself. "What?"

"Jaeger just got notified by a buddy at the port authority in the Emirates. Seems there's a pretty stiff welcome wagon waiting for us to dock."

"How the heck do they know where we are?" He turned to tell Kasra, but saw her already kneeling at her satchel.

"Unknown." He shrugged. "You and the missus need to bail.

We've got a Zodiac you can take, but you have to go now. If you aren't past the harbor by sun-up, they'll see you and interdict."

In a matter of minutes, they'd shouldered their gear and followed Renner down to the main deck where they met Wire and another guy halfway down. Wire nodded a greeting then took their gear. Stuffed it in a Zodiac and tied it down.

"Anything else on you that shouldn't go in the water?"

"Negative," Range said, taking the lifejacket he offered and passing it to Kasra.

Her lips parted as she stared at him. "Wha ... You know I can't swim."

"With that, you don't have to. You drop in, relax, let it bring you back to the surface. Just kick your feet."

She faltered, and he knew her anger from their conversation was getting in the way of her hearing him ... again. "No." She shoved it back at him.

"Kas—"

"I can't."

Range shifted in front of her. "We'll drop in together." Gently, he threaded her arms into the lifejacket and secured it. "Only thing I need you to do is cover your nose and keep your mouth sealed." He showed her how to pinch her nose and clamp her mouth.

Her expression was one of stark terror. "I. Can't. Swim."

"I'll be the one swimming," he said with a nod. "When we hit the water, don't panic and don't fight me. That's a quick way to drown us both."

"No." She shook her head hard and backed up into a wall. "No, I'm not—can't! I'll drown. I don't know how to swim. I can't!"

Range cupped her face. "Kas ..." He waited for her gaze to meet his, noticed her chin bouncing as she fought the tears and panic. "If they find us, we're dead. It won't end any other way.

You can do this. You're strong. I wouldn't have married you otherwise."

Anger flared through her eyes. "Not funny."

He pursed his lips. "It kinda was."

"What if you hit your head and are unconscious?"

"Then Renner will come in after us."

Kasra glanced at the former SEAL who winked at her. "I … can't."

Inching closer, he lowered his mouth to her ear, so only she could hear. "Ten minutes ago, you wanted me to make love to you."

"That's different."

"It involved trust, and that's what we need here. To keep us alive."

Her gaze trounced around the main deck of the tower. "Sex is one thing, but *this* …" she hissed.

Range frowned. Felt like he'd been sucker punched. Had that been all it was to her? Maybe it was a good thing he hadn't said he was falling in love with her.

Behind her, Renner cocked his head to the water, telling Range to just take her in.

Tempted to do that, he worried she'd panic and flail. "Hand near your face," he said, guiding her to the edge. Used a carabiner to attach her vest to his belt, then inched them closer to the edge. Hooked his arms around her and gripped her vest. "Now."

Though she tensed and whimpered, she complied and pinched her nose.

Holding her tight, her head to his chest, he shoved off the deck.

CHAPTER
TWENTY-ONE

Pakistani Reefer, Persian Gulf

ICY WATER YANKED her into its suffocating grasp. Hearing went garbled. Pressure smothered her. Kasra fought the instinct to panic, to gasp. Had to remind herself that Range was there. How he had maintained his hold on her, she could not fathom. Her mind was thrashing as she felt them sinking ... sinking ...

Why was he not kicking them upward?

He must have fallen unconscious or something.

No. Could not have—he was still holding her. But it had been so long. They were going to drown!

Her lungs pounded from the deprivation. Pulse throbbed at her temples.

Breathe.

No!

A sudden upward tug jerked her sideways. Her hand slipped from her nose. She gasped.

A mistake!

Water filled her nostrils ... throat. She gagged. Felt it—

Air smacked her.

Kasra coughed hard, sputtering as she tried to haul in greedy breaths.

"Easy. Steady," Range huffed, one arm hooked across her chest and the other slicing into the water, swimming them toward the boat.

Fighting tears of relief, she clung to his arm, remembering his warning not to fight him. She did not know how to best help him except to kick her legs, too.

"Here," he huffed again. "Catch the boat. Climb up."

She glanced over and saw they were there. Holding him tightly with one hand, she caught a handle with the other. Found another and tried to pull herself over … and started sliding back—

Range unceremoniously shoved her backside up.

She flopped into the rubber boat like a fish. Scrabbling around, she reached to help Range. But he was already halfway over the side. Skilled and strong. It was impossible not to notice the way his dark shirt was plastered to his sculpted torso. Recalled when she had thought to let him have her. Give herself to him. And he'd stopped. Called it and her a mistake. It hurt. So very deeply. Did he not understand that she had *never* given herself to anyone like that? She had never *wanted* to make love to someone before?

Aware of her own clothes stuck to her, she suctioned them free, but it was of little use with them so wet.

Range moved to the back and powered up the motor. After a signal to the ship that they were good, he steered them away from the ship. He was a marvel. No hesitation. Nothing he could not do. Why would he think beautiful women did not choose him? She had. Would.

Maybe she should stop thinking that way. He clearly did not deem her worthy enough.

They zipped along the waters, the boat slapping the waves with determination.

Kasra settled in the bottom, holding the handles and shivering so fiercely her teeth clacked. The deafening whir of the motor, the howl of the wind as they tore into the Persian Gulf, made it impossible to chat. Not that her clacking teeth would let her. She burrowed down, doing her best to hide from the wind. She knew not how long it took them, but Range was skilled and masterful at navigating over the black void that was the ocean.

Lights blinked in the distance.

She looked back to Range, who gave a grim nod where he knelt, steering them. They navigated around the Hawar Islands. A while longer and a little farther delivered them into the dusky maw of a small inlet without a real dock. Fishing boats lined the shore.

He drove them right up to the edge and hopped out, pulling the boat ashore. "Grab your gear." On the gravelly stretch, they unloaded their belongings, then he made quick work of stowing the boat in a covered grill area with a half wall. Perfect for hiding the boat. "C'mon."

They hurried through the rapidly lightening morning. Thanks to the speed of the boat and hours on the water, their clothes were mostly dry and would not draw undue attention. With dawn not yet fully proclaiming herself, most people would likely still be sleeping. Would they take another car? There were plenty here to choose from.

She had no sooner wondered that than she noticed him checking vehicle windows. No, not windows—locks. Finally at an older pick-up that looked like many of the others around, he nodded to her.

Understanding his meaning, she hurried to the passenger side. Stowed her bags in the back. Climbed in. Even as she buckled in, the engine turned over. Range pulled into traffic and in under an hour, they were outside the nearby limits.

She couldn't help but admire him. With his brooding blue

eyes, his muscular body, and his intense focus ... it was no wonder she ... Loved him?

"... *that's not all that love is* ..."

Range had been talking about sex. But why had he mentioned love? Was he thinking about it? No, impossible. He would not love her. It was impossible this fast, was it not? He implied there was more to love than sex, but ... what was it? What *did* it look like?

That question kept her company as they drove to Al Hofuf, east of Riyadh. She wondered what Atia would do when she saw her. They had not spoken or seen each other in over two years. How would she convince Zahir to release Atia to her after all this time?

"You okay?" Range asked, as the sun climbed into the sky and threw a warm glow across his blue eyes.

"Zahir has raised Atia these last two years. I worry he will not easily let me take her." It had taken much pleading for him to accept her in the first place. But after two years, she was sure there was a bond ...

"If that happens, we warn him that bad people are coming for the girl. And if he keeps her, he will need to prepare for violence."

The words stole her words. She eyed him. "That is true, is it not?"

He smirked. "We aren't going out of our way to secure the kid just for fun, right?"

No, not for fun. But ...

"Hey. Meant to tell you—you did good in the water."

"I panicked and nearly drowned."

"But you didn't."

"Only because of you." In so many ways ... because of him. She was here in Saudi, where she had not dreamed of ever coming again, about to be reunited with Atia. Free—at least, so far. But with the way Range handled dropping into the water, commandeering the boat, getting them here … she had every confidence her freedom would happen. As said, because of him.

"Something I should know?" Range asked, frowning at her.

"What?"

"You did that thing again—went quiet. You worrying about something?"

It should not surprise her that he could read her, especially with the way she could read him, but it was … strange. "It is nothing."

"Does this Zahir use computers?"

Kasra frowned. "I do not—"

"Wondering if they might've seen the video from the mosque."

"Oh no …"

⸺⸺⸺

He had a bad feeling about this. Something was off—Kasra hadn't been the same since they'd hit the beachhead. She'd ended up ticked at him on the ship, but that seemed to fall away as a greater worry plagued her. As he pulled up to a gray two-story structure that looked like a giant cube with a walled courtyard and one-vehicle garage, he noticed she was holding her hands in a tight fist. And it kinda ticked him off.

"Want me to just go in and get her?"

She startled. "No!" Then waffled. "Zahir … he is very … devout. Strict."

In other words, all the guy saw was her past. She was the victim—no, the *survivor*. Fighter. She shouldn't have to prove anything. Rather than doubting or questioning, people should be helping and praising her for enduring the unimaginable.

And he had no idea when his view of her had changed so radically. Maybe it'd been that moment in the tower, looking out at the water. Maybe it'd been that first kiss. Or the liquid fire that poured through his gut seeing her held at gunpoint. Or when he'd nearly said he was falling in love with her.

"I'm so scared," she whispered, then flinched.

Range reached over and placed his hand on hers. "You've got this. You're kick-butt Kasra." Did that sound as corny as he thought it did? "And I've got your six."

She wrinkled her nose. "Six?"

He smirked. "Your back. I've got your back."

Eyes puddling, she leaned back against the headrest. In a strange but cool way, her eyes seemed like some of the exotic lakes he'd seen. "Why are you being so nice to me? Helping me."

"Why wouldn't I?" Guess that was what he was doing, but it was also about nailing Hellqvist's butt to the wall.

"I know you said being with me would be a mistake—"

"Kasra—"

She lifted his hand to her lips and kissed it. "I love you."

Something happened in his gut right then. Startled him. The girl never chose him. It wasn't supposed to happen here either. She was the madam he was supposed to take down. Bring to justice. "You're riding adrenaline. Under a lot of stress. Don't mix-up—"

"No." Her eyes blazed with meaning. "I've never known a man like you. And I know, after this, every man will pale by comparison."

Huh. No idea how to process those words. Things like that—this—didn't happen to him. This violated the whole pretty-girls-don't-choose-him belief. No, it didn't. Because she wasn't just pretty. She was beautiful. With a whole lot of hurt and if he misspoke, mistook his own adrenaline and action-drive for love …

Does that really make sense in that thick skull of yours?

"It is okay," she said. "I know you cannot love someone like me."

"Hold up." His hand slipped to her face. He caught the back of her neck. Thumbed the small scar on the right side of her cheek. He'd given her that when they'd sparred six months ago. "Just because I need time to figure things out ... don't disqualify me."

Her expression shifted, surprised by his words. Hope smoothing out the torment in her beautiful face.

Say it. Say you're falling in love with her.

Nah, it'd just jinx things. Every time he stepped out and confessed his feelings, his face was shoved in a pile of manure.

Her gaze shifted past him. "Oh. There he is."

Range saw a man standing to the side, holding open an opaque door that led to a courtyard. "That's a pretty mean scowl."

"Like you, yes?" she teased. "Zahir does not know any other way." She unbuckled. "Allah, help me convince him ..." Snatching up a scarf, she opened the door. Wrapped the scarf over her head and neck. Climbed out. "*As-Salaam alaikum,* Zahir."

Not liking the timidity in her tone and posture, Range slid a weapon to the holster at the small of his back, and got out. Waited by the car, feeling like this was something she had to do.

Wary eyes met Range as the man spoke to Kasra. "*Wa-alaikum as-salaam,* Kasra." He frowned at her. "What are you doing here? Why did you bring *him*? Are you trying to get us all killed?"

So he knew about the video.

"Can we please move out of the street?" Kasra kept her head high.

Though Range was tempted to clock the guy for the way he talked to her, he let her run this show. She was more than capable. But he moved in behind her to let the guy know she had back-up.

Zahir shifted, then huffed and moved out of the way. But he didn't go into the house.

"I never knew you to be rude, Zahir," Kasra challenged him. "But since I am not wanted here, I will take Atia and be on my way."

The man's face reddened. "She is not here."

Kasra faltered. "What? *Where* is she?"

"With my father at his home."

"Why did you send her to him? He is not—" She drew up. "This was Hasna's doing, was it not?"

"She did not think it proper for our children to be with Atia."

Kasra growled. Pounded a fist on his chest. "You *promised* me you would protect her!"

Though chagrined, Zahir did not seem the type to suffer a woman's beating.

Range shifted to the side, reaching for his weapon.

"That is what I did," Zahir hissed. "You do not know … it was much better for her to be with an old man than a bitter woman." He faltered, seeming to regret his words. "You must go. Hasna will be in an uproar if she finds you here."

In a blink, she had the guy on his backside. "It is a shame your wife is more a man than you are." She pivoted and stalked out of the courtyard.

Range couldn't help grin. Felt proud of her. He gave the guy a cockeyed nod. "Lady's got a point."

"If you truly love her, get her out of here," he sneered. "They will slaughter her and her daughter!"

Smile vanished, Range froze. *Her daughter …?* In a daze, he returned to the truck. Eyed her. Couldn't process the bomb that had just been dropped. He got them back on the road. "Assuming you know how to get to this other man's house."

"I cannot believe this!"

"Yeah …" And by this, Range meant the whole 'daughter'

business. Then that connection fired in his head—her daughter ... was Hellqvist's daughter. He needed to puke.

She gave him an appreciative look. "He's in the middle of nowhere. Just west of town."

He headed in that direction, heat of anger thrumming in his veins. "Your daughter. Atia is your daughter."

Kasra stilled. "He told you."

"Explains why you dreamed of her." Why wasn't he more ticked? "Shouldn't be surprised. You said you were the Hellqvist's favorite." The thought of that jerk getting her pregnant ... "He knows you're the mother?"

She nodded. "He is the reason I had to get her away from Roud. He threatened to use her against me. To force me into silence and into more ... compliance. To the captain, she was not an innocent child but a tool, a pawn. Like everyone and everything else."

The entire time he'd been with her, Range wondered what to do with the experiences she related. Then with his out-of-nowhere feelings. Her saying she loved him. Now this—she'd had a kid by that piece of work.

"You are mad."

"Yeah." There was a big chunk of angry, but he understood she hadn't been able to trust anyone her entire adult life. "Wish you had trusted me with it." But clearly that wasn't on the table for them. "I mean, I get it. She's your daughter."

Man, that was bitter on his tongue. She had a kid. By a client from Roud.

"I am sorry, Range. I have told no one outside Roud that she is mine. It was too dangerous." She seemed unusually contrite. "After all that has happened between us, I am sorry that I did not tell you."

He sighed, wanting to redirect this. "Is this old man bad news? You seemed angry Zahir sent Atia to him."

"He is old and not the nicest man. Not terrible, but Zahir promised to raise her for me, and I knew he had a good job and home. A family for her to have siblings. I wanted that for her. I wanted her protected and loved, since I could not do that for her."

She was a mother who wanted the best for her child …

The trip out took them a half hour. He pulled up to the plaster home, the unpaved road laden with chasm-sized holes. Four structures straddled a pen that looked like it had a couple goats and chickens. A man sat in a rickety chair out front, gray-white hair and beard scraggly about his head as he smoked a pipe. He didn't seem to care that a car was coming up to his house.

"That him?" Range asked. Why did he have an entire armory? Maybe that was just his irritation over this whole revelation. Nah. Something …

"There she is!" Kasra pitched herself out of the car.

"Wait!" Danggit. Range parked and stepped out, leaving it idling in the hopes this wouldn't take long. Palmed the weapon at his back, watching Kasra hurry toward where a child of about four or five was playing. In the pen. With the goats. Penned up. Like a freakin' animal!

He wanted to strangle someone. Specifically that old man sitting in a chair smoking a pipe. Who still hadn't moved or spoken.

Stay back. Let Kas handle this. He leaned on the truck.

Kasra lifted the little girl into her arms, shooting the man a glower and a few stern words.

A large spider scampered across the road in front of Range, drawing his attention. Thought to kill it, but the thing wasn't hurting anyone. He watched it skitter down the—

He stilled. Tire track. He studied the ground and space around him. Saw evidence of grass trampled by vehicles. Two or three. Recent. Skated a look in the direction of the buildings.

"Kas," he called in warning, drawing his weapon. "Might have—"

Crack! Pop!

"Down! Down!" Range started for her, but a barrage forced him back.

Crouching, moving backward, he fired in the direction of the shots: the lean-to. Needed a better weapon. He double-checked and spotted Kasra hopping from one location to the other with the kid, working her way back to him. The old man—he hadn't moved. He was dead, probably had been all along. They'd walked straight into an ambush.

He ripped open the door and ruck. Extracted the rifle and vest. Taking a knee, he kitted up. "Kas? You okay?"

A child's scream rent the day.

Range sighted down the road. Saw Kasra laid out. *No!* Blood stained her back. "Kasra!" He started for her but the spray of gunfire and logic yanked him back. He had to get to her and the only way he could was with the truck.

With a curse, he whipped into the truck. Kept low. Shifted it into DRIVE. Leaned out the driver's side.

Ping-ping! Crack! Pop!

As the truck rolled forward, he peered under the open door as he steered. Couldn't veer too far right or he'd expose himself. Too far left, he'd run her over. Coasting, he watched her body slide into view beneath the door. Shifted into PARK.

He scrabbled over her. Knelt at her side.

Bullets struck the truck. Cracked the windshield.

Range shoved himself out and crouched at her side. "Kas." Eyed the bullet wounds—three. Non-responsive. He pressed two fingers to her carotid. Thready.

Raven-haired Atia screamed, wriggling to get out from under her mother. Got on all fours. Dust erupted near her.

Range yanked the girl back to himself. She howled her

protest even as he tried to wrangle her into the truck. "Stay," he barked in Pashto and Arabic.

Wide brown-green eyes, streaked with dirt and tears, fastened onto him.

He repeated the command and she stuck the two fingers between her pinky and forefinger into her mouth and sat down on the floorboard.

Can't believe that worked. He whipped back to Kasra. She needed immediate life-saving measures, but the situation was too hot. Dangerous. They had to get out of here. But moving her was a risk with the bullet wounds.

Ping-ping-ping-crack!

Rocks and dirt crunched behind him. He glanced back and saw an SUV barreling toward them. He snapped up his M4 and fired at the SUV. the rounds bounced off the windshield. Armored.

Are you freakin' kidding me? They were screwed. Dead.

A whistle streaked through the air. Another.

He knew that sound. Threw himself over Kasra.

Boom! Boom-boom!

Range saw an orange flash as the SUV flipped into the air. Flames roared from the lean-to. What the heck?

That's when he heard the thunder. Saw movement, a man emerging from the consumed lean-to. With a weapon.

On one knee, M4 tucked into his shoulder, Range fired several rounds until the man thudded into the dirt, his head bouncing off the hardpacked ground. A Black Hawk whizzed overhead and circled back, hovering over them. Rotor-wash chewed the air and spit out dirt and rocks.

Range covered Kasra's body as the bird set down. Had no idea who'd come to his aid. And didn't care. The bird seemed to back off, letting him focus on saving her.

"Kasra." Stabilizing her head and neck, he shifted her onto

her side, then eased her onto her back. A trail of blood slid down her temple. Exit wounds on the right side of her chest and lower abdomen. The third hadn't exited. Not good. Made CPR tricky. A miracle the kid hadn't taken one of the bullets that exited.

On his knees, he pressed two fingers to her carotid and lowered his ear to her mouth to check for breathing. Nothing—no breathing, no pulse. Focus warred with panic. "C'mon, Kas," he muttered as he began compressions, monitoring the abdomen wound and how much it bled. "C'mon, c'mon. Don't do this to me."

Hands threaded on top of each other, he did thirty compressions. Then opened her airway and pinched her nose. Gave two full breaths. Back to compressions. "Kasra! C'mon!" In his periphery he heard the kid crying. Boots thudding toward him.

After tilting her head back and opening her airway, he blew into her mouth. After two more breaths, he glanced toward the bird. A half-dozen men had poured out of it. Nearly on him.

Range snapped up his M4 and aimed.

"Blue, blue!"

He saw the face—nearly faltered. Canyon. No time. He refocused on Kasra.

Counting ... breathing ... Counting ... breaths.

Two men slid to the ground with large packs. Others started prepping a litter.

"Sit-rep," a big burly black man demanded.

"No pulse, not breathing."

Two men shouldered in next to him.

"She's not breathing. No pulse."

A familiar form shoved into the fray. "Hey," Canyon said. "Move over. Let me—"

"Get off!"

"Hey!"

Range grabbed his brother's shirt with a bloodied hand. "She doesn't die."

That familiar cocky smirk slid away as Canyon gave a sharp nod. Went to work with a masterful repetition. His blue eyes met Range's for a second as he administered breaths with better equipment and skills because he was a combat medic.

"Patch him up," Canyon barked, nodding to Range.

Only then did he feel the searing pain in his shoulder. But as large hands touched him, he threw it off. "Don't worry about me—save her!"

"Stand down," the man's deep voice boomed in the chaos. Griffin Riddell, AKA: Legend, was only doing his job, but Range wasn't leaving Kasra's side. "She's in good hands. I need to make sure your injury—"

"It's fine."

"That's shock talking." He held his gaze. "Clear?"

Range gave a nod, shifted back, watching as a third guy—was that Azzan?—threaded an IV into Kasra's arm.

"We need to be wheels-up," another shouted. "Unfriendlies incoming."

Range spotted brown-green eyes peer from behind Griffin. The kid. Frantic, he pulled Atia from the truck. The team was up and moving, Kasra in a litter with Canyon hustling alongside, still doing rescue breathing and compressions.

Two men jogged from the direction of the lean-to.

Range met them, not surprised to find Leif among them.

His little brother gave him a shoulder hug.

"How many?" Range shouted over the rotor wash.

"Two bodies."

"White male?"

Leif shook his head. "All Middle Eastern," he shouted above, then pointed to his shoulder with the silent message to get it looked at.

They climbed into the helo, and though he felt the terrorized screams of Atia through the rise and fall of her chest and the rigidity of her body, he pressed her close to his chest. Climbed aboard.

On the deck, he noted Canyon wasn't performing breaths or compressions anymore. Was she breathing? Heart beating? She looked pale, her lips lacking their light-raspberry coloring.

But she was being tended by at least one combat medic. The real problem, the one that left an anchor in his gut was that the men who'd died here were all local fighters. Which meant Hellqvist was still out there. Could still come for her. Kill her.

CHAPTER
TWENTY-TWO

LANDSTUHL REGIONAL MEDICAL CENTER, LANDSTUHL, GERMANY

AFTER BEING PATCHED UP, Range snagged his dirty, bloodied shirt and stalked out of the bay to the objection of the nurse and staff. He prowled down the hall toward the surgery bay. Saw a team working on someone. Alarms were blaring and doctors were barking orders.

Range stilled. He'd thought she'd stabilized.

"Hey. Loverboy."

He pivoted. Spotted Canyon standing near a door he thumbed toward.

Stalking there, Range was haunted by the words Kasra had spoken, the decision he'd made about his brother and said-grudge. But he didn't have the words. Had only one focus: Kasra. He stepped into the room and slowed.

She had color back, but still looked as if she'd been through the grinder. At her bedside, he rested his hands on the rail. Trailed the tubes and IV. Scanned the monitors. *Kas* ...

"She's stable," came Canyon's soft words. "If you hadn't started basic life-saving measures, she wouldn't have made it."

The bruises from the imam's beating had faded into the

background with the knot on her temple.

"One of the bullets ricocheted off a rib, cracking it, then hit her lung," Canyon said. "They were able to remove all fragments and repair the lung, but it'll feel like she's eating fire every time she moves."

Range felt like he could breathe now. At least, a little easier.

"You should get some rest. I'll stay with her—"

"No." He wasn't sure he'd ever leave her side again. Which was whacked, considering where he'd started when he hit Roud almost a month ago. But there wasn't time for rest or complacency. "We have to get out of here. She's being hunted." He felt his brother's gaze, the curiosity over his attention but said nothing. Didn't look at him.

"We need to talk—"

"Just"—he bit back the familiar rage and conflict—"give me a sec." He forced himself to look at Canyon. "Please."

Arching an eyebrow, his brother gave a hesitant nod. "I'll be in the hall."

Once he heard the door close, Range reached down and took Kasra's hand. Wondered where Atia was. "Sorry I broke my promise." She'd almost died. "I should've been there ... done more ..." He squeezed her hand. "Just ... don't die on me, okay?" Why did his throat feel so thick?

"I love you."

Yeah ... me, too. What did he know about love? Except that he was sure if she'd succumbed out there, he wouldn't have wanted to come back either. He bent over the rail and leaned down. "Come back to me, Kas." He pressed his lips gently to her forehead and straightened. Thought he saw movement near the window—probably Canyon watching. But when he stepped out, he found Canyon talking with Griffin, Azzan, and Leif.

The brawny black guy pulled him into hug. Patted his back so hard he almost sent him into next week. Azzan shook his head in apology for the situation.

"What do you know?" Canyon asked.

"About the attack? Nothing—they were waiting for us. No idea how they found the place. Kasra didn't know the girl was with the old man until today."

"Know who's behind the hit?" Leif asked, arms tucked under his armpits.

"Suspect Calvin Hellqvist, an Army captain. The kid's father. Frequent patron to Roud."

Canyon's eyebrows lifted.

Range nodded. "Kasra said the captain worked with Taweel Abdul-Ghulam, who owns the compound and runs the Trench. Gave him favors."

"You mean girls," Leif growled.

Another nod.

"And all this over a kid?" Canyon frowned.

"Not really," Range said. "Kasra knows names—specifically, the real name behind Viper."

Griffin let out a low whistle.

"Nobody knows that name," Azzan argued.

"*She* does." Range couldn't stop the swallow his throat processed. "He … visited her."

Canyon's gaze sharpened. He was all over that. All over the way Range swallowed. The way he said little, chose "visit" rather than any other rancid term or phrase.

"Then he's right," Azzan said. "We need to get them out of here ASAP."

"Stateside," Range insisted. He'd all but promised her. "And the kid—Kasra is her mother."

Leif and Canyon exchanged a look, and Range didn't care. Beyond the window, he saw Kasra. "She's awake." He shoved into the room. "Hey …" At her side, he smiled. "How are you doing?"

With a hooded look, she grimaced. Groaned. "Hurts …"

"Yeah, but at least you're alive."

Her eyes widened. "Atia!"

"Safe." He caught her hand. "She's here, safe."

Her eyes slid closed and she released her stress. Sighed. "Where are we?"

"Landstuhl," he grunted. "Germany."

Kasra hauled in a breath. "No!" Came up—and yelped in pain. Dropped against the bed, and though she was in obvious pain, her panic wouldn't let her rest. "No. We cannot be here."

When she gripped the rail, as if to climb out of the bed, he stopped her. "Whoa. Wait. Stop, Kasra." He held her shoulders. Pushed her back. "You can't—"

She grabbed his arm. "Range. You don't understand. He is here."

"Who?"

"Adler. Adler Roth lives here." Her gaze met his and she slumped, tears forming and her chin trembling. "Viper!" She was again coming out of the bed. "He will find us. I can't be here." She started crying.

Gut clenched, Range steadied her. "Canyon!"

The door burst open, his brother's expression fierce as he entered, trailed by the guys and all their mission readiness. "Viper is Adler Roth."

"Are you kidding me?" Leif balked. "*The* Adler Roth, the fashion titan?"

"And partner to Germany's Prime Minister," Griffin added.

"Stay with her," Range ordered. "I'm going to get Atia and we're ditching this place." He opened the door.

A weapon aimed into the room.

"Gun!" Ranged shouted as he dove forward. Thrust hands up as gunfire cracked against his ears. Felt the bullet whiz past his head. He drove into the man's gut. They went down, slamming into a concrete pillar. A notable crack sounded. Range drew up, fist ready to coldcock the guy. Saw the face.

Hellqvist.

Only then realized the guy wasn't moving. Saw the odd angle of his head.

He pushed onto his haunches, realizing the trajectory and impact of their collision had snapped his neck. Though he hadn't meant to kill the captain, he wasn't sorry. Especially considering the man had just tried to kill Kasra.

She'd be safe now ...

"That's one way to solve things," Canyon said as he helped him up. "You okay?"

On his feet, Range nodded. "Yeah." His right ear was ringing. "That's Hellqvist."

Azzan joined them. "Likely sent by Roth to finish the job."

Griffin gave a deep grunt. "Definitely time to vacate the premises."

"Yesterday."

***

Private Jet Over Northern Virginia

It was too much to believe. Amid throbbing pain in her ribs and a burn in her lungs, Kasra was on a plane for a nine-hour flight from Germany to America. Thankfully, the plane had room for her to lie down as being upright wracked her back. The men flying with them were the same ones who had been there when Range killed the captain.

There was such relief in her breast that she had thought her lung was torn again because she could not breathe. She wished she could say she had not willed death on that man, but it would not be true. Still, she did regret the loss of life. At least he could no longer torment her or Atia. Her daughter would not have to grow up under the shadow of such a man.

On the flight, she watched Range interact with Atia and take care of them both. Once Atia had fallen asleep, he shifted onto a seat near where Kasra reclined and smirked. "Making me do all the hard work, huh?"

"It is a good change."

He chuckled. "I'd say that's mean, but maybe you're right."

She gave him a warning look. "You are being nice again."

His expression slipped. Those blue eyes considered her. "It's—"

"Nice."

He faltered. A smile pinched the corner of his eyes. "I'm glad to hear you say that." He took her hand. Eyes still on her, he kissed it. "Because I plan to be nice a lot from now on." Angling in closer, he had an intent expression. "Remember on the ship when you got mad at me?"

She winced.

"What I wanted to say then that I struggled to say … It seemed unreal to me …"

"You said the pretty girls did not fall for you, but you were wrong."

He smirked. "Good, because I think—no." He cocked his head. "I *know* I'm falling in love with you."

Her heart did this little pitter patter that she had never felt before. A blossom of hope, a promise of love. "I never dreamed this could happen."

"Same." He leaned over and kissed her.

"Beginning descent into Dulles. Prepare for landing," the captain droned over the intercom.

When they landed, two SUVs were waiting that delivered them to a large hotel that they called a lodge. There were trees, a pool, mountains with snow-capped peaks. "It is beautiful."

A broad-shouldered man in a cowboy hat—*must be his brother Stone*—waited as the vehicles pulled to a stop in front of him, where he stood with his arm wrapped around a woman who was pregnant. Beside them was an older woman with a warm smile.

"*Spey, spey!*" Atia exclaimed, her toes stretching as she tried to push herself up to see over the window sill.

A dog? Where?

Sure enough, a large black dog trotted across the grass and sat beside the cowboy.

"His name is Grief," Range said in Pashto.

"What a strange name for a dog," Kasra said quietly, the effort to talk still painful. And an odd thing happened in her chest as she took in the scene. Realized … this was Range's family. His mother, brothers, sister-in-law … Though this lodge was not his home, he was home.

Home.

She had neither a home nor a family.

"Wait here," he said over his shoulder to Kasra. "I need to find out the most direct route to your room." He and Canyon climbed out of the truck.

Your room. Not their room.

She watched him hug his mom, who held him tight, swayed and patted his pack. Touched his face with such tenderness as Kasra had never known. Pulled him down and planted a kiss on his cheek.

The big man—Stone—pulled him into a hug, the slaps on the back loud enough to hear inside the Suburban. Introductions continued, this time to the wife. Finally, Range turned to the SUV.

Kasra's heart hiccupped. It was her turn. She watched him come to the door and open it.

"Ready?"

She smiled her answer, not sure if she was ready for this. It felt like so much expectation. What must they think of her? Range said they knew her story. A nice way to put the horrible truth of her past. Zahir and his father hated her, rejected her. So had the imam of her village and her own brother. She could not expect his family to treat her any different than her own had.

But for him, that their love was so obvious, she was glad for him.

A wheelchair appeared and Range directed her toward it.

"No," she said, catching his arm. "I want to meet them on my feet."

Range held her gaze. "They won't care if you're standing or sitting."

The words made he breath catch in her throat. Moved her with emotion. "On my feet."

He lifted an eyebrow. "Then in the chair after."

She could tell he wouldn't budge, so she nodded.

Head cocked, he gave her a warning look. "None of your sly shrewdness with the non-answer. Promise."

She couldn't help the laugh, which pinched. "Promise." They turned toward the family, and Atia gave a shout, impatient to be freed from her car seat.

"On it," Canyon said, hurrying to the other side to rescue her impatient daughter.

Arm around her shoulder to assist her made it hard for Kasra to think. She felt a blush creeping into her cheeks, but focused on walking forward. On avoiding their gazes and finding the same admonishment she met everywhere.

"Stone, Mom—this is Kasra. My wife."

She faltered. Gasped.

"Of a sorts," he said with a smirk that made her smile.

"I am so glad to meet you, honey." His mom rushed toward her.

"Mom!" Range warned. "Easy—she's been wounded."

But the woman's arms ensconced her. Hugged her. Not an ounce of pain or pressure. Just ... acceptance. Warm, affectionate acceptance. "Welcome to the family!"

Tears burst from her eyes. Fears burst from heart, never to return again.

CHAPTER
TWENTY-THREE

ONE MONTH LATER

Reston, Virginia

"I AM massively out of my depth." Range paced in the conference room.

Looking relaxed and entirely too in control, Stone threaded his fingers and swiveled the chair toward him. "Makes sense."

"No," Range balked. "Nothing makes sense—that's the thing. What if he comes back and says it's fake? What the heck do I do? How do I tell Kas? No way on God's green earth I let her go back there or—"

"Hey. Nobody's going to let that happen. Regardless what Caruthers finds out, she stays." Stone tilted his head to the side and squinted at him.

Range caught Canyon's notorious smirk. "Last thing I need is crap from you."

On his feet, Canyon blocked his path.

"Get out of my face, man."

"Calm down. Just want to say you're doing the right thing."

"Like I need you to tell me what's right." Range felt too

confrontational, like his skin was crawling. He shook his head. Turned away to pace again.

"Have you figured out yet that you're in love with her?"

"I don't need you to tell me what I feel."

"Don't you?" Canyon edged in closer. "You seem to be looking everywhere except here"—he stabbed a finger into Range's chest, directly over his heart—"for the answer on what to do."

Range grabbed his finger. Yanked his arm backward and shoved into Canyon. Pinned him against the wall. "I have one thing to say to you"—anger tremoring, heart racing, all he could hear was Kasra's soft but firm voice, " ... *lives go on, and you are left behind bars that keep your grudge safe and nursed ...*" that made his anger bottom out—"you're right." He stepped back. "I owe you an apology."

Canyon lifted his eyebrows and drew back. "Say that again?"

Though he wanted to punch is brother for milking this, Range was done fighting ... everything. "I owe you an apology— for the whole Dani thing, for holding a grudge. For almost taking you down just now—"

With a barked laugh, Canyon stepped back. Smirked. "*I let you vent some steam.*"

At the nonstop rivalry and banter, Range sniffed, then his thoughts swung back to his brother's challenge. "And yes, I do know that I love her. But she's been to Hades and back. She doesn't know what love is or what it looks like." He considered his older brother. "I'm afraid ... Pretty sure I'm the first guy to treat her with respect. What if she gets down the road and realizes I was just a nice guy? That what she feels now isn't love but ... gratitude?" He shrugged. "For getting her out of A-stan, out of that life?"

"Stop underestimating her now. Before you officially put a ring on her finger," Stone said and folded his arms. "Kasra has a lot of healing to do—how can she not after the lives she's endured—but trust her to be smart enough to know the difference between love and someone being nice."

"*People are only nice when they want something.*"

Range grunted. "She has pretty dark views on people being nice."

"But she does not have dark views on you," Canyon said with a cockeyed nod. "I've seen the way she looks at you. She trusts you for advice and safety—with all she's survived, that says a lot."

The door to the conference room swung open and in filed Stone's lawyer and his admin.

Gut tight, Range tried to gauge the man's face, which was like granite. Oh no …

Mr. Caruthers handed him a manila folder.

Stone eyed the folder as Range took it. "What's the verdict, John?"

Bexar-Wolfe Lodge, Northern Virginia

Her heart hurt. Not for herself—but for Atia.

No, Kasra supposed that was not entirely true. Sitting at the kitchen island as she peeled apples, Kasra had kept a close eye on her daughter, sitting on the floor by the fireplace in Stone's cabin and petting his dog. In her short life it seemed she had found more friendship and connection with an oversized dog than with children—or even Kasra. Another life impacted and damaged by Kasra's life … If only Atia had known stability and love, had parents …

Laughter erupted to her left where Dani, Iskra, Brighton and Mrs. Clara were prepping dishes for a family barbecue. The men had gone into the city for some business, but would be back by dinner. They were so happy, so pretty, so— This whole scene was so domestic and ... perfect.

I should not be here.

"I know that look," Brighton whispered as she shifted closer to Kasra and lightly bumped their shoulders. She smothered butter over the pan of cinnamon rolls.

Self-conscious, Kasra tucked her chin. Focused on the apple-peeling. "What look?"

"The 'I don't belong here' look, the one that shows up when you feel like you're ... less. Damaged." Her bright eyes took her in, then she set a hand on Kasra's. "They're lies. *You* belong here."

"I would not be so sure."

"All of us, except Mrs. C, have been where you have been."

"It is a sweet thought, but no, you have not." Her eyes burned but she could not stop the words. "What I have done ... I do not deserve to be here. To be a part of ... this." A family. This family of heroes and heroism.

When an arm came around her shoulders, she found blue eyes framed by short, silvery-blonde hair. "My dear, before God, all our sins are the same. And believe me, we—all of us—have sinned."

In her many talks with Range's mom, Kasra had asked about God. Learned a lot. "That ... cannot be true. How can a liar have the same punishment as a murderer? Or one who sold their body the same as those who make others do it?"

"Because," Mrs. Clara said, brushing Kasra's hair back in a sweet, loving way, "sin is sin is sin." She turned to face her and smiled. "When you hang a blanket over a door, it does not matter if it is a wool blanket or a cotton one. They both are a barrier that blocks fresh air and sunshine. The person in the house who hung the blanket may have less light or air with a wool blanket, but the sun's power is not altered by the material.

Like the blanket, sin—no matter the type—blocks *us* from God, and He hates that because it keeps us from Him."

Absorbing that truth, Kasra tried to accept it. "I would very much like to believe that …"

"Then believe it, Dear Daughter," Mrs. Clara said. "And let go of the self-condemnation. It is harder for us to forgive ourselves than it is for God to forgive. More than anything, He wants to know and love you, and vice versa. Let Him. Just as you're letting Range know and love you."

Heart in her throat, she gazed up at his mother.

It had been a month since she and Range arrived. Five weeks since they had been married by the imam. Five weeks since he refused to accept the marriage as legitimate. Five weeks in which she had fallen more in love with him. Five weeks in which she ached for their marriage to be real, to find healing in his arms and with his name, his family. For Atia who had begun to bond with—

"Range!" Atia leapt up from the so-called sleep and bolted to the door, the large Malinois trotting behind her.

"I guess the men are back." Mrs. Clara gave her a hug. "Let's see what they found out."

Found out—the marriage.

Suddenly feeling sick, Kasra stayed at the island. Watched as Stone and Canyon entered, hugging their wives. Then Range … he immediately lifted Atia into his arms, and she wrapped around him like a monkey. His gaze searched and found Kasra's.

And her breath caught at the concern in his eyes.

Oh no … it was not real. He would ask her to leave. Send her back.

Range passed Atia to his mother, who took her to the fireplace where Grief was once more snuggled up on his bed.

Kasra focused on the apples. A dozen apples she had not managed to peel in twenty minutes!

He stepped into her personal space, one hand finding the small of her back. The other sliding a folder onto the island.

"It … it is okay," Kasra lied. "Please … Just … please do not send me back."

Range edged in closer, his breath skidding along her cheek. "We need to talk."

CHAPTER
TWENTY-FOUR

BEXAR-WOLFE LODGE, VIRGINIA

"WHAT DO YOU MEAN, if I want to explore my options?"

Range lowered his head as they sat in Mom's apartment, which she had loaned out to Kasra and Atia until they figured out what was going to happen. He had taken a room down the hall. "I just ..."

"What did the lawyer say?" she demanded. "Are we legally married?"

Letting out a deep breath, he nodded. "We are. What happened in Wesh is legal. But it can be annulled, if that's what you—we want." He met her gaze. "You are free now, Kasra. Free to do what you want. Date whom you want—"

"*Date?*" She drew up and shook her head. "I came here because of you!"

"I don't want you to feel trapped or—"

"I do not! I *love* you."

His heart thudded. "Do you? Or are you just in love with the idea of me?" He started forward, seeing her expression darken. "And I do not mean that in a bad way. I just—"

"You are the best man I have ever known. Why would I downgrade?"

He huffed a laugh.

"You gave everything to protect me, to protect my daughter. When you could have turned me in, walked away." Arms folded, she hugged herself as she moved to the island. "You tell me—do you want to marry me? This woman who has had sex with countless men, ran—"

"Hey." Range stood and went to her. Held her shoulders. "I need a promise from you right now."

She lifted her chin defiantly.

"Never speak of yourself that way again."

"Why, does it embarrass you? Do *I* embarrass you?"

"No. But that is not the whole of who you are. You're strong, fierce, compassionate, and brave. So very brave." He framed her face. "You have had few decisions in your life that were wholly yours to make. This one—it's completely yours. Me? Yes—I want to marry you. That night on the ship when we ..." He cocked his head with a telling smirk. "Well, if that didn't show you what I felt, hear me now: I don't want anyone else. But neither will a forced marriage by a psychotic imam define our future."

She searched his face. "Do you mean it—that you want me?"

"Yes ... How many ways do you want me to say it?"

Her eyes were bright with meaning. "Only one." Her voice was small, the request large.

There was one thing Range realized he had never vocalized. He framed her face again. Wanted to kiss her, but more than that, wanted her to understand his feelings could stand apart from arousal or passion. "I love you."

"Then the decision is done."

Two weeks later, armed with a marriage certificate arranged by Stone who had a connection to someone who promised to bury the filing of that until Adler Roth was in jail or dead, they stood at the hearth in Bexar-Wolfe Lodge and willingly, heartily became man and wife.

EPILOGUE

TWO WEEKS LATER

Somewhere in Taiwan

CHRISTMAS HAD ALWAYS MEANT department stores and bellringers plying the guilt of customers to spend-spend-spend. It meant pressure from staff for time off—*paid* time off—and for family to get together. *"It's one holiday—please, dear. Won't you try?"* Mom would try with her sweetest voice. Every year she had dreaded it. Hated it.

Except this year.

Christmas had to be close. Brooke wasn't sure exactly how close—she'd lost track of the days when she'd lost her phone.

Correction: when she'd thrown it into a river once she realized they were tracking her.

In a courtroom, she learned to be savvy. See the weakness of the other side to control the narrative, drive the conviction in the favor of her client. Her machinations and ability to set aside emotion built her into a master. A sought-after trial attorney. Got her to New York. Surpassed men who felt with her looks that she was better suited in their bed than at a litigation table.

And she'd proven them wrong. Stepped on them to reach the top of the proverbial ladder. Been named partner, her name—she'd taken her mom's maiden name, Mulroney—on the plaque gracing the Manhattan high-rise.

So how had she so thoroughly failed here?

The subtle splash sounded from the right.

Brooke darted away in her bare feet, a move she'd made to conceal her steps. She had to get back to the hotel. My purse … She cursed herself. She'd lost it when the guy tried to accost her outside the restaurant. Used it to knock him away, then bolted, not even thinking that it had her ID, her credit cards … her phone!

She wouldn't give up, though. Couldn't. Lives were at stake.

Exhausted, she slumped against a wall, listening for the two men following her. She had to get back to new York. She'd been gone longer this trip than any other. But she'd been on a mission for Mazin. It seemed the least she could do, considering how Dad had completely failed him. Now, a little boy was depending on her.

A tinkling noise came from behind.

Sucking in a breath, Brooke whipped a look over her shoulder. Tried to blend into a corner. A shape moved a few yards away. Something glinted.

Gun!

She slid around the corner and sprinted down the darkened street. Rocks and glass cutting her feet, but she did not care. Could not stop. The people who had taken Jihan and Caliyah would not stop. Would make sure she was silenced.

She rounded a corner.

Light exploded, blinding her. Arms up to shield her eyes, she barely saw the vehicle before it plowed into her.

GET INVOLVED

Looking for a way to get involved and help combat human trafficking? Here are a couple of organizations that could use your help, either through volunteering or donations.

OPERATION UNDERGROUND RAILROAD

To the children
who we pray for daily, we say:
Your long night is coming to an end.

Hold on. We are on our way.

And to those **captors and perpetrators,**
even you monsters who dare offend God's
precious children, we declare to you:
Be afraid. We are coming for you

To Those Who Have Read This Far
we plead with you: Donate to our cause

Donate. We can't do this without you.

MORE INFORMATION ON OPERATION UNDERGROUND RAILROAD

Within the Metcalfes Series, you will meet Cord Taggart and his organization, Mission: Liberate Everyone (MiLE), an organization I've loosely modeled after Tim Ballard's Operation Underground Railroad. A couple of years ago, I stumbled upon a video about a young boy name Gardy (check out Gardy's story here https://ourrescue.org/blog/search?search=gardy), stolen from his church in Haiti's Port-au-Prince and from his father, who has never given up the fight to find his son. The heart-wrenching story gripped me and wouldn't let me go. I watched hours of videos, which invariably led to Tim Ballard and his backstory, and his organization, Operation Underground Railroad. This fight against trafficking wouldn't leave me alone. So, I reached out to O.U.R. and asked if someone would talk to me, so I could be sure to write with accuracy and authenticity. I was in awe of how responsive they were, how willing they were to share their organization and their hearts. Not to brag on themselves. But rather to add to the voices screaming out against trafficking. O.U.R. has my heart. I can't venture around the globe, but I can write. And that is my contribution to O.U.R.'s endeavor and the fight against monsters selling people for sex. PLEASE. DONATE.

From the O.U.R website (www.ourrescue.org):

WE WORK WITH LAW ENFORCEMENT TO FREE SURVIVORS OF HUMAN TRAFFICKING AND EXPLOITATION. THEN WE WORK TO BREAK THE CYCLE.

Operation Underground Railroad currently supports operation and aftercare efforts in 22 countries and 34 U.S. States. Since our group is privately run, we are able to quickly respond to foreign government requests and institute investigative measures, develop intelligence and assist in enforcement operations and rescue efforts.

The O.U.R. Ops Team primarily consists of highly experienced and extensively trained current and former law enforcement personnel. Other members have a background in either the military or in intelligence work. Our goal is to develop long-term relationships with foreign governments and their law enforcement agencies responsible for combatting human trafficking and child sexual exploitation; working closely with O.U.R. Aftercare in anticipation of their rescue.

O.U.R. does not conduct or participate in investigations, operations or enforcement action in the United States. This important work is conducted by the brave men and women in law enforcement.

Domestically, O.U.R. develops relationships with law enforcement agencies and offers resources to assist them in their local efforts against human trafficking and sexual exploitation.

THE PROCESS

1. Assess the feasibility of rescue. This must take into account the willingness of local authorities to work with us since we not only want to save the children but arrest the perpetrators as well. We also want everything to be done legally and above board.

2. Research the location, the children and the background of those who are running the sex ring. We also search for vetted care facilities that will take the children once they are rescued and not only give them food and shelter but rehabilitate them as well. In some instances the children are able to return to their families.

3. **Design a strategy** for rescuing the children. This is the logistical part of the process. As former CIA, Navy Seals, Special Agents, etc., we have a very unique skill set to make this happen safely, efficiently and legally. We provide local law enforcement training to support and sustain anti-trafficking operations.

4. **Take action.** Obviously this is the most dangerous part of the operation but one well worth taking. In some instances we go undercover and arrange to "buy" a child as if we were a customer. After the purchase, we move in with the police, arrest those responsible and rescue the children. In other cases, we may act as a "client" looking for favors, etc. Again, we work with local authorities to make sure everything is done to protect the children and that the perpetrators are arrested.

5. **Recover the children.** These children's lives will never be the same. Their innocence has been stolen and they need help to readjust to a better world. Therapy can be provided as well as food and shelter at a pre-screened facility.

6. **Arrest, try, and convict the perpetrators.** We follow this process every step of the way to make sure they don't traffic children again. In many cases the perpetrators were sex slaves and victims of trafficking themselves and know no better way to survive. We hope to break this cycle.

EXODUS CRY

HTTPS://EXODUSCRY.COM/OURSOLUTION/

Exodus Cry has worked both nationally and internationally training abolitionists in outreach, hosting governmental screenings of our documentary *Nefarious*, and reaching women bound in sexual exploitation. Here's the impact we've made since starting in 2008.

Exodus Cry is committed to abolishing sex trafficking and breaking the cycle of commercial sexual exploitation while assisting and empowering its victims.

Our international work involves **uprooting the underlying causes in our culture** that allow the industry of sexual exploitation to thrive and **helping those who have been sexually exploited.**

We fight sex trafficking and all forms of commercial sexual exploitation.

Trafficking is one component of a much larger system of *violence, exploitation,* and *gender inequality* known as the **commercial sex industry.** Our strategies are designed to assist, empower, and help bring freedom to those who have been victimized, while also fighting to uproot the larger system of injustice and exploitation that made it possible.

OUR BATTLE PLAN

Exodus Cry fights sexual exploitation in the sex industry in three strategic ways:

Shifting our culture – Working to shift the culture with powerful messaging through films, videos, podcasts, conferences, and the written word.

Changing Laws – Advocating for laws that uproot commercial sexual exploitation and defend those who are sexually exploited for profit.

Reaching Out – Engaging with those who are currently bound in sexual exploitation and lovingly offering them a way out.

HOW WE'VE MADE AN IMPACT

Exodus Cry has worked both nationally and internationally training abolitionists in outreach, hosting governmental screenings of our documentary *Nefarious*, and reaching women bound in sexual exploitation. Here's the impact we've made since starting in 2008.

We've started the fight.
You can strengthen the movement and bring freedom to those caught in the commercial sex industry.
Donate
Join the movement. Sign the pledge.
Become an Abolitionist.

THE METCALFE CHARACTERS

BOOKS FEATURING CHARACTERS FROM
THE METCALFES

Range Metcalfe
Willow (The Metcalfes #2)
Crown of Souls (The Tox Files #2)
Wolfsbane (Discarded Heroes #3)
Lygos (Discarded Heroes: A Novella)

Willow Metcalfe
Stone (The Metcalfes #1)
Willow (The Metcalfes #2)
Wolfsbane (Discarded Heroes #3)
Lygos (A Discarded Heroes Novella)

Stone Metcalfe
Stone (The Metcalfes #1)
Willow (The Metcalfes #2)
Wolfsbane (Discarded Heroes #3)
Lygos (A Discarded Heroes Novella)

THE METCALFE CHARACTERS

Canyon Metcalfe
Stone (Metcalfes #1)
Willow (Metcalfes #2)
Kings Falling (The Book of the Wars #2)
Soul Raging (The Book of the Wars #3)
Nightshade (Discarded Heroes #1)
Digitalis (Discarded Heroes #2)
Wolfsbane (Discarded Heroes #3)
Firethorn (Discarded Heroes #4)
Lygos (Discarded Heroes: A Novella)

Danielle "Dani" Metcalfe
Kings Falling (The Book of the Wars #2)
Soul Raging (The Book of the Wars #3)
Wolfsbane (Discarded Heroes #3)
Lygos (Discarded Heroes: A Novella)

Leif Metcalfe
Stone (The Metcalfes #1)
Willow (The Metcalfes #2)
Storm Rising (The Book of the Wars #1)
Kings Falling (The Book of the Wars #2)
Soul Raging (The Book of the Wars #3)
Thirst of Steel (The Tox Files #3)
Wolfsbane (Discarded Heroes #3)
Lygos (A Discarded Heroes Novella)

Azzan Yasir
Stone (The Metcalfes #1)
Digitalis (Discarded Heroes #2)
Wolfsbane (Discarded Heroes #3)
Firethorn (Discarded Heroes #4)
Lygos (Discarded Heroes: A Novella)

THE METCALFE CHARACTERS

Griffin Riddell

Stone (The Metcalfes #1)
Storm Rising (The Book of the Wars #1)
Kings Falling (The Book of the Wars #2)
Soul Raging (The Book of the Wars #3)
Nightshade (Discarded Heroes #1)
Digitalis (Discarded Heroes #2)
Wolfsbane (Discarded Heroes #3)
Firethorn (Discarded Heroes #4)
Lygos (Discarded Heroes: A Novella)

Clara Mulroney Metcalfe

Stone (The Metcalfes #1)
Wolfsbane (Discarded Heroes #3)

WHAT'S NEXT?

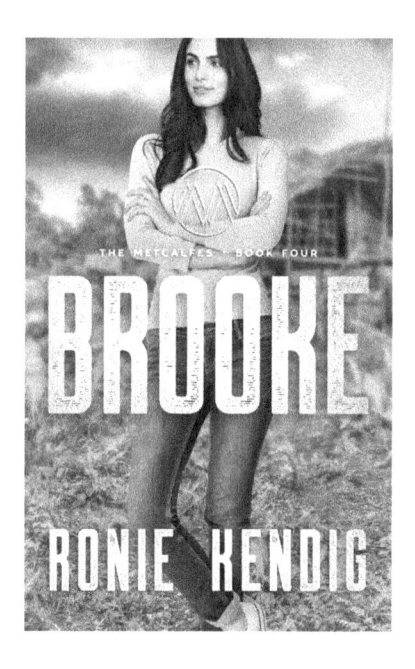

She has conquered a male-dominated field, toppled corporate giants, and gained world-wide notoriety and recognition for her prowess in law. But Brooke Metcalfe Mulroney is ill-prepared for the human-trafficking fight that has dragged her across the globe ... and straight into the well-muscled, tattooed arms of thick-skulled black-ops operator Cord Taggart.

Oh yeah ... This is gonna be just great.

ACKNOWLEDGMENTS

Many thanks to dear friends who helped bring this book to fruition: Rel Mollet and Kim Gradeless. Thank you, Bethany Kaczmarek, for proofing this story and your amusing comments that kept me from tears (mostly).

Thank you to Jenny of Zemanek Designs for such perfect covers for The Metcalfes.

Again, a million thanks to Jessica Mass and Tyler Schwab of Operation Underground Railroad for taking the time to talk to me and share from your hearts. A heartfelt thank you to Ali from Unbound Waco (unboundwaco.org) for meeting with me and sharing your heart and thoughts about trafficking and survivor work. You are all warriors!

ABOUT THE AUTHOR

Ronie Kendig is an bestselling, award-winning author of over thirty books. She grew up an Army brat, and now she and her hunky hero have returned to their beloved Texas after a nearly ten-year stint in the Northeast. They survive on Sonic runs, barbecue, and peach cobbler that they share—sometimes—with beloved Benning the Stealth Golden. Ronie's degree in psychology has helped her pen novels of intense, raw characters.

Website: www.roniekendig.com
Instagram: www.instagram.com/kendigronie
Facebook: www.facebook.com/rapidfirefiction
Twitter: www.twitter.com/roniekendig
Goodreads: www.goodreads.com/RonieK
BookBub: www.bookbub.com/authors/ronie-kendig
Amazon: www.amazon.com/Ronie-Kendig/e/B002SFLGQ2

ALSO BY RONIE KENDIG

The Metcalfes

Stone

Willow

Range

Brooke (Winter 2022)

The Discarded Heroes

Nightshade

Digitalis

Wolfsbane

Firethorn

Lygos: A Novella

The Book of the Wars

Storm Rising

Kings Falling

Soul Raging

The Tox Files

The Warrior's Seal

Conspiracy of Silence

Crown of Souls

Thirst of Steel

The Quiet Professionals

Raptor 6

Hawk

Falcon

Titanis: A Novella

A Breed Apart

Trinity

Talon

Beowulf

The Droseran Saga

Brand of Light

Dawn of Vengeance

Shadow of Honor

War of Torment (April 2023)

Abiassa's Fire Fantasy Series

Embers

Accelerant

Fierian

Standalone Titles

Operation Zulu: Redemption

Dead Reckoning